PUFFIN BOOKS
Editor: Kaye Webb

FURTHER ADVENTURES OF THE FAMILY FROM ONE END STREET

The seven Ruggles children are already famous. Their first appearance in *The Family from One End Street* won a Carnegie Medal for their creator, Eve Garnett. In this new book Mr and Mrs Ruggles are as short of money as ever, the children are just as engaging. When the story begins three of them go down with measles, but this turns out to be a Blessing in Disguise, for as a result Kate, Peg, and Jo are sent on a convalescent holiday to a dream house in the country called the Dew Drop Inn, where they are looked after by Mrs Wildgoose, who must be the kindest landlady ever invented.

But as well as the excitements of the train journey and the joy of discovering the habits of the countryside, the family have other adventures, like the time Lily Rose is a bridesmaid, or when Mr Ruggles gets sent the wrong pig, or when Baby Ruggles sees a pussy-cat at the kitchen window and it turns out to be an escaped tiger.

A charming book for ages 8 to 11.

D1147537

By the same author

IS IT WELL WITH THE CHILD?
*(with a Foreword by Walter de la Mare
and a Preface by Marjorie Bowen)*

and for children

THE FAMILY FROM ONE END STREET

IN AND OUT AND ROUNDABOUT

A BOOK OF THE SEASONS
An Anthology

HOLIDAY AT THE DEW DROP INN

TO GREENLAND'S ICY MOUNTAINS:
The Story of Hans Egede,
Explorer, Colonizer, Missionary

LOST AND FOUND: four stories

Further Adventures of the Family from One End Street

WRITTEN AND ILLUSTRATED BY EVE GARNETT

PUFFIN BOOKS

Puffin Books, Penguin Books Ltd, Harmondsworth, Middlesex, England
Penguin Books, 625 Madison Avenue, New York, New York 10022, U.S.A.
Penguin Books Australia Ltd, Ringwood, Victoria, Australia
Penguin Books Canada Ltd, 41 Steelcase Road West, Markham, Ontario, Canada
Penguin Books (N.Z.) Ltd, 182–190 Wairau Road, Auckland 10, New Zealand

—

First published by William Heinemann Ltd, 1956
Published in Puffin Books 1963
Reprinted 1965, 1967, 1969, 1971, 1973, 1974, 1975, 1976

—

Copyright © Eve Garnett, 1956

—

Made and printed in Great Britain
by Cox & Wyman Ltd,
London, Reading and Fakenham
Set in Monotype Baskerville.

This book is sold subject to the condition
that it shall not, by way of trade or otherwise,
be lent, re-sold, hired out, or otherwise circulated
without the publisher's prior consent in any form of
binding or cover other than that in which it is
published and without a similar condition
including this condition being imposed
on the subsequent purchaser

TO ALL WHO ENJOYED

The Family From One End Street

AND ESPECIALLY

'S'WARK'

CONTENTS

Foreword   9

1. *Trouble at One End Street*   11

2. *Ways and Means*   25

3. *Kate Has a Plan*   39

4. *The Journey*   52

5. *The Dew Drop Inn*   69

6. *Country Days and Ways*

    (i) *Exploring*   87

    (ii) *An Invitation*   110

    (iii) *Four Farthings*   121

7. *A Day of Disasters*   127

8. *The Wedding of Uncle Albert*   157

9. *Mrs Ruggles Gets a Surprise*   201

10. *Mr Ruggles Buys a Pig*   217

11. *Ten Little Nigger Boys*   232

12. *The Return*   244

FOREWORD

IN 1941 my father's property was totally destroyed by fire. Amongst the few things saved was a box containing letters and other papers, and the notes and manuscript of this book. The manuscript and notes, particularly, appeared far too badly charred to be readable but were left lying with the other, less damaged papers, in the hope that a few fragments might perhaps be legible and provide sufficient clues to rewrite the book.

Some years later, going through the contents of the box, I found to my surprise that actually only the notes and the outer layers of manuscript – a chapter previously published in the *Junior Bookshelf*, were completely unreadable. Deeper layers, though very badly burnt, proved with difficulty, and much patience, to be decipherable.

This deciphering began, and in 1950 some chapters were completed and published in *Collins Magazine*, and then, for various reasons, the work had to be put aside. Now, at long last, it has been completed. Here are the Ruggles again and I hope those who have met them before, and those who meet them now for the first time, may enjoy this further recording of their small day-to-day fortunes – and misfortunes.

EVE GARNETT

Sussex
December 1954

CHAPTER ONE

Trouble at One End Street

LILY ROSE, the eldest of the Ruggles children, sat up in bed one morning feeling Rather Queer. Her head ached, she felt hot and cold by turns, while the wall-paper – a beautiful trellis-work design, with bunches of pink and yellow roses – which covered the walls of the small room she shared with her sisters, Kate and Peg, seemed behaving in a *very* peculiar manner! First the trellis-work seemed to be slanting to the left, then to the right, while the bunches of roses appeared to be hurling themselves towards one and then as suddenly retreating.

'I think I'm going to be ill!' said Lily Rose to herself – for she was a considerate girl on the whole, and the others were still asleep. She lay down again to see how she felt that way, but it seemed to make matters no better – in fact, rather worse! The trellis-work was leaning more than ever in alternate directions, and as for the roses – well, it was difficult, really, to say what they *were* doing!

'I think I *am* ill!' said Lily Rose, and crawling out of bed she made her way over to the dressing-table to take a good look in the glass and make really sure. It was a surprise, and certainly a disappointment, to see, in the image reflected back at her, instead of the 'haggard face, white as death', which her romantic imagination had already conjured up, her usual round, fat countenance, wearing, perhaps, a rather anxious expression, but by no means white, not even pale, but bright – bright *pink*, and covered all over with small red spots!

Lily Rose gave a gasp, clutched the dressing-table tightly with both hands and whispered: 'Scarlet fever!'

Yes, it must be! And immediately her mind was filled with visions of Fever Hospitals, Death Beds, Beautiful Funerals, and Sorrowing Parents! Lily Rose felt suddenly very much worse, and crawled back to bed as quickly as possible, for at least she knew that with scarlet fever it was *most* important to keep warm . . . though perhaps, even now, it was too late . . . ! She lay down and drew the bed-clothes tightly over her; the trellis-work was whirling madly round in circles now . . . she closed her eyes for a moment, then opened them, and, giving one look at her sleeping sisters, decided she could be considerate no longer, and turning over buried her face in the pillow and wept loudly!

A minute later her sister Kate, who shared the bed and was one of those people who, when they wake, wake up all over at once and not, like many of us, in instalments, sat up, flung her arms wide apart, and casting her eyes up to the ceiling, began to recite in a loud whisper, but with great fervour:

> 'Go, for they call you, shepherd, from the hill!
> Go, shepherd, and untie the wattled cotes!
> No longer leave thy wistful flock unfed . . .!'

One might almost have suspected that Kate had been taken ill, too, but this was not the case; she was merely what her mother called 'getting her homework', for Kate had won a scholarship from the Council to the Secondary school, and at times her homework was overwhelming! A great deal of it seemed to consist in learning by heart long pieces of poetry and passages from the Bible. Kate had a good memory, but she did not believe in overworking it, and she had invented a plan by which this could be avoided. Taking the book containing the lesson to be learnt to bed with her, she would alternately read and learn until she became throroughly sleepy, then, pushing the

book beneath the pillow, she would fall asleep murmuring the half-learnt lines, waking, in some incomprehensible way, almost word-perfect in the morning! Though science might have offered another explanation, Kate maintained it was the book under the pillow 'as did it', and 'Certain something does', Lily Rose would say, 'for you never knows it one bit at night!'

> 'Here will I sit and wait,
>   While to my ear from uplands far away
>   The bleating of the folded flocks is borne . . . .'

continued Kate, then paused for a word and suddenly
became aware of the sobbing Lily Rose beside her! Explanations followed, and a few minutes later Peg was sitting
up in the bed opposite gazing with round eyes and intense
interest at her afflicted sister, while Kate, her head round
the door of her parents' room, was announcing, with
great importance, that 'Lily Rose had come all over
queer-like'.

'Quite correct, Mrs Ruggles, it's measles all right!' said
the doctor a few hours later. 'Third case I've had this
week – "she's had it before" – that's nothing – and it's a
mild attack so far; but you can't keep her here, you know
– nowhere to isolate her and no time to look after her if you
had; it's the isolation hospital for measles these days. I'll
have the ambulance round in half an hour and someone
to disinfect that room for you. "The others?" no, they
certainly can't go to school, but don't you worry, they'll
probably all have it in a few days and be off your hands in
hospital, too! Put them to bed at the first sign of anything
and let me know – yes, go down to the hospital this evening
if you like but they won't let you see her.' And picking up
his hat from the kitchen table and threading his way
between the airing sheets (for Mrs Ruggles took in washing
and yesterday had been ironing day), he made for the
door, let himself out, and the next minute had shot off in
his car round the corner of One End Street and was lost
to view.

'Not ten minutes,' said Mrs Ruggles to herself, glancing
at the clock, 'easy money, I calls it; *I* knew it were
measles!' and taking a look through the back kitchen
window to make sure that William, the baby, was still
asleep in his pram in the yard, she went upstairs to break
the news to Lily Rose.

Lily Rose had stopped weeping, but she almost began again when Mrs Ruggles said it was measles and not scarlet fever, for there was something romantic about scarlet fever, somehow, whereas anyone and everyone got measles, and when she heard about the isolation hospital she *did* begin again! Mrs Ruggles was sympathetic but firm, and told Lily Rose to remember as she was near fourteen, and too big to cry – not even very ill, neither, and didn't she remember as Mary Mills, what had the diphtheria last year, couldn't hardly be got to leave the place, she'd had such a good time there? Mary Mills was a school friend of Lily Rose's, and she did remember something about it now – going with Mary's auntie one day to take Mary a bunch of violets. Perhaps someone would do the same for her. It would be very grand to receive flowers all to oneself! ('How is Miss Ruggles today?' 'Nicely, thank you.' 'Please give her these flowers and say I called.') Lily Rose quite cheered up, and when she was bundled downstairs in blankets by two ambulance men an hour later, and saw all the neighbours gaping at the shiny white ambulance drawn up outside their door, she felt rather important and almost excited and waved 'good-bye' to Mrs Ruggles with great vigour, crying: 'O.K., see you tonight, Mum,' as the men closed the doors. Ten minutes later she was being tucked up in a bed at the hospital, while at home in One End Street Mrs Ruggles was serving the dinner and anxiously regarding the rest of her family – who had returned from an enjoyable morning in the park, spent in undisputed possession of the sand-pit and swings – for a sign of a sneeze or spot!

They all appeared in robust health, and, with the exception of Kate, in the highest spirits. Kate declared that she didn't want a holiday – not one bit – at least not *now*, and how long did Mum think they'd be away from school and would it be more than a week? because if so she'd have no chance of winning the form prize at the end of the term, 'and I *had*, you know', she added, confidently. Mrs Ruggles was not feeling particularly sympathetic towards higher education at the moment, and she told Kate to 'stop worrying, do', while Mr Ruggles, who was a dust-man, and had just come in from a rather depressing morn-ing among the rubbish-bins (someone had left a litter of drowned kittens in one and this always made him gloomy), said he wouldn't be surprised if it didn't 'run on like', and they weren't in quarantine for six weeks or more!

'Six weeks!' exclaimed Kate, aghast. 'Why, school'll be over by then – it was half-term two weeks ago!' Her ten-year-old twin brothers, Jim and John, looked at her in disgust! Though they liked school well enough, even enjoyed it very much at times, they would never have

dreamt of objecting to any kind of holiday – especially six weeks added on to the usual Easter one, and they pinched each other under the table, for they belonged to a secret society called the Gang of the Black Hand, membership of which called for constant adventures, and six weeks' free time – *coo*! Jo, aged seven and three-quarters, said nothing. He loved school, nearly always, and just now his entire being was absorbed in a large plasticine map of England his class were making between them. Next week they were going to 'do' the mountains and rivers, and the thought of the others rolling out the green and blue plasticine while he, Jo, was not there to take a hand, was agonizing – and the teacher had promised him the Isle of Wight all to himself! 'Curse measles,' muttered Jo under his breath, but he took good care not to say it out loud, for Mr Ruggles would have been terribly shocked. Peg, who had only just started school, seemed to share his unspoken thoughts and murmured indignantly: 'No dolls' house? No shop?' for so far Peg's educational activities had been chiefly concerned with these delights, and there was neither dolls' house nor shop at No. 1 One End Street. As for William, school and holidays were, as yet, all one to him, but feeling himself neglected he flung the greater part of his dinner on the floor, and having in this way success-fully attracted his mother's notice, set up a loud wail and secured her undivided attention for the rest of the meal!

Nearly a week went by. Lily Rose was reported to be 'going on nicely, thank you', at the hospital, and though the ambulance had called at three other houses in One End Street – one only that morning – Mrs Ruggles began to have hopes that the doctor had been wrong and it would not be seen outside her door again. But, alas! Mrs Ruggles's

hopes were short-lived! That very evening Peg com-
plained of a headache, and next morning she, too, had a
pink face covered all over with red spots, and by the afternoon was lying in a cot at the hospital beside Lily Rose.

Lying, perhaps, was not quite the right word, for Peg
had refused to lie at all and remained sitting up, clutching
the bars of her cot and screaming with a persistency that
would have done credit to William! This awful behaviour
so upset Lily Rose that her temperature, normal for two
days, went up, and very soon every child asleep in the
ward was awake, half of them wailing in sympathy.

'Yes, we know you want to go home!' said the matron,
summoned in desperation by the young nurse in charge,
'but you can't go today. Lie down now like a good girl and
think how nice it is to have your big sister in the bed there
beside you!' But Peg took not the slightest notice and only
wailed louder! 'Come, come,' said the matron, losing
patience, 'you're waking up all the other children! You'll
be able to go home soon.' 'But I don't *want* to go home!'
cried Peg, surprisingly. '*Not till I get my bear – I want* MY
BEAR!'

'Oh, dear!' said Lily Rose, 'that's it – of course she
won't lie down!' and she explained how Peg, in all her
five years, had never, never gone to bed without her bear,
adding that she was sure Mrs Ruggles would never have
forgotten to send it and it must have got left behind in the
ambulance!

'Well, we've no time to be looking for bears and things
here,' said the matron sharply. 'Here's a beautiful rabbit;
you lie down like a good girl and talk to *him*.' And she put
a large long-eared rabbit, dressed in a beautiful pair of
blue velvet trousers from which his fluffy white tail stuck
out like a little flag – a rabbit to be proud of – on Peg's cot
and walked away. Peg took one look at the rabbit, then

seized him by his long ears and flung him into the middle
of the ward! 'I want my *bear*!' she shrieked, 'not a *rabbit*!
I — WANT — MY — BEAR!'

'I shall take no more notice of you,' said the matron
coldly, and turning back again, she picked up the rabbit
and disappeared with it through a door at the end of the
ward. But the young nurse, who hadn't been long at the
hospital and become so used to tears, asked Peg what her
bear's name was, and said if she would only stop screaming
and lie down nicely, *at once*, she would perhaps try to find
it. Peg was really only too glad to do so, for screaming so
long, especially with measles, was awfully tiring, but how
else was she to get her bear? She half-smiled at the nurse
and whispered that the bear's name was Buttonhook, and
then lay down quickly, only giving a sniff occasionally and
very soon fell asleep. When she woke, Buttonhook, rescued
from somewhere by the nurse in her short time off, his
elderly moth-eaten appearance looking strangely out of
place against the shining white cot bars and clean red
blankets, was staring at her with the boot-button eyes
with which Mrs Ruggles had long since replaced his
original glass ones. The matron, passing through the ward
some time later, saw what she considered 'a most unhygienic toy' cuddled up in Peg's arms; she said nothing,
however. 'But, my word!' said Lily Rose to herself, 'can't
she *look*, and I bet that nurse don't half get ticked off,
neither!' Lily Rose had never liked the matron much, she
thought, and now she decided she didn't like her at all,
but the young nurse was a sport all right – even if she *was*
a nurse! But Peg, every time the matron passed her cot,
would look at her out of the corners of her eyes and mutter
in the dilapidated ear of the 'unhygienic' Buttonhook,
'We'll tell our mum of her, we will!'

Jo was the next victim! He felt funny when he woke up next morning, and not much like breakfast, but he was determined he was not going to be ill – no measles or hospital for *him* – for wasn't he thinking about that map every day? It was over a week now since he'd gone to school – they'd have done the rivers by this for sure – perhaps the mountains as well, and what, oh *what* was happening to the Isle of Wight? Fearfully Jo peeped at himself in a mirror; not a sign of a spot, but he certainly looked rather white. 'I *won't* have measles!' he muttered furiously, and taking a nail-brush he scrubbed his face vigorously, hoping that the beautiful pink glow produced would last through breakfast and deceive the sharp eyes of Mrs Ruggles. A cup of hot tea assisted matters, and Jo did his best with a slice of bread and treacle, though a good deal of it found its way into his pocket. Mrs Ruggles's attention, however, was centred on William, who was what she called 'fretty'. It had been bad enough Peg going off to the hospital – poor little thing – but a tiny mite like William . . . ! Mrs Ruggles had no thoughts for the rest of the family that morning, and Jo slipped out unnoticed and made his way to the park.

It was a hot day and he felt very tired by the time he got there. He sat down on a seat wondering what to do. It was very odd; there lay the whole playground in front of him, all to himself, and he didn't feel like doing anything! He looked at the swings – too hot; the 'stride'? he felt too tired; the sand-pit? it wasn't much fun alone, and somehow it reminded him of that map. Jo shook himself angrily. He didn't feel like anything; he only felt cross and cross *because* he felt cross! He looked over at the 'shute' – perhaps a slide down head-first would liven him up! He went slowly towards it. Too hot to climb up the ladder he decided, when he reached it, and yet, somehow, he felt

rather cold – sort of shivery, and *very* thirsty, though it was
not so long since he'd had breakfast . . . but, of course, it
was a hot day. He turned round and went over to the
fountain in the middle of the park, where, in place of the
old-fashioned tin cup attached to a chain, a neat button
was provided which, on being pressed, spouted a jet of
water into one's mouth, or, as all the Otwell children knew
well enough, anywhere else one might choose to direct it!
Jo took a long drink; he felt better almost at once. A
minute later he was busy scooping a hole in the neat
gravel path, filling it with water from the button (getting
extremely wet in the process), and making what he called
'a paddly-pool'. He had just taken off his shoes and socks
and was enjoying the coolness of the water and the squishy,
gravelly mud between his toes, when he saw a park-keeper
approaching. Hastily picking up his belongings, Jo ran off
as fast as possible in the opposite direction, for 'paddly-
pools' and the makers thereof were highly unpopular with
the park officials. Jo hid behind a bush, but whether it
was the running, the effects of the 'paddly-pool', or the
fear of the park-keeper, his head suddenly began to ache
violently and he felt even funnier than he had when he
woke up! He decided he would very much like another
drink and peeped cautiously round the bush. The park-
keeper had given up the pursuit and was apparently occupied in chasing two stray dogs out through the main gates.
Jo shook himself and stood up, when, to his surprise, he
saw Kate coming towards him. Kate looked very pleased
with herself! She had three books under her arm and was
looking about for a quiet place to read in. Her form-
mistress had called yesterday, remarking there was no
need to be idle or waste time, and left her some work to
get on with. Kate was feeling much happier and wondering, if they all kept well now, whether she might not have

a chance of that prize after all! When she came close to Jo, however, she felt less hopeful. He looked very odd – 'white as a sheet'. Kate studied him closely. No. No spots.

'Why are you all wet?' she demanded, 'Been messing about with that fountain, I suppose? You'd better go home and get dry or you'll have the measles – if you haven't got 'em now – you look so queer I believe you might have,

though I can't see any spots on you. Oh, Jo, you *are* a nuisance if you have got them – that'll be *another* week to go!' And Kate gave a big sigh, for although she was fond of her small brother she was also fond of learning things, for she wanted to get on in life, and when your father was a dustman and there were seven of you, 'learning things' seemed about the only way of doing it!

'I *haven't* got measles,' cried Jo, indignantly, 'there's no spots on me so I can't have – and I'm not going home till I *want*,' he added.

'All right,' said Kate, 'but you'll have worse measles if you've got measles if you stay wet.' And she walked off. Jo stood looking after her . . . perhaps it *would* be better to get dry and, as the sun seemed to have gone in now, home seemed the only place to do it in. He put on his shoes and socks and set off slowly in the direction of One End Street. 'But I haven't got measles all the same,' he said to himself as he trudged along, 'and I *won't* have them, neither!' But it was no good. By dinner-time, spots or not, it was quite obvious Jo had *something*.

'I've *not* got measles!' he wailed, as Mrs Ruggles undressed him and put him to bed. 'It's summat else – pendy-citis, perhaps, like Tony Towner down to West Street had!' And Mrs Ruggles said well, perhaps it *was*, and they'd see what the doctor said. The doctor said Jo was a very sick boy, and told Mrs Ruggles downstairs it was always worse if the spots stayed in, and the sooner Jo was in hospital the better!

'I *won't* go to hospital – I *won't*,' screamed Jo, as half an hour later the ambulance men stood waiting to carry him downstairs. 'I haven't got measles, I tell you! It's pendy-citis – people don't go to hospital with pendy-citis; Tony had his in the kitchen! I *won't* go!' And he tore off the blanket one of the men had wrapped round him, and threw it on the floor.

'But your sisters are at the hospital,' said the other ambulance man, who was beginning to know the Ruggles household. 'You'll like to see them, won't you?' Jo only scowled at him and screamed louder 'I won't go, I tell you. I won't!' Mrs Ruggles was at her wits' end and the men were getting tired of waiting. Suddenly one of them picked up the blanket from the floor, rolled Jo round in it like a sausage – only the tip of his nose sticking out – and the next thing he knew he was inside the ambulance and a nurse was *un*rolling him!

'I *won't* go to hospital,' he wailed, as soon as his mouth was free of the blanket. 'I haven't got measles – I've got pendy-citis and you can have it at home!' 'Pendy-citis?' said the nurse, tucking the blanket round his neck. 'So that's it, is it; well, well, we'll soon cure that – quicker than at home, too!'

Jo stopped wailing. 'Will you?' he sniffed – 'and quicker than measles?'

'Oh, much quicker,' said the nurse.

'Then I'll come,' said Jo kindly. 'But what,' he added after a pause, 'what would you do if I got measles, too?'

'Well, we cure good boys very quickly,' said the nurse. 'Of course, bad boys who scream and things like that, take longer.'

'I'm a good boy,' said Jo virtuously, 'but I can't stay long because of the Isle of Wight.'

The nurse looked at him curiously and decided Jo was a bad case, but she only said, 'I'm sure you're a very good boy and not one of the screamy sort at all.' And when the ambulance drew up at the hospital and the men came to lift Jo out she told them what a good boy she'd got inside. They both laughed.

'Come out better than he went in, then,' one of them remarked.

Jo scowled at them each in turn. But he smiled to himself. He knew better!

CHAPTER TWO

Ways and Means

LILY ROSE and Peg recovered very quickly, but Jo was not so lucky. For several days he was, as Mrs Ruggles described it, 'Real Bad', and on one alarming morning she was suddenly summoned to the hospital. She went off in a great flutter, leaving Kate with instructions to take William to the park, and the Monday morning wash Here, There, and Everywhere!

Kate, left alone with William and the washing, felt very melancholy and immediately decided Jo must be about to die! Putting William (who had never ceased to wail since Mrs Ruggles left the house) into his push-chair, and successfully quieting him with a large slice of bread and jam, she set forth at a great pace – *not* to the park, however, but towards the middle of the town, never stopping until she reached a small shop at the far end of the High Street. Here, in a gloomy window devoted to tombstones of every description, urns, weeping angels, and wreaths of artificial flowers, discreet, black-framed notices announced, 'Funerals Furnished Throughout'; 'Mourning Orders Promptly Executed'; 'Wreaths Procured In Half an Hour.'

It was a depressing display, and before Kate had stood there very long, trying to decide between the merits of the various tombstones and the beauties of wax or granite wreaths, she found herself beginning to weep bitterly. Oh dear! this was dreadful – crying in Otwell High Street! She gave a big sniff and began desperately to search for her handkerchief. First in one sleeve, then in the other; then her knicker legs; inside her belt; down her front – it was nowhere! She gave another sniff and at that moment

the door of the shop slowly opened, and a very elegant
gentleman dressed entirely in black (as no doubt befitted
his gloomy calling), and with a face which somehow reminded Kate of one of the wax flowers in the window,

bent towards her, his head slightly on one side, and, gently
rubbing his hands together, inquired, in a hushed whisper,
'whether there was any way in which he could help her
today?' Kate rubbed her eyes, gave another sniff, took
one further look at the elegant, waxy-faced gentleman;

then, seizing the handle of the push-chair, set off at a furious pace up the street, bumping William straight into the first pedestrian they met!

'Mum-Mum!' cried William, joyfully waving the remains of his bread and jam, '*Mum-Mum*!'

Sure enough it was Mrs Ruggles *and back from the hospital already*! . . . Jo . . . ?

'Whatever are you doing-of up here!' she exclaimed, 'and William with his face all over jam – I never seen such a sight! Didn't I tell you to take him straight to the park? – you aren't no more to be trusted than a baby; and what're you cryin' for?' she added, giving Kate a little shake. 'Are you hurt or summat?'

Kate shook her head. 'No,' she said at last, between a couple of *very* large sniffs. 'No, I'm not hurt; it . . . it were just . . . just that fu . . . funeral shop – I b . . . been looking at a wreath for Jo!' And suddenly she began to cry again, harder than ever!

'Wreath!' exclaimed Mrs Ruggles, '*Wreath?* Why, whatever will you think on next? – you surely are a strange child and no mistake! Jo's all right – he was better again afore I got there – just worritin' over some nonsense at school and makin' hisself worse – they thought as I might know what it was but they wouldn't let me see him above a second and I couldn't make head nor tail of it – summat to do with the Isle of Wight – *You* don't happen to know nothing about it, I suppose?'

Kate shook her head. 'Well, I told him the teacher's writing a letter to say everything's all right – whatever on earth it is,' continued Mrs Ruggles, 'and he settled down nice. (I'll have to go along to the school this afternoon and see as she *do* write it or the fat'll be in the fire!) Matron says he'll be over the worst in a day or two now if he stops this fussing, and Lily Rose and Peg'll be home next week.

"Wreath" indeed! It's not a wreath the child'll be want-ing but a square meal from the look of him! Here, take this handkerchief and dry your face and then give it me back to clean up William – the idea of my baby going about the town all jammy – don't you never *think*?'

'I *was* thinking,' answered Kate, giving a final sniff and handing back the handkerchief, 'but about Jo more than William. Coo! Mum, I *am* glad he's not going to die!'

'Well, no one ever said he was as I knows of,' replied Mrs Ruggles dryly, 'and suppose you tries thinkin' of one thing at a time in future,' she added, licking a corner of the handkerchief and giving a final scour round William's mouth. 'There! Now can I trust you to take him *straight* to the park and look after him proper while I gets back to my washing, for I'm all behind like the cow's tail this morning, or are you going to go off dreamin' of funerals and wreaths and suchlike and push him straight into the first person you meets?'

Kate looked surprised. 'Funerals and wreaths' – why, she'd stopped thinking of them *minutes* ago – she was busy now planning a tea-party for Lily Rose and Peg to cele-brate their return home . . . Kipper-paste-and-chocolate-biscuits? . . . No . . . Kipper-paste-and-an-ice-brick-each? . . . *No* . . . Kipper-paste *and* an-ice-brick-each *and* chocolate-biscuits . . . Or perhaps. . . .

'Did you hear what I said?' asked Mrs Ruggles sharply.

'Yes, I heard; Mum! Listen! How about a tea-party for Lily Rose and Peg when they come home . . . kipper-paste and ice-bricks and . . .' Mrs Ruggles' reply was to take the handle of the push-chair herself. William, she decided, in spite of the lack of fresh air, would be better at home in the back yard that morning!

Lily Rose came home first. Always a stout child, she

now appeared almost square and Mrs Ruggles remarked that no one could say as she'd been *starved*, anyway; and her estimation of hospitals, which was low, rose somewhat in consequence.

Lily Rose was full of importance as well as good food. She had been one of the older children at the hospital and during her convalescence had assisted with some of the dusting, brass-cleaning, and the making of beds. She was soon instructing Mrs Ruggles in the correct performance of these duties.

'A *little* Brasso does better than a lot, Mum,' she remarked, watching her mother labouring at the door-bell and knocker the day after her return. And presently, upstairs, helping with the bed-making, she explained how important it was that the button-ends of the pillow-cases should all face in the same direction – away from the door, while the sheets should be turned over and tucked in at a neat angle at the corners of the bed – if they must be tucked in at all – but, of course, the *proper* way to make a bed was to tuck in neither sheets nor blankets, but fold both neatly back a few inches from where one's feet came! As to dusting . . . ! Well, of course, what they *really* needed in the kitchen was rounded corners so that the dust didn't stick, though even so, with coal fires . . . and how about Mum and Dad starting to save up for an 'electric'?

'Now listen to me, my girl!' said Mrs Ruggles, who at first had been faintly amused but was now beginning to get annoyed. 'I dusted, cleaned, and made beds, long afore you was born – or thought of for that matter. I've had no complaints about the results so far, and I'm not goin' to start receivin' of 'em now. If you think I've time to see whether the pillow-cases has their backs or their faces or whatever it is to the door or no, and your Dad's going to sleep in a bed with his feet stickin' out uncovered, you'd

best think again! All this here's all right in hospitals and
suchlike where it's all on the rules and part of the trim-
mings, but in an ordinary, human home it's out of place.
You remember that. And the idea we should save up and
put in the electric! You'd best realize it's savin' up for
doctors' and chemists' bills we've got to be afore we
thinks of anything else. Peg and Jo's got to be fed up with
malt-and-oil when they comes out, and Jo's that pulled
down the doctor says as six weeks in the country'll barely
set him up – though where it's to be goodness alone knows,
for it's not as if we'd any relaytives as was any use and could
take him in – why, I shouldn't be surprised if your Dad
didn't have to use nearly the whole of the Pig Money . . .
and you goes talkin' about savin' for an electric!'

Lily Rose felt crushed. When there was talk of touching
the Pig Money it always meant things were in a bad way,
while nearly the *whole* of the Pig Money . . . ! !

For as many years as she could remember Mr Ruggles
had talked about keeping a pig, but until quite recently
the idea had always been firmly discouraged by his wife.
Their back yard was already overcrowded, and the
neighbours, if not the sanitary inspector, would most
certainly object, while their allotment, out London Road
way, was cultivated to the last inch – there was hardly
room for another cabbage – much less a pig-sty! The only
thing would have been to rent another or larger allotment
and put a sty on that. Renting two allotments, however,
or even a larger one, was a costly business – to say nothing
of buying both pig and sty – and no sooner had Mr Ruggles
put by a little money in the old cocoa-tin which was his
savings bank, than something not allowed for in the weekly
budget would occur. A relative would die and a wreath or
perhaps a black tie must be bought; a saucepan would
start to leak beyond repair and have to be replaced; or the

children would be extra hard on their boots and shoes and the visits to the little shop round the corner for soles and heels and 'tips' be even more than usually frequent! Or one of them would fall down, get a cold or a sore throat and sixpennyworth of something have to be procured from the chemist's! Out would come the cocoa-tin and cheerfully, without complaint, but with an inward sigh, Mr Ruggles would hand over the necessary amount to his wife.

During the last year or two, however, the tin had begun to grow a little heavier. Mr Ruggles had had a windfall or two. A little left over from the reward when he found the bundle of notes in his dustbin last year; a little from William's prize at the baby-show. There were little bits of overtime too, and sometimes, in a mood of excessive virtue, Mr Ruggles would refrain from a glass of beer or a smoke and a few pennies would find their way into the tin. Only just before the measles started he had remarked one day he really thought he had almost enough at last! And now most of this precious hoard was going to be used to pay for doctors and chemists and malt-and-oil! No wonder there was nothing for an electric and Mum was fed up!

'Never mind, I'll be earning soon, Mum,' said Lily Rose presently. 'Not much more than six months now!'

'*If* they don't raise the school-leaving age,' replied Mrs Ruggles, 'though I'm not agin it for one. I'd rather do without the little bit you'd get another year and keep you home and fed proper whilst you're still growing.'

'Oh, *Mum*!' cried Lily Rose aghast, 'you wouldn't – not *really*! Why, I'm just *living* till I'm fifteen!'

'Well, you live and let live and get on with the dusting – even if the corners in the kitchen aren't round,' said Mrs Ruggles dryly.

And Lily Rose, who, as I said at the beginning of this

story, was a considerate girl on the whole, seized a duster
and set to work with a will.

A week later Mrs Ruggles fetched Peg and Jo home
from the hospital. 'And no one could say as *they* looks as if
they'd been overfed!' she declared to Mr Ruggles that
evening. Mr Ruggles said no they couldn't and it was a
pity Lily Rose couldn't spare a pound or two for each of
them. Mrs Ruggles agreed and said well she hoped the
malt-and-oil as the doctor had ordered would soon set
them up.

'Come along,' she said to them as soon as breakfast was
cleared away the next morning, 'Come and take this nice
malt-and-oil as I got for you at the chemist's yesterday.'
And she opened the cupboard under the dresser and put
the bottle and spoon on the table. Peg and Jo looked a
little depressed; anything from the chemist's sounded
suspiciously like medicine and they'd both had enough
of that!

'Come along, now,' repeated Mrs Ruggles, holding a spoonful out to Jo. 'It's not medicine nor yet oily – more like soft toffee, Mr Preston told me' (she did not, however, mention that the chemist had also said that though some children loved it, others could not be induced to touch it!) Jo felt encouraged; he took a taste – it *was* like toffee! He took a second – a bigger one this time, then a third; finally he licked the spoon all round, back and front. 'More, please, Mum!' he demanded.

Mrs Ruggles was delighted. Thank Heaven he liked it! Now for Peg. Peg approved even more than Jo – in fact she almost wept when Mrs Ruggles refused them both second helpings, screwed up the bottle, and put it away 'till next time'.

Well, that was one problem settled and she wished the more important one of sending Jo (and Peg too, if possible, the doctor had said yesterday) away for a change of air could be as easily arranged. If *only* they had some useful relaytives in the country! Mrs Ruggles began to go over a list of her own and Mr Ruggles's as she washed up the breakfast things. There was 'Grannie' – her mother – old Mrs Moss, crippled with rheumatism poor soul and living – well, you couldn't rightly call it country – nor yet town either for that matter. What *was* it they called them places? – suburbs – that was it; in a suburb. The trains ran past the house at the back and the trams in front; there was a gasworks at the end of the street, and although it was a penny ride to the centre of the town and they was building a nice recreation ground on the dust-dumps opposite, you couldn't rightly call it real country – not much better than Otwell, come to that, and Grannie with her rheumatics ... no, that was no use!

Then there was Gert – her only sister, married to a signalman and living in a big town up North ... no use

either. Her three brothers? Jack, 'somewhere abroad' –
written home exactly twice these last eight years! Fred?
Well, Fred lived in the country it was true; earned good
money, too, from all accounts – though what his job was
she'd never rightly heard. But Fred's wife! A good-for-
nothing young woman if ever there was one, while as to
their house – a new council one, too – no better than a pig-
sty – she wouldn't send her children there if they paid to
have them! That left only Albert, her youngest brother,
and where Albert was nobody knew and, after that little
affair he'd had with the police a while back, nobody liked
to inquire! Anyway Albert wasn't married and had no
home to offer children. 'A poor lot!' muttered Mrs Ruggles to herself, seizing a saucepan and scouring it vigorously.
What about Jo's folk? His mother as had passed away
afore they was married, poor dear – Ah, she'd have been
the one and no mistake! A wonderful woman from all
accounts (a fact which Mr Ruggles was rather too frequently given to asserting); lived in the country too; Mrs
Ruggles sighed. There were the Charlie Ruggles of course,
who'd given them such a good time in London last
Whitsun Bank Holiday. *They'd* have been all right, but
there, London was no good. She went rapidly over a list
of her husband's remaining relatives and decided that,
with the exception of his eldest sister who had died last
year, they were an even poorer lot than her own! And
some people had *such* useful relaytives, she thought as she
finished the saucepan and began to scrub down the sink!

She happened to remark on this fact and the difficulty
of finding a suitable place to send Peg and Jo to her friend,
the fat cook at Mrs Beaseley's in Sycamore Road, when
she called for the laundry next morning.

'Well, if that isn't a co-in*ci*dence!' exclaimed the cook.
'Only this morning I had a letter from my sister what lives

in Kent – Mrs Wildgoose – you've heard me speak of her?
– saying as the children she usually has there of a summer
won't be coming this year and asking me when I was
thinking of taking my holiday as she'd have a room and
all to spare. It so happens,' she continued, 'as I've
arranged to go to my brother's in Birmingham. Now how'd
it be if you was to arrange to send your two to *her*? She
don't charge much for the little "Holiday Children" as
they calls 'em – five shillings a week I think it is, and she'd
do yours for the same if I said as you was a friend of mine.
She's real fond of children tho' she's none of her own and
she'd look after 'em well. Keeps the village Public her
husband does. "The Dew Drop Inn" they calls it. Nice
old house it is too, and you couldn't wish for a prettier
village – not so very far from here neither, tho' it's a bad
train service I'll allow. You think it over, Mrs Ruggles,
and I'll find out definite what she'd take 'em for. The fare?
Funny now, I don't seem to remember exact – something
round about ten or eleven shillings I think – not more I'm
certain – but I'll find out for sure when I writes and let
you know.'

It certainly did seem a co-incidence. Mrs Ruggles
thought it over all the way home, doing little sums in her
head as she went; in fact she became so absorbed in her
arithmetic that she forgot all about the traffic lights at the
cross-roads near One End Street and was only saved from
being run over by a large lorry by a kindly gentleman who
grabbed her coat just as she was about to step off the pavement right under its front wheels! For a moment Mrs
Ruggles felt quite faint! The lorry-driver's language, however, soon revived her and she told herself to be more
careful in future. Had she not told Kate only the other day
to think of one thing at a time, and here was she attempting to deal with half a dozen at the same moment? She

did a few more little calculations when she reached home, and that evening, when the children had gone to bed, she talked the whole matter over with her husband.

Mr Ruggles said slowly he was not *agin* it – not if Mrs Wildgoose's terms were as reasonable as her sister had said, though he'd have preferred as she didn't keep a public-house. The railway fares, he was afraid, were going to be a bit of an item, for although Peg and Jo would travel for half price, Mrs Ruggles or someone would have to take and fetch them, and there was a pound or so gone bust straight away as you might say. Mrs Ruggles nodded.

'I'm afraid it's going to mean a lot of the Pig Money, dearie,' she said sympathetically. Mr Ruggles sighed and said it looked rather like it, but he added heroically that Peg and Jo were, after all, more important than a pig.

A few days later Mrs Beaseley's cook called in on her day out; the fare, she said, was nine and tenpence return and her sister had written to say she would be pleased to take in Peg and Jo and look after them *proper* for five shillings a week each, any day after next Monday Mrs Ruggles cared to send them. No, she wouldn't come in for a cup of tea, thanks . . . yes, she'd had the measles but still you never knew. . . .

Mrs Ruggles thanked her very much and said no, you never did, and she'd tell Mr Ruggles about the fares and all soon's he came in. . . . And when the cook had gone she drank an extra cup of tea herself to assist in the telling, for, Pig Money or no, she reckoned those fares was going to be a 'bit of an item' and no mistake!

That evening, as soon as supper had been cleared away, and the children were all safely out of the way in bed, Mr Ruggles sat down at the kitchen table, produced a small stub of pencil, and spreading out the remains of an old paper bag, settled down to do some arithmetic. Now arithmetic was not Mr Ruggles' strong point, nor, for that matter, was writing, and he was a long time about his calculations.

'Fare. Mother. Going,' he wrote, first moistening the stump of pencil between his lips, and holding the paper bag down firmly with his left hand, '9s. 10d.'

> Fare. Mother. Coming Back, 9s. 10d.
> Fare. Peg. Going, 2s. 5½d.
> Fare. Jo. Going, 2s. 5½d.

At this point the grain of the kitchen table seemed to be coming through the paper bag rather badly, so Mr Ruggles got up and fetched a couple of sheets of the *Otwell Gazette* to put under it, then moistening his pencil again he set to work afresh.

> Fare. Peg. Coming Back, 2s. 5½d.
> Fare. Jo. Coming Back, 2s. 5½d. he wrote.

Then:

> Board. Peg. Six Weeks, £1 10s.
> Board. Jo. Six Weeks, £1 10s.

After this Mr Ruggles paused for some time. He seemed to be thinking deeply.

'EXTERAS?' he wrote at last, and making a really *very* good question-mark he regarded it with pardonable pride for a moment. Then drawing a rather shaky line under the column of figures, he prepared to add them up. This took a long time because Mr Ruggles counted everything on his fingers, very slowly, and often two or three times over in order to make sure there was no mistake.

'Four pounds, nine shillings and sixpence, Rosie,' he announced to his wife at last, 'just for the fares and keep.

Comes to a bit less than I thought for, but what about exteras – I've wrote down exteras – there'll be some things wanted I suppose? Shall I say five shillings for the exteras?'

Mrs Ruggles put her hand on his shoulder. 'I'm afraid five shillings won't go far there, dearie,' she said gently. 'That there malt-and-oil's expensive stuff; a half-crown bottle don't last no time, not with two of 'em takin' it three times a day; it'll be summat like ten shillings for that alone and then there's boots and shoes to be mended, afore they goes – I can manage the clothes somehow I think; and we'll have to let Mrs Wildgoose have a few shillings in case there's anything she might have to get for 'em. I'm afraid it's going to come to over a fiver, Dad,' said Mrs Ruggles almost in a whisper.

Mr Ruggles said nothing, but he sat rather still for a moment or two; then he stood up, pushed back his chair and went slowly upstairs. He took the Pig Money tin from its hiding-place in an old boot under his bed, and carefully counted out five pounds ten shillings in half-crowns, shillings, and sixpences, and the new-fangled 'three-pennies' which weighed a lot but meant so little. The tin felt strangely light when he put it back in its hiding-place again and he sighed deeply. It would take a great many pipes and glasses of beer and bits of overtime to replace that little hoard. The possibility of ever buying a pig seemed very remote indeed to poor Mr Ruggles that evening.

CHAPTER THREE

Kate Has a Plan

WHEN Peg and Jo heard they were going to the country they became wildly excited and Mrs Ruggles declared they looked better at the very idea. She had expected all the other children – especially the twins – to be envious but, to her surprise, with the exception of Kate, they took the matter very calmly. The twins were much occupied with each other these days, for ever whispering in corners

or suddenly pinching each other and bursting into wild fits of giggles. 'Up to some mischief,' Mrs Ruggles said to herself, and determined to keep a sharp eye on them. As for Lily Rose, she declared that a week, much less six weeks, spent looking at 'silly cows and fields' would send her 'bats'; indeed, the very thought of it made her feel 'goosey all over'!

No, it was Kate who was the envious one! Peg and Jo going to the country! And not just for the day either, but to *stay – a whole six weeks in the country – real* country; country she, Kate, had been wanting to go to for as long as she could remember; where it was so important she, of all the family – the one who was 'going on the land' (as soon as she'd got a scholarship to that Agricultural College place she was always dreaming about) – *should* go! Oh dear! it did seem hard. Of course, Peg and Jo had been ill and she hadn't ... and for the first time Kate began to regret having escaped measles. Was there, she began to wonder, a hope, a tiny chance, she or the twins or William might yet develop it – just two more days' quarantine to go? Oh, if only *she* could! She began to wonder if she was really quite well. She shook her head violently to see if it was inclined to ache at all, but she only felt rather giddy and that soon wore off. She peered at herself in the glass for spots but all she could see appeared to be an extra large crop of freckles. She thought she detected a slight ache in one of her legs but it turned out to be due to an old bruise. As for William and the twins, they had never looked better. Was there *anything* to be done? Could she possibly catch cold somehow? A cold might perhaps lead to measles – 'start them off like?' And although she felt somehow that it was rather a wicked thing to try to get a cold on purpose (as indeed it was!), Kate decided she was going to try. She had just *got* to get to the country somehow!

She thought hard for a bit, and after tea when the others were all out of the way, and Mrs Ruggles busy upstairs with William, she took off her stockings, held them under the cold tap in the kitchen for a minute or two, then wrung them out and put them on again. Damp stockings 'dried on you', she had always heard, were the one thing absolutely certain sure to give you a really *shocking* cold! By the time she went to bed they would be dry; next morning she would, she hoped, awake with a *streaming* cold, and measles no doubt would follow immediately!

But alas! she woke up feeling remarkably well – not even the tiniest hint of a cold, and, in spite of this disappointment, in the highest spirits. Time, however, was slipping by; only twenty-four hours now to go! She must think of something else, and think quickly too!

It was in the middle of breakfast that the great idea came to her, and as soon as she had helped with the washing up and seen her mother busy getting in coals, she dashed out of the house and round to the next street where her friend Patricia Watkins's mother kept a newspaper and stationery shop. Patricia had gone off to school, having escaped measles, but Mrs Watkins was in the shop leisurely flicking over the stock with a feather-brush and chirruping to the canary in the back room as she dusted.

'Morning, Kate,' she cried. 'Some days since we've seen any of you – still all right, then? – I was only saying to Patricia this morning as your quarantine must be about up – can't be much longer now, surely?'

'No, Mrs Watkins, there's only tomorrow to go now – unless one of us gets it before then – there's still the twins and William haven't had it, besides me,' replied Kate.

'Only tomorrow to go? Oh, you'll surely be all right now,' said Mrs Watkins. 'Come for a paper?'

'No, Mrs Watkins, not today. I've come . . .' Kate hesitated a little, 'I've come to buy something; and I'm afraid I haven't got enough money to pay for it,' she added 'but could you possibly wait till I go back to school and gets my dinner money again, do you think? I can't ask for any at home because it's a secret.'

Mrs Watkins laughed. 'You mustn't go buying things with your dinner money,' she said, 'or you'll be getting thinner than ever! What is it you want? Is it something very expensive?'

'Not *very*,' replied Kate, 'it's . . . it's just a bottle of ink – *red* ink – just a *tiny* one – I think they're threepence.'

'Whatever kind of a secret can it be!' said Mrs Watkins. 'All right – don't you worry,' she added quickly, noticing the look of alarm on Kate's face, 'I won't say nothing about it. But you needn't buy a bottle – there's one here open – Patricia's had it for something – you can let me have it back some time if you don't want to use it all.'

'Oh, I only want a *very* little!' said Kate, 'of course I'll bring it back. Thank you *ever* so much, Mrs Watkins – I know you won't tell.' And she took the bottle which Mrs Watkins put in a bag and wrapping it round carefully with her handkerchief to hide it completely, she ran back to One End Street.

At the front door she stopped to listen and make sure Mrs Ruggles was still out at the back, then she stole quietly upstairs, paused for a moment to listen again, then stealthily turned the door-handle of her mother's room and went inside. A second later she was out, carrying Mrs Ruggles's imitation ivory hand-mirror, and tiptoeing across the little landing she opened the door of her own room and went in, shutting it *very* quietly behind her!

Once safely inside Kate put the mirror and the bottle of ink down carefully on the dressing-table and, with many anxious pauses to listen lest Mrs Ruggles should take it into her head to come upstairs, opened a drawer and took out her school pencil-box from which she extracted two small paint-brushes. Next she unwrapped the bottle of ink, took out the cork and selecting the smaller of the paint-brushes, sucked it into a neat point and dipped it gently in the ink. She then picked up the hand-mirror from the dressing-table and gazing earnestly into it began very slowly, and with great precision, to decorate her face and forehead with small, red spots! !

It was surprising how effective that red ink was! And what fun it was putting on the spots! But Kate was an artist. 'Mustn't overdo it,' she said to herself, and putting one on her chin for luck she corked up the bottle and hid it

under some stockings in a drawer, put away the paint-brushes, and sat down on the bed, fanning herself with a piece of old newspaper to make the ink dry quickly. It took a long time and Kate was in terror lest at any moment Mrs Ruggles should appear to make the beds or dust. At last, after what seemed an interminable time, she finally decided she was dry, and opening the door *very* quietly and taking a final look in the mirror, she returned it to her mother's room.

But now, although well-pleased with her efforts, Kate

suddenly began to feel rather nervous – all hot-and-cold-like! Suppose Mum wasn't took in after all, and, awful thought, even if *she* was, were the doctor and the hospital going to be? She'd done it all in such a hurry she really hadn't considered this possibility very carefully, and now it seemed to her extremely unlikely that they would be. Well, it was too late now – she'd have to chance it ... Coo! she did feel nervous – quite shaky! Was it – could it be the measles – the wet stockings 'working' after all? Kate's spirits rose a little. She crept downstairs, hesitated a moment outside the kitchen door, then, screwing up her courage, opened it and walked boldly in.

Mrs Ruggles had come in from the yard and was busy at the sink, her back to the door.

'That you, Kate?' she cried, filling a saucepan under the tap as she spoke, 'wherever have you been to? – I sent Lily Rose to look for you and she couldn't find you no-wheres; I've had to send her with the little ones to the park, the twins is off somewheres and there's some collars waiting to be took round to the Vicarage – they're wantin' 'em this morning particular. Just you pop off with 'em now, quick; the parcel's there on the dresser.'

'All right, Mum,' said Kate slowly, but she didn't move. This was *dreadful*! She couldn't go out all spotty! Why, oh why, didn't Mum turn round and see! She stood waiting for a moment or two. But Mrs Ruggles had dived under the sink for a bag of potatoes and was busy peeling them.

'Get on, do!' she cried presently, but still without turning round. 'I never knew such a child for dawdling!'

There was no help for it; she'd have to go. But she must hide the spots – someone would notice for sure and then the whole plan might be spoilt! Kate thought quickly. A cap wouldn't be any use – her forehead would show too much. A hat was the thing! And taking a big straw one belonging to Lily Rose off a hook on the door, she pulled it well down over her forehead, took the parcel from the dresser and set forth. She kept well on the shadowy side of the street, her head bent down, but there were few people about, most of the inhabitants of One End Street being out or busy with their housework. The same seemed to apply to the Vicarage and she put the parcel inside the open back door, rang the bell, and fled down the drive without seeing anyone.

It was a very hot day and by the time Kate neared home again the hat pressing tightly down on her forehead was almost unbearable. As soon as she turned into One End Street (which still appeared deserted) she pulled it off.

Just as she was approaching No. 4, however, the door opened and out came Mrs 'Nosey-Parker' Smith to shake a mat!

Like all the Ruggles children, or, for that matter, almost every child in One End Street, Kate detested Mrs Smith. She seemed always ready to criticize or to have some unpleasant remark to make. Today was no exception.

'Good morning, Kate Ruggles,' she remarked, giving the mat a good bang against the kerb and raising a cloud of dust half across the street. 'How's that little brother of yours – shocking ill he looks to me – and Peg – she don't look much better neither? I seen 'em go by with Lily Rose a little while back. My word! what a big girl she's gettin' – measles don't seem to have done *her* no harm; but all that fat's no good to her – not healthy at all – I wonder your Ma don't do something about it.' And she gave the mat quite a vicious shake.

'You all right?' she continued as Kate skipped aside to escape another cloud of dust. 'Yes, you keep out of the way – we don't want none of your measle germs here! Oh yes,

you may be out of quarantine tomorrow *but you're not today*!
I've known many a one go down at the last minute,' she
added, giving the mat a final bang before throwing it
down inside her door.

'*Have* you, Mrs Smith?' asked Kate hopefully, drawing
nearer again. 'Really! *Many?*'

Mrs Smith bent down and kicked the mat into place
with her foot. '*Many!*' she replied grimly as she straightened herself up; and she stood in the doorway, her arms
folded, looking disapprovingly down at Kate. '*Many!*' she
repeated. Suddenly her expression changed. She bent
forward (evidently forgetting all about germs!) and
grabbed hold of Kate, peering intently at her through her
glasses.

'My word!' she exclaimed. '*My word* – if you ain't got it
on you now I do believe! *Covered* you are! Whatever is your
Ma thinking of to be letting you run about the streets,
giving of it left and right to everyone! Disgraceful I calls it
– she ought to be learnt better. Here, you come along home
at once!' And seizing Kate by the arm she half-pulled,
half-dragged her up the street and banged loudly and
wrathfully on the door of No. 1.

Mrs Ruggles put her head out of an upstairs window.
'What is it?' she inquired; then, seeing Mrs Smith
clutching Kate by the arm – 'Mornin', Mrs Smith –
what's the matter *this* time – what's Kate been doing –
something as she shouldn't?'

'Well, the child's hardly to blame I suppose,' replied
Mrs Smith primly, 'but I'm surprised at you, Rosie
Ruggles – indeed I am – letting of her run about in the
state she's in – spreadin' measles right and left – you'll
have the health authorities after you if you don't take care
– and rightly too! Just look at her!'

Mrs Ruggles banged down the window. She came

clattering downstairs, duster in hand, and flung open the front door.

By this time Kate had managed to wrench herself free from Mrs Smith. She was hot and breathless with the struggle; her hair was all over her face, her frock split on the shoulder, while a hole in the knee of her stocking was rapidly laddering down to the ankle. She pushed her hair out of her eyes as her mother opened the door. Heavens! What *had* happened? Her hand was all over red! The 'spots'? The precious 'spots'? Alas! 'the spots' had 'run'!!

'Funny measles, Mrs Smith!' said Mrs Ruggles a few minutes later, holding up her duster which she had used to scrub Kate's face. 'Them glasses of yours don't seem to help you much; I should see about getting some new ones if I were you!' And pushing Kate before her into the house, she slammed the door.

'Interferin' old parrot!' she muttered.

As for Kate, she sat down on the nearest chair, buried her face in her hands and burst into tears.

'Whatever is the matter with you now!' exclaimed Mrs Ruggles sharply. 'Regular cry-baby you're gettin' these days – slightest thing and you're weeping! Get up and stop acting silly at once and tell me how you come all over that red – it's not off you proper yet!'

It took Kate a long time to stop crying and tell, between many sniffs, what she had meant to do. It was all so terribly disappointing, while the fact that Mrs 'Nosey-Parker' Smith, of all people, should bave been the one to spoil everything seemed to make matters even worse. Mrs Ruggles, however, was too amused to be really angry.

'You beat all, you do', she said when Kate finally came to an end. 'Whatever you'll think on next I don't know! You've took Mrs Smith in fine – I'll say that – your Dad

won't half be amused when he comes home! All the same,'
she added, 'you're a naughty girl; there's illness enough
in the world without people making of it up. When *I* were a
little girl,' she continued impressively, 'I used to be told
as punishment always comes. If you *should* get the measles
afore tomorrow it'll be only what you *deserves* – and there
won't be no country holiday attached, so don't you think
it.' And with this comforting assurance Mrs Ruggles
picked up her duster and returned to her work upstairs.

The rest of the day, however, passed uneventfully and
Kate, William, and the twins all awoke well and smiling
next morning. Mrs Ruggles said she felt like hanging out
a Union Jack, while Mr Ruggles said *he* felt like a 'cele-
bration' – and returned at dinner-time with two large
bottles of beer!

The next day a letter came from Mrs Wildgoose
suggesting, 'if convenient', Peg and Jo should go to her
the following Wednesday.

Kate found it dreadfully hard not to mind when Mrs
Ruggles began mending and tidying up their clothes and
sometimes she could hardly bear to be in the house. Going
out, however, was nearly as bad because it meant passing
Mrs Smith's door, and Kate would run like a rabbit every
time she had to do so. If only she could rush off to school
and be away most of the day, but the holidays had begun
now and that meant nearly three weeks at home!

On Saturday morning Mrs Ruggles insisted on her
helping to carry the laundry basket to Mrs Beaseley's and
although Kate looked hard at the other side of the road as
they passed No. 4, she felt certain, somehow, that 'Nosey
Parker' was glaring at them from behind her kitchen
curtains! And when they reached Mrs Beaseley's if Mrs
Ruggles didn't have to go and tell the whole story to her

friend the cook! They were both laughing heartily while Kate was beginning to feel more and more miserable, when Mrs Beaseley herself, who was doing some gardening happened to pass the open kitchen window.

'Good morning, Mrs Ruggles!' she cried, putting her head inside, 'you sound very merry in there! . . . Is that Kate I see – *she* doesn't look very cheerful! Is she one of the children who's getting over measles and going to Mrs Wildgoose's – she certainly looks as though she could do with some country air?'

It was the last straw! Kate's eyes filled with tears. Oh dear! Mum was right! She was getting a regular cry-baby and no mistake; but why, oh why, should Mrs Beaseley say that, of all things!

Mrs Beaseley noticed the tears but she was very tactful.

'How about a cup of tea, Mrs Ruggles?' she said hastily before Mrs Ruggles had time to reply, 'and perhaps Kate would like to come out and help me pick some gooseberries while Bertha gets it for you?'

Mrs Ruggles said thank you – a cup of tea was just what she *would* like, and Kate hurriedly dried her eyes – thank goodness she'd remembered her handkerchief today – and followed Mrs Beaseley into the kitchen garden. But, try as she might, the tears *would* come and very soon Mrs Beaseley had the whole story out of her.

'Don't cry any more now,' she said kindly, 'and I'll see what I can do. Who is going to take Peg and Jo when they go next week?'

'Mum is,' replied Kate.

'Do you think she'd let you go with them instead – stay with them too, perhaps, and bring them home?'

Kate shook her head. 'I don't think she would,' she replied, 'she'd never trust them with me – she says I *dream* – and . . . and there wouldn't be any money for me to stay too – as well as go there and back,' she added, getting very pink.

'Well, we'll see what can be done,' said Mrs Beaseley. 'You stay here and pick me that basket full of gooseberries while I go and have a talk with your mother,' and she disappeared in the direction of the house.

Oh! wasn't Mrs Beaseley marvellous! Oh! if only she *could* do something! Overcome with emotion Kate sat down among the gooseberry bushes.

Mrs Beaseley seemed gone a long time; was it a good sign, Kate wondered? She sat straining her eyes in the direction of the house, completely forgetting about picking any gooseberries! Suddenly she became aware of the empty basket beside her. She jumped to her feet and hurriedly began to pick, scratching her hands considerably and including almost as many leaves as gooseberries in her anxiety to fill the basket quickly.

She picked all the gooseberries off two bushes, the basket was full; still Mrs Beaseley did not come. What *could* be happening? Kate began to feel almost sick with suspense!

'It'll come to less than your own fare, Mrs Ruggles,' Mrs Beaseley was saying, 'and I'll give you something for her keep. Let her go – *do*. I'm sure she's quite to be trusted to take the children, and she really *does* look as if she'd be better for some country air, and there's still nearly three weeks of the holidays she tells me, so it would only mean her missing about two weeks of school if they went at once.'

'I'd like her to go, of course,' said Mrs Ruggles slowly, 'but she's missed near half a term's schooling as it is, so I don't know what they'd say – her with a scholarship and all. But it isn't that so much,' she went on, '**it**'s whether I could trust her with the little ones – I don't really know as

I *could* – she's a real dreamy child Kate is,' she added mournfully.

'Those sort of people can be very practical sometimes, you know, Mrs Ruggles,' said Mrs Beaseley. 'Especially when they feel they've someone dependent on them. And it's an easy journey – only one change and you could get the guard to see to them. Look! Here's something towards her board – just think it over – there's the telephone, I must go,' and putting down a pound note on the kitchen table, Mrs Beaseley hurried away.

'Well, I don't hardly know what to say,' said Mrs Ruggles, sitting down and turning to the cook. 'I really don't. I don't feel as I *could* trust Kate to get 'em there safe – and I don't like taking the money, for all Mrs Beaseley's so kind!'

'Well, you knows best, Mrs Ruggles,' replied the cook, 'but I'd chance it if I was you. That child looks real washed out, indeed she does, and look how she wants to go, painting her face and all! Oh dear! that did make me laugh that did!' and the fat cook chuckled. 'One thing I can tell you,' she added, 'it 'ud be a help to my sister to have an older child as well – she'd be useful looking after the little ones.'

By the time Mrs Beaseley came back from the telephone, Mrs Ruggles was almost persuaded.

'What about your husband, Mrs Ruggles?' she asked. 'What would he say?'

'Oh, he'll be for it all right,' replied Mrs Ruggles, fingering the pound note. 'He were all for her going when he heard about the "spots" – it were more a question of the money like with him – he don't know Kate's ways like I does; no, he won't say "no", I'm sure of that.'

'And you won't either?'

Mrs Ruggles hesitated, then she smiled.

'Of course you won't!' cried Mrs Beaseley before Mrs Ruggles could say anything further. 'That's settled then! I'll fetch Kate in and tell her.' And she went off down the kitchen garden.

'I spent a pound note, this morning,' said Mrs Beaseley to her husband at dinner that evening, 'to see a child smile!'

'Rather excessive, wasn't it?' he remarked, putting down his soup spoon and regarding her over the top of his glasses in his best professional manner. (Mr Beaseley was a barrister.)

'Perhaps,' replied his wife absently. She was thinking of Kate's little freckled face grinning from ear to ear – her whole expression one huge beam.

'You see, it was rather an excessive smile!' said Mrs Beaseley.

CHAPTER FOUR

The Journey

To Kate, Peg, and Jo, it really seemed as if the day fixed for going to the country would never come. To Mrs Ruggles, however, it seemed to come far too quickly. There had been a little difficulty with the school authorities about Kate. A doctor's certificate, however, had eventually worked wonders, but it had all caused a good deal of delay; and there *was* so much to be done before they went. Instructions to be written to Mrs Wildgoose; shoes to be soled at the little shop round the corner; clothes to be washed and mended – even some new ones to be made. This consisted chiefly in cutting down old ones and making them up again – and what Mrs Ruggles couldn't do in this direction was hardly worth considering. 'Makes a yard go where three ought, my missis does,' Mr Ruggles would sometimes proudly remark to a neighbour, and really the results sometimes *were* astonishing!

However, by machining until after twelve o'clock one night, and sending notes to some of the more important of her customers to explain that the laundry would be a day late this week, and would they please excuse it, everything was ready in time, and on a glorious sunny morning Mrs Ruggles, Kate, Peg, and Jo actually stood on the platform at Otwell Station awaiting what Jo called 'the country train'.

'And not much time to spare, neither,' remarked Mrs Ruggles, glancing at the station clock as she thankfully put down the bulky suitcase she had carried all the way from One End Street.

The children looked happy and their eyes reflected their happiness according to their dispositions. Kate's dreamy, Jo's bright and excited, and Peg's big with awe and inquiry. Mrs Ruggles, however, looked worried. Could she *really* trust Kate to see 'em there safe? Only one change and the train the same platform . . . still . . . if she'd five shillings to throw away she'd have goed as far as that with 'em, but there it was. . . . She glanced at the clock again – another two minutes and the train would be in. . . . Had they got everything? The paper 'carrier' with the new, large-sized bottle of malt-and-oil, their washing things, and a jumper that simply *refused* to go in the suit-case; Kate's little cardboard attaché-case with a 'surprise' for the journey inside; Peg's bear; the umbrella; yes, it was all there. Mrs Ruggles picked up the bulky suitcase once again – they must have a porter for that, she must tell the guard, and some coppers to give him. Turning to Kate she slipped sixpence into the pocket of her blazer. 'And

mind you don't go dropping them out,' she added when
she had given instructions how and when they were to be
bestowed. 'Nor go off in one of your dreams and forget all
I've told you; just remember as you've got two little
children dependent on you and you'll never forgive yourself if anything should happen to 'em. Is them keys and
the bag with the money and the tickets safe round your
neck? ... don't keep pulling at the ribbon like that or
you'll have 'em off ... and mind what I've said about
door-handles and not putting your head out of the
windows ... and *whatever* you do don't go speaking to no
strangers nor taking food from them – you understands
now?'

Kate nodded solemnly. She felt very important and a
little awed. 'Two little children dependent on her!'

'Don't you worry, Mum,' she said, 'I'll see 'em there
safe all right,' and seizing Jo by the collar she pulled him
farther from the edge of the platform by way of asserting
her authority and impressing her mother. Jo was still
protesting loudly at this treatment when the train came
thundering in. It was a very long one and its final destination was London, a fact, it seemed to Kate, of which the
engine was fully aware, for it swept through the station
with a haughty air, as though it considered stopping
at a place like Otwell-on-the-Ouse greatly beneath its
dignity.

Mrs Ruggles selected a carriage which said, 'No
Smoking', and contained a Nice Quiet-looking Middle-
aged Lady; gave many instructions to the guard to see
they got out at the station where they were to change (and
not the station before or the station after it); counted the
luggage once again, and kissed them all several times.

'Come along, missis, come along!' cried the guard impatiently, 'we're late already. Don't you worry,' he added,

slamming the door after Mrs Ruggles as she jumped
from the carriage, and preparing to wave his flag, 'I'll
see to 'em all right.' A moment later he blew a piercing
blast on his whistle. Three faces, their noses flattened like
squashed button-mushrooms against the window-glass,
peered out; three pairs of hands waved wildly; the
haughty engine shrieked and snorted, and the train
steamed out of the station.

'Now,' said Kate, turning away from the window as
the train curved round a bend, 'you can't see Mum no
more so it's no use looking, and you've got to be very good
and sit quite still till we get to the station where we change.
And she picked up first Peg and bumped her down in a
corner of the carriage, and then Jo. Both protested at this
summary treatment, Jo with his fists, Peg with wails.

'I want to go 'ome. I want my Mum!' she howled. But
Kate was prepared. 'Don't you "but" me,' she said
sternly to Jo, 'or you won't see the surprise I've got in my
case. And you can't go home,' she added, turning to Peg,
'you've only just started; stop crying now and see what
I've got!' And sitting down beside her sister, Kate prepared to open a very small and battered attaché-case. Jo
leant forward; *what* was the surprise? But Kate held the
lid half-shut.

'Are you going to be a good boy or not?' she demanded.

'I *am* good,' replied Jo sulkily, 'if you don't boss me
about.'

'I'm bossing you for your own good,' said Kate primly.
'Sit still now and I'll give you the "surprise",' and she
dived into the case and abstracted a coloured 'comic' and
three large oranges.

'I'll peel the oranges while you look at the pictures,'
she said kindly, and dividing the highly coloured sheets
between them she produced a small pen-knife, and

carefully spreading an old newspaper over her knees for fear her school uniform clothes (which she was only allowed to wear for school and on *very* special occasions) might be hurt, she set to work.

She had been busily engaged for two or three minutes when she suddenly became aware that the Nice Quiet-looking Middle-aged Lady opposite had put down her newspaper and was speaking to her.

'Little girl!'

'Little girl!' – she, Kate Ruggles, aged twelve-and-nearly-nine-weeks!

'Little girl, *must* you eat oranges – the smell is *quite* dreadful! If you *must* eat something I can let you have some chocolate instead.'

Kate looked up in surprise. 'Smell?' Surely no one could possibly object to orange smell! She was about to reply when she remembered Mrs Ruggles's warning. A stranger! And a stranger offering food too! Ah! This was where one was on one's guard! Where one kept one's head!

She looked down again and continued with her peeling operations. There was a pause and then the lady spoke again.

' I'm afraid you didn't hear me,' she said. '*Must* you peel those oranges? – the smell is *frightful*,' and then, after a second or two as Kate made no reply, 'You seem to me a very bad-mannered little girl! All the expensive education you get today doesn't seem to teach you to be polite; you should *answer* strangers when they speak to you. However, if you *won't* stop peeling those disgusting things will you please open the window and at least let some of the smell out of the carriage!'

Oh dear! thought Kate. Now it's the window and I promised I wouldn't touch one! What awful luck! Straight away three things Mum warned me about! And what a horrid lady – my manners are as good as hers – better – I wouldn't say nothing if *she* ate oranges! And what's she know about my education, anyway! And getting very pink Kate bent lower and lower over the newspaper and the peelings. . . .

Two oranges were ready now. Tucking paper handkerchiefs under their chins, and avoiding the lady's eye, Kate handed the fruit to Peg and Jo with instructions not to be 'messy' and returning to her seat began to peel an orange for herself.

But it was too much for the Nice Quiet-looking Middle-aged Lady! She sprang to her feet and, pushing past them, furiously slammed down the window as wide as it would go!

Jo looked at her reproachfully.

'We have to eat oranges,' he said quietly. 'They're full of things called vitimins what's good for your insides. We've just had measles in *our* insides,' he added proudly.

'Hush!' said Kate in a loud whisper. 'You're not to speak to strangers.'

The lady regarded them angrily, each in turn. She seemed very agitated.

'You've "just" had measles did you say!' she exclaimed. 'How long ago may I inquire? Oh, it's scandalous!' she continued, receiving no answer, 'scandalous allowing you to travel – simply scandalous. *How* long is it since you had it?'

'Oh, only just a little time ago,' said Kate, stung at last to reply; 'they're quite all right now,' she added, pointing at Peg and Jo, 'and I haven't even had it!'

'I shouldn't be surprised if you weren't sickening for it now!' said the lady. 'You're very pink. I shall complain to the Railway Company about it!' she added a moment or two later, 'Oh, most certainly I shall complain. Its really *quite* scandalous!'

Peg and Jo gazed at her a moment with round, solemn eyes. They then returned to their oranges. Kate, pinker than ever, gazed out of the window. (She had put her orange back in the attaché-case; with the lady looking on so disapprovingly she did not feel she would be able to enjoy it!) There was silence except for the chugging and clanking noise of the carriage wheels and the squishy sound of orange-sucking. A few minutes later the train slowed down and drew up at a small country station. The lady glanced out of the window, then hurriedly seizing her suitcase and umbrella from the rack, opened the carriage door, got out, and disappeared up the platform. She did not return.

'Well *that's* a good thing!' said Kate presently as a whistle sounded, a porter slammed-to the door and the train steamed on again. 'Now we've got it all to ourselves; and you'd better hurry up with those oranges,' she added, 'because we'll have to get out next stop.'

Peg and Jo needed no further encouragement, but they had only just finished and had their hands and faces wiped (under protest) when the train stopped again and a minute later the guard opened the door, lifted out first Peg (clutching her bear), then Jo, and then the bulky suitcase, leaving Kate to follow with the little one, the umbrella, and the paper carrier containing the precious malt-and-oil. He put Peg and Jo down on a bench with the bulky suitcase beside them.

'Now you all stay here – do you understand?' he said, turning to Kate, 'and the next train *but one* on *this side's* yours – don't you go getting into the next, nor yet one on the other side of the platform or you'll find yourselves at the back of beyond; you see that porter there – I'm telling

him to put the suitcase in for you. Now good-bye – you've
twenty-five minutes to wait – it goes at five to the hour –
so don't go wandering about and getting into mischief.'
And he hurried away. Kate saw him speak a few words to
a porter, indicating them with a backward jerk of his
thumb, and a moment later he had waved his flag, blown
a shrill blast on his whistle, and jumped nimbly on to the
moving train, waving to them until he was a tiny speck in
the far distance. Peg and Jo waved back but Kate felt to do
so was rather babyish and a little beneath her dignity.
Truth to tell she was rather annoyed with the guard for
telling the porter to see to their suitcase for them. She had
looked forward to engaging a porter *herself* – in fact she had
rehearsed the scene several times . . . 'only a small amount
of luggage . . . in the rack I think, please, and the small one
can go on the seat', and bestowing on him the sixpence
Mrs Ruggles had provided for the purpose. She would
still have the thrill of doing this, she supposed, but the
guard was an interfering old man all the same! And did he
really suppose anyone as old as she – anyone twelve-and-
nearly-nine-weeks – was going to remain for twenty-five
minutes sitting on that bench!

'You two stay quiet here for a minute,' she said, putting
down the attaché-case and the umbrella. 'I'm going to
look at something.' And grasping the paper carrier and
feeling if the keys and the bag with the tickets and the
money were safe round her neck, she got up and strolled
a little way down the platform just to show her indepen-
dence.

On the opposite platform was a large, green notice-
board with 'Haywards Heath', the name of the station, on
it in big, imposing white letters.

Kate stood gazing at it for some minutes. Who, she
wondered, was Hayward – and why did he have a Heath?

She stood staring, staring – turning this problem over and over in her mind, when suddenly, 'snap', went one of the handles of the carrier! Out fell the bundle of washing things with a flop, followed by the jar of malt-and-oil with a frightful bump! *Most* surprisingly it was unbroken and went rolling gaily away along the platform. Kate tried to grab it but alas! before she could seize it, it had vanished over the edge, crash, smash, on to the line where it broke into a dozen pieces, malt-and-oil spreading and oozing in every direction over the shiny rails!

Oh, how dreadful! The precious malt-and-oil – an extra large jar, too, to last all the holiday – *a whole 8s. 6d. worth!* What *would* Mum say? and what would Peg and Jo do without it? – probably get ill – get measles again – perhaps die this time – a second attack so soon! Kate's imagination rushed wildly ahead, as she picked up the bundle of washing things and stuffed them back in the damaged carrier.

'What's the matter?' said a voice. 'Been sick on the line?'

Kate turned round. It was the porter. 'Sick on the line' – what a *disgusting* man! Kate was almost too angry to speak.

'Of course not!' she replied furiously, 'it's the bottle of malt-and-oil that's gone and broke itself – the handle came off the carrier – look!' and she held it up.

The porter was sympathetic but irritating.

'Waste of good stuff, that is,' he said. As if Kate didn't know!

'Expensive stuff too, I shouldn't wonder!'

'*Very* expensive!' said Kate, now almost weeping, 'and what my babies are going to do without it I don't know. I won't be able to buy any where we're going – there's no shops; are there any shops near here – I believe I'd have

time to get some – that clock there says there's twenty
minutes afore our train goes.'

'There's a chemist just across the road outside the
station,' replied the porter, glancing at the clock. 'You've
got plenty of time if you hurries – here, give me the bag
afore you drops any more things out of it – and what about
yer babies as you calls 'em? *I* can't sit lookin' after 'em
while you're gone!'

'I'll take Jo,' said Kate decidedly – 'he wouldn't stay
anyway, and he can run nearly as fast as I can, and I – *I'll
tie Peg to the suitcase!*'

And without waiting for the porter to reply she rushed
back to the bench, hastily removed the belt from her dress,
passed it round the waist of her astonished sister, and
buckled it through the handle of the suitcase almost before
Peg had time to utter a protest.

'Now you just stay quiet there, like a good girl, for five
minutes,' she cried, holding up a warning finger, 'and I'll
bring you some chocolate!'

And seizing the astonished Jo by the hand, she set off,
tugging him after her, in the direction of the subway.

'What's-the-matter? Where's-you-going? Let-go-my-
hand!' protested Jo as she pulled him after her along the
platform.

'To a chemist's to get malt-and-oil,' Kate panted over
her shoulder. 'I dropped it. The bottle's broke! Come
along, don't drag like that or we'll miss the train!'

The malt-and-oil broke! Jo was appalled. This was
serious indeed! He wasted no further breath in questions.

Down the long flight of stairs to the subway they panted;
along a passage, down more stairs. . . .

'Tickets, please!' said the man at the exit gate. Kate
fumbled for the bag round her neck – her fingers seemed
to tie themselves in knots. . . . Ah, there they were. . . .

'Three – there's only two of you?' said the ticket collector, leisurely regarding the small pieces of cardboard held out to him.

'Oh, give it back, quick; give them *all* back, quick, *please*!' cried Kate, 'or we'll miss the train – I've got to go to the chemist's – which way is it, please?'

'Round to the right and straight in front of you,' replied the collector. 'And mind how you cross the road, or it's the Hospital you'll be in – not the chemist's.'

Kate seized the tickets and put them carefully back in the bag.

'Now, hang on, Jo,' she said, holding out her hand as they stood a minute later on the kerb, waiting to cross the road. 'You don't want to be under a bus.'

Jo felt the need for care. No indeed! He had no wish to be in a hospital again. How dreadful to start off on a holiday to the country and find yourself in Haywards Heath Hospital! . . .

Would the traffic *never* stop! . . . 'Not for a minute,' said Kate, looking anxiously both ways; then, a moment later, '*Now!*' And they dashed across.

There were three people in the chemist's shop and none of them seemed at all in a hurry. First Kate and Jo waited while a lady chose a hot-water bottle. *Oh*, the time she took! Was the chemist sure it was a good, *lasting* kind? Did he *really* think boiling water spoilt a rubber bottle – of course, it always *said* so on the label, but she was afraid she always *did* use boiling water – a bottle never *really* kept hot unless one did, did it? . . . The price? . . . Four and sixpence. *Four and sixpence!* Oh, she *never* paid that! At Blight and Timkins where she lived, you could get beautiful bottles, exactly that size, for three and elevenpence!

'I'm sorry, madam,' said the chemist, 'but that is our

price for these bottles. Yes, sir,' he turned to a stout, elderly gentleman, 'what can I get for you?'

Kate was in agonies! Oh, these people! She pushed in between the hot-water-bottle lady who, muttering something about small shops always charging more, was preparing to depart, and the third customer, a spotty-faced youth who looked as if he needed many of the remedies advertised with such frankness and confidence all around.

'Please! . . .' she began, but the stout elderly gentleman was speaking.

'I want a tooth-brush,' he announced.

'Certainly, sir; hard, medium, soft? These are pure bristle, sterilized, guaranteed made in Great Britain – nothing to touch the British tooth-brush!'

'Please!' said Kate again, 'I want . . .' The chemist looked coldly at her through a pair of horn-rimmed glasses.

'*Children,*' he said severely, 'must *wait.* Try this one, sir – it's not quite so hard.'

But the stout elderly gentleman seemed very hard to please. If he felt one tooth-brush he felt a dozen! Finally the one he selected had a green handle.

'Dear, dear – that won't do!' he said, just as the chemist was about to wrap it up. 'Never be forgiven if I took home a green-handled tooth-brush! Nothing green allowed in our house – my missis thinks it's unlucky – got a real kink about it. Find me another, please – blue – yellow – anything but green!'

The chemist retired to the back of the shop and the stout gentleman turned his attention to the weighing machine.

'*Please!*' shouted Kate at last, in desperation. 'Can I take this or we'll miss our train?'

And flinging down a half-crown and two sixpences on

top of the cash register, she seized a bottle of malt-and-oil from a pyramid on the counter and held it up.

'Catching a train, are you?' asked the stout gentleman, slowly turning round on the weighing machine. 'Hi! Mister,' he called to the chemist. 'Serve this kid, she's in a hurry.'

'Children should *wait*,' said the chemist again as he reappeared. 'Put that bottle down at once, little girl, or you'll have the whole lot over. What is it you want – malt-and-oil? What make and size? That'll be three shillings and sixpence . . . be careful how you carry it,' he added as he picked up the money from the cash register. But he

spoke to the stout gentleman and the spotty-faced youth only. Kate and Jo had vanished like streaks of lightning!

Back they raced, Kate clutching the malt-and-oil against her chest with both hands; across the road (carefully); past the ticket collector; up a flight of steps; along the subway; up another, longer flight of steps! Breathless, they arrived on the platform. A train was drawing in; they were *just* in time! All was well! Kate glanced at the station clock. But alas! instead of pointing at the hour of departure – five minutes to three – the hands were pointing at five minutes *past* that hour! All was *not* well – indeed, far from it! Their train had, in fact, been gone *ten minutes*!

And Peg? Where was Peg? What, oh what had happened to Peg? For Peg was no longer sitting on the bench where Kate had left her, attached to the suitcase – in fact the suitcase itself appeared so have vanished too; likewise the attaché-case, the umbrella, the bear, and the remains of the carrier! Further up the platform a small group of people were standing. Kate dashed towards them, Jo panting after her. There, in the middle of the group, sitting on a luggage barrow, her bear under her arm, a piece of chocolate in her hand, while a lady hovered near holding a glass containing the remains of some milk, was Peg! The porter stood leaning against the handle of another barrow surveying the scene. Peg had evidently been crying, and crying hard. A tear or two still rolled down her cheeks but she appeared to be making headway with the chocolate.

'Here I am, Peg!' cried Kate breathlessly rushing up. 'Here I am *at last*!'

'Well, you've been a tidy time!' remarked the porter, straightening himself up for a moment. 'Know you've

missed your train, I suppose?' he added cheerfully. Kate
nodded.

'Is this your little sister?' inquired the lady holding the
glass of milk.

'Yes,' replied Kate. Oh dear, *another* stranger – with
food too! Well, it was evidently too late to do anything
now.

'Do you realize she was nearly having convulsions?'
asked the lady severely. 'Why, the poor little thing was
almost black in the face when I came along,' she continued. 'How *could* you be so unkind as to leave her tied up
like that!'

'Unkind!' repeated Kate. 'Why, whatever else could I
do with her – I had to go to the chemist's and I couldn't
take her with me – there wasn't time!'

'Surely you could have asked someone – some lady – to
look after her while you went? Really, the child might
have had a fit! What your parents are thinking of to leave
two small children in charge of a little girl like you I don't
know! How old are you – you can't be more than ten I'm
sure?'

Well *really*! What *next*! Suddenly and completely Kate
lost her temper! She was hot, tired, and everything seemed
to be going wrong.

'*Ten!*' she cried furiously, stamping her foot. 'Ten!
Why, I'm twelve – turned twelve – I'm twelve-and-
nearly-nine-weeks!'

'Dear me,' said the lady. 'But surely you are *very* small?
However, if that is so, I think you ought to know better.
And there's no need to lose your temper!' she added
reprovingly as Kate looked ready to stamp again.

'I've been told special,' said Kate (and her voice now
sounded suspiciously as though tears were not far off),
'*special*, not to speak to strangers!'

'I see,' said the lady, and she spoke more kindly, 'that makes a difference, of course. Well, never mind; your sister's all right now, but I think,' she continued, 'you'd all better go and sit in the waiting-room until your train goes. How long is it, porter, they have to wait till the next one?'

The porter leant sideways and regarded the clock. 'Close on an hour,' he replied. 'I'll see 'em safe into it,' he added, 'if they'll promise to stay in there,' and he indicated the waiting-room with a jerk of his head, 'till I comes for 'em.'

'You hear what he says?' asked the lady. 'Will you *promise* to stay quietly in there – all of you – till he comes?'

Kate had calmed down now. She was already regretting stamping her foot. 'Yes,' she replied meekly. 'I promise. We won't none of us move an *inch* till he comes.'

'Let us go then,' said the lady, and taking Peg by the hand, she led the way to the waiting-room, Kate and Jo following, while the porter brought up the rear with their belongings, dumped them down just inside the door, shook a warning finger, and departed whistling.

'And now I'm afraid I must leave you,' said the lady, 'or I shall miss my own train. I do *hope* you'll all arrive safely! Of course, your mother's quite right to tell you not to speak to strangers,' she added, 'it's all very difficult – very difficult. And now I *must* say good-bye.'

Kate suddenly began to feel quite sorry the lady was going; now they were to be left all alone in the waiting-room she seemed almost like an old friend! And she'd really been very kind, giving Peg milk and chocolate and all. Suppose Peg *had* had a fit, or, almost worse, gone black! Just imagine arriving at the Dew Drop Inn with a little black sister!!

She seized Peg by the arm. 'Did you thank the lady for

giving you the milk and the chocolate?' she demanded.
Peg shook her head.

'You ought of, then; say it now; say thank-you-for-the-nice-milk-and-chocolate. Say it!'

'Thank-you-for-the-nice-milk-and-chocolate,' said Peg
obediently, swallowing the last remnant of the latter and
looking earnestly at her knees.

'That was very nice!' said the lady, patting her on the
shoulder. Then she held out a hand to Kate.

'Good-bye,' she said. 'You *will* remember your promise
won't you? I'm giving the porter sixpence and he'll see to
your suitcase,' she added as she opened the waiting-room
door. 'Good-bye!' A moment later they were alone.

Kate sat staring at the closed door. In the pocket of her
blazer she turned two pennies over and over ... Was
anything going to go right today, she wondered?

CHAPTER FIVE

The Dew Drop Inn

MRS CHARLIE WILDGOOSE propelled herself through
the door of Mr Washer's taxi and plodded into the station
at Upper Cassington. 'Afternoon, George!' she called to
a gentleman who appeared to combine the roles of station-
master, signalman, booking-clerk, and porter. 'Train not
in I hopes?' George shook his head. 'You'm just on time,
Mrs Wildgoose,' he replied, 'her's this minute signalled.'
Mrs Wildgoose sat down on the nearest bench. She was a
stout lady; hurrying always somewhat flustered her, and
really, she had thought Mr Washer's taxi would never
get up the hill to the station! 'Grit in the plugs,' he had
kept muttering. 'Just grit in the plugs.' But why, in the
name of fortune, didn't he dust, wash, oil – or whatever
one did to plugs, before starting? There was always *something* wrong with Mr Washer's taxi, reflected Mrs Wildgoose. Truth was, it were wore out . . . and Mr Washer
too mean (certainly not too poor) to get a new one. No
Competition – that's what it was – No Competition, or
he'd get a new one quick enough – have to; as things were,
however, it was Mr Washer's taxi – or walk; and well Mr
Washer knew it! . . . She could only pray it 'ud hold out
till she got back safely with the children – she hoped they
wouldn't bring much luggage . . . but it wasn't likely . . .
her sister had said. . . Ah, here was the train!

Mrs Wildgoose got to her feet as the engine came puffing under the bridge. It chug-chugged slowly into the
station and drew up at the far end of the platform, four
coaches wheezing and jolting after it. Mrs Wildgoose
looked anxiously at each one. A solitary passenger alighted

but there seemed no sign of any children. . . . Perhaps
they could not open the door? She bustled forward,
peering into each compartment in turn. But the train
appeared practically empty. There was certainly not a
vestige of a child!

Oh dear! What *could* have happened! They were most
decidedly not there! As the train steamed on again she
turned to George for comfort and advice. (George knew
all about Mrs Wildgoose's expected guests. His home was
only a few doors from the Dew Drop Inn, and in Upper –
to say nothing of Lower – Cassington most people knew
their neighbour's business as well, if not better, than their
own.) Could they have missed the train, did he think?
Should she telegraph to their mother? George thought the
former quite possible and advised against the latter . . .
there was another train in just an hour; they might come
by that; it would be best to wait and see . . . Mrs Wildgoose agreed. But what about Mr Washer? Could *he* wait
– and if he could, *would* he?

She went out to where he reclined in his taxi, reading a
paper and apparently totally unconcerned with anything
but the news of the day. Mrs Wildgoose explained the
situation and suggested that perhaps he might care to fill
in the time by calling at a garage to see about 'the little
something wrong with his engine'? Mr Washer bristled
with indignation and replied that repairs of *that* sort he
saw to himself. He had no objection to waiting he added;
he had no other appointment that afternoon. He would,
of course, have to charge for his *time* – Mrs Wildgoose
would understand *that*? Time, after all, was *time*. . . . Mrs
Wildgoose understood perfectly. She returned to the platform and sat down on the bench again. Oh dear! She did
hope those children were all right! Lucky it was such a
nice afternoon. . . . If only the weather would be kind for

their stay. . . . Poor little dears, measles was a nasty thing.
. . . They'd want lots of sun and feedin' up thorough she
didn't doubt. . . . Well, she'd see to the feedin' all right. . . .

It seemed a very long hour! Mrs Wildgoose read all the
advertisements on the station. Advertisements for sausages, cigarettes, lipstick, disinfectant, cattle-cake; notices
about a forthcoming race-meeting, a concert in London,
and an agricultural sale in a neighbouring parish. George
occupied himself weighing and labelling various boxes
and packages, pausing occasionally to make some remark.
Mysterious bells rang, and he popped importantly in and
out of doors answering them. Finally, after what seemed
more like two hours than nearly one, he disappeared over
the bridge and into the signal-box, and a minute or two
later a train came in at the opposite platform. There was
no one to get in, and no one got out. The engine steamed,
and some of the steam blew across to Mrs Wildgoose and
deposited several large smuts on her clean white blouse.
George became a porter and put in a couple of parcels and
a crate of cabbages; exchanged a few words with the
engine-driver, and the train puffed away.

'Only five minutes now!' he shouted, and Mrs Wildgoose straightened herself up, flicked away the smuts on
her blouse, and took heart. Oh, she did hope they'd be on
this one all right!

They were! A head wearing a hat with a school band
looked out of a window as the train came to a standstill
and, before Mrs Wildgoose could reach the carriage, the
door was opened, and out stepped Kate clasping the new
and doubly-precious jar of malt-and-oil, closely followed
by Jo, while Peg stood in the doorway clutching her bear
and waiting to be lifted down to the platform.

'Well, well! Better late than never!' exclaimed Mrs
Wildgoose hurrying up to them. 'Let me see; this is Kate?

This, Jo? and this' – lifting her down and giving her a kiss – 'this is Peg? Is that right? Oh, and here's a beautiful bear! No one told me about him! I wonder what *he's* called? Any luggage, my dears?' she continued. 'Just what you've got in here? Don't worry, the porter will bring it along for us. My word, I'm glad to see you all safe!' she went on, 'I was beginning to think you were all lost! How is it you're so late – did you miss the train?'

'Yes,' said Kate, hardly above a whisper. She had been dreading this moment! Mrs Wildgoose, she felt sure, couldn't fail to have been terribly fussed when they didn't turn up, and probably very angry at having to wait about! But oh, the relief! She didn't appear angry at all! She seemed *very* kind. She just said, oh well, these things *would* happen, and they must tell her all about it in the taxi.

Jo pricked up his ears! Taxi? Were they going in a taxi? Coo! That 'ud be something to tell his brothers – something they *hadn't* done. He swelled with satisfaction.

'Here's my new family, George!' called Mrs Wildgoose. 'That's all the luggage – will you bring it along for us? Come, my dears, this way.' And taking Peg by the hand she led the way out of the station.

Mr Washer was still immersed in his newspaper but on their approach he folded it up, put it under the driving-seat, and started up his reluctant engine. It spat and spluttered alarmingly and Mrs Wildgoose regarded it with much apprehension. Mr Washer, however, took not the slightest notice and directed his energies into deciding how best to accommodate his passengers. Jo, to his great joy, was selected to sit beside him while Mrs Wildgoose, Kate and Peg were relegated to the back. George strapped the suitcase on to the luggage rack and then handed in the umbrella and the attaché-case.

Putting the malt-and-oil down on the seat, Kate

fumbled in the pocket of her blazer. Now was the great moment! For one awful second she thought the contents must have fallen out, but no, all was well. Turning to George and blushing furiously she held out six very hot and sticky pennies to him. 'Thank you,' she said. 'Thank you very much!' But George shook his head. 'You keep those for sweeties,' he said, giving her a kindly wink, 'thanking you all the same. Mind your hands now!' and he slammed-to the door. Before Kate had time to know what to think, Mr Washer released his brake, put his foot on the accelerator, and the next minute the taxi shot forward with a jerk, pitching her right on top of Mrs Wild-goose!

If she hadn't felt so shy, or Lily Rose had been there to join in, Kate was sure she would have got the giggles! As it was she said, 'Oo, sorry Mrs Wildgoose,' and the next minute Mr Washer drove happily over a brick and she was shot back into her own corner again, narrowly miss-ing the precious malt-and-oil jar!

'Shan't be long now,' said Mrs Wildgoose, outwardly optimistic, if inwardly anxious, 'it's only a matter of three miles. Tell me how you came to miss your train?' So while the taxi rattled and spluttered its way along past rows of little houses that gradually thinned out until there was only an occasional cottage, and they seemed to have reached real country, Kate related the sad story. Mrs Wildgoose was very sympathetic – especially about the malt-and-oil, and said she could see from the look of Peg and Jo how important it was, but mark her words, before the three of them had been a week at the Dew Drop Inn, eating the eggs from her ducks and hens, good farm butter, and drinking milk from Mr Digweed's cows, they wouldn't know themselves! And here they were; here were the beginnings of the village, and there, coming back from milking, the very animals she'd mentioned! And sure enough, just ahead, was a herd of strange black-and-fawn-coloured cows being driven across the road from a farm to a field opposite. Mr Washer slowed down with a great deal of grumbling, his engine wheezing horribly. 'Drat them plugs,' he muttered angrily, and Mrs Wildgoose inwardly dratted them too. . . . Only a very little way now though, she consoled herself.

Kate sat squeezing her hands together. This was Real Country all right! The very cows were different from the ones round Otwell! Whatever sort were they? 'Jerseys,' said Mrs Wildgoose. 'Not seen none before? Oh, you'll have to make love to Mr Digweed and ask him to let you see them milked.'

'Could *I* milk one, do you think?' asked Kate breathlessly. 'Would Mr – Mr Digweed let me?' (What a queer name – and how suitable for a worker on the land!) Mrs Wildgoose smiled and said well, stranger things had happened, and at that moment the last cow went through the gate and the taxi plunged forward again.

'You couldn't wish for a prettier village,' Mrs Beaseley's cook had said, and she might have added, 'or a more unusual-looking one'.

There was no doubt Upper Cassington, and Lower Cassington which almost joined it – the two being separated by the grounds of a big estate – *were* very pretty, and most certainly uncommon. 'Coo!' exclaimed Kate, who was beginning to feel less shy every minute, 'I never seen houses *that* colour before! Are they all like that?' For the cottages they were passing were a strange yellow – a pinky, orangy sort of yellow – something the colour of a Dutch cheese.

'Well, not all,' replied Mrs Wildgoose, 'but most of 'em, and more down to Lower Cassington than here. It were

the old Colonel's idea – Colonel Ayredale-Eskdale as was
– him as owned most of the land hereabouts; some reason
he had for it – you'll have to ask my husband, he knows all
about it – a great one for information is Mr Wildgoose;
always got his nose in a book of some kind.' Kate was
interested to hear this and thought Mr Wildgoose sounded
a man after her own heart! Funny, she wouldn't have
thought a man that kept a pub would be interested in anything much but beer and suchlike. . . .

'Most of the tenants seems to like it well enough,' went
on Mrs Wildgoose, referring to the colour of the cottages

again, 'and just as well seein' they've got to live with it;
and it always pleases visitors. I can't say I'm partial to it
myself and I'm glad the Dew Drop's a nice plain cream –
and here it is!' she added as Mr Washer turned a corner
almost on two wheels and the taxi came to anchor with a
thankful snort of its uneasy engine.

The Dew Drop Inn was almost too good to be true! It
looked like a cross between a picture on an old-fashioned
grocer's almanack and a house-agent's dream. The roof
was deeply thatched; early roses and honeysuckle climbed

over the porch and up to the latticed windows, while the wealth of oak beams within was almost unbelievable! Over the porch a green notice-board swayed to and fro in the breeze. On one side was painted in large white letters, 'THE DEW DROP INN,' and on the other, 'DO DROP IN.' Could anything be more inviting?

They all got out of the taxi. Mr Washer unloaded the suitcase, dumped it down, and with a surly 'good evening' departed with his unhappy vehicle. Kate stood gazing, entranced, while Jo thought (very privately) he must be mixed up in some strange dream; even perhaps, a fairy story. As for Peg, landscape, cows, or picturesque inns represented one thing and one thing only. Clutching the beloved Buttonhook more tightly and pointing towards the Dew Drop Inn, she whispered in his delapidated ear, 'Look! There it is – there's The Country – we've *come*!'

There was no garden in front of the Dew Drop Inn, but on the gravelled sweep outside were a couple of old settles and a trestle table. On one of the settles three old men were seated sunning themselves and waiting for opening time, while a couple of children stood near regarding the newcomers with steady, unblinking stares.

A thin man with spectacles, wearing a very gay pullover, his shirt-sleeves rolled up, and a green baize apron over his trousers, came out of the porch. This was Mr Wildgoose. They had missed the train, he supposed? Well, well! But like his wife he did not seem in the least annoyed.

'Welcome to the Dew Drop!' he said, shaking hands solemnly with each of the children in turn, 'and may your shadows never grow less – in fact may they grow considerably more – as they undoubtedly will after a week or two of my missis' cooking. You mustn't go by me,' he added, smiling at Jo who appeared to be regarding him a little doubtfully, 'I'm what they call one of Pharaoh's lean kine!' And he picked up the suitcase and carried it into the porch. And Jo, who had learnt about Pharaoh and his doings at Sunday School, smiled back and decided he was going to like Mr Wildgoose.

'Come along, my dears,' said Mrs Wildgoose holding out a hand to Peg, 'Come along; this way.' And feeling very shy under the scrutiny of the staring children and the three old men, Kate and Jo followed her into the house.

Mrs Wildgoose led the way upstairs – and such stairs! Steps of dark, solid oak; uncarpeted, polished, and *very* slippery; stairs that twisted first to the left, then to the right; then lengthened out and became a little landing and then stairs again with more twists and turns, and finally a narrow, oak-panelled passage. All along this passage were little sheep-skin mats, so small and so many that one was reminded of stepping-stones – in fact Kate felt compelled to treat them as such but quickly discovered this was unwise for the floor both beneath and between, was so slippery that one was liable to be precipitated on to one's nose. They were the sort of thing her mother, she was sure, would have immediately labelled 'Highly Dangerous'; all the same there was something very endearing about them.

'Nearly there!' said Mrs Wildgoose, pausing at the end of the passage and smiling down at Peg and turning to see if the others were following.

'Think you'll ever remember the way back again?' she asked. It was exactly what Kate and Jo *had* been wondering; Jo from the start having been doing his best to remember various 'landmarks', which he had heard his brothers say was the proper thing to do if you ever felt in danger of being lost, while Kate had just decided there could be no possibility of forgetting the stepping-stone mats. But she did not like to say this for fear of hurting

Mrs Wildgoose's feelings. At the end of the narrow passage there was another staircase; steep, narrow little stairs this time, with a carpet down their middle, and a rope on the wall side to help yourself up. At the top was a small landing with three solid-looking, low-lintelled, brown-painted doors opening on to it.

'Here we are!' cried Mrs Wildgoose, a little breathlessly after the steep stairs. 'Here we are!', and she opened the second of the brown-painted doors.

The room inside was not very big but it was certainly a very great deal larger than any at No. 1 One End Street. The ceiling sloped in much the same way as the bedroom ones did there, but there was no paper on the walls – just plain whitewash, which after the roses and trellis-work she was used to at home Kate thought decidedly dull (she was to think differently very soon); there was a dark red carpet on the floor, and a very black, shiny old-fashioned little fireplace with a cupboard on either side. In the middle of the room was a big soft-looking bed covered with a white knitted quilt which hung down on either side ending in a fringe of bobbles.

Kate looked round. There was no other bed; were they all three to sleep in that? – of course it was big enough – easily – but she'd hate to sleep three in a bed, and . . . But Mrs Wildgoose was opening one of the cupboard doors by the fireplace, and – it wasn't a cupboard at all! It was another room – a very small one it is true – some people might say it *was* a cupboard – but it had a window all to itself, and it was furnished. There was a bed, and a chair, and a table; and across one corner a curtain behind which you could hang your clothes. Sprays of honeysuckle and clusters of roses swayed in the breeze and tapped against the open window, sending queer, greenish shadows skimming over the whitewashed walls.

'I thought the two little ones in together, and this room leading out, for you,' said Mrs Wildgoose to Kate. 'That seemed the best arrangement to me, but you change about if you like – how's it to be now?'

Kate was enchanted! A room to herself! And fancy being *asked* which she would prefer! She assured Mrs Wildgoose it was the best possible arrangement.

Fortunately Peg and Jo liked the idea of sleeping in such a big bed after their own tiny ones at home.

'Coo! Isn't it *soft*!' murmured Jo pressing it with his elbows.

'That's my feathers!' said Mrs Wildgoose. 'My *hens*' feathers I suppose I ought to say! You must come and see my hens when you've had your teas – and talking of teas, everything'll be ready and waiting right now, so we'll just take your coats and hats off here and come to the bathroom next door and have a nice wash, for I'm sure you must feel like it after those dirty old trains. Never mind the washing things,' she added as Kate began rummaging in the paper carrier, 'there's towels and soap, and a nice new face-flannel all there waiting for you.'

To many people the bathroom at the Dew Drop Inn might have appeared rather old-fashioned and not particularly attractive, but to Kate, Peg, and Jo who had never seen a bathroom at all it seemed a truly magnificent apartment. Peg and Jo were so entranced with the size of the bath; the large shiny taps, and the plug that lifted out with a long gold chain, that they could hardly be persuaded to get ready for tea; while Kate, who was already busily writing a letter to Lily Rose in her head, immediately added its glories to the splendour of a bedroom all to oneself. At last, however, all three, washed, and with neatly combed hair, followed Mrs Wildgoose along the passages and landings and down the twisty stairs again, finally arriving at a room leading off the kitchen where a young woman with dark hair and pink cheeks, whom Mrs Wildgoose introduced by the name of Elsie-as-helps-me, was putting a plate of scones on a table already loaded with food. Bowls of corn-flakes, boiled eggs, mugs of creamy milk, honey, fruit – there seemed no end to it, and all set out on a gay blue-and-white checked cloth with a big bowl of pink tulips in the middle.

What a big kitchen! thought Kate. Why, you could put theirs at home inside twice over and have room to spare! And how lovely it looked out there through the window. Apple trees ... and tulips ... and the *dearest* little tiled path. ...

'Now you must all make a good tea, my dears,' said Mrs Wildgoose, 'or Elsie here will be very disappointed, for she's took a deal of trouble getting it all ready.'

Now Peg and Jo had not really cared very much about food since they'd had measles, and for the last day or two Kate had been too excited to take a great deal of interest in hers; so whether it was that twelve o'clock dinner at One End Street seemed a very long time ago, or that they didn't want to disappoint the pretty, dark-haired, pink-cheeked Elsie who had taken so much trouble; or just that the food looked so good it simply *asked* to be eaten – whatever it was, no sooner had they sat down round the blue-and-white checked table-cloth than they all felt tremendously hungry, and one by one bowls of cornflakes, boiled eggs, milk, scones, honey, and fruit began rapidly to disappear. Mrs Wildgoose was delighted and the pink-cheeked Elsie smiled more than ever. At last no one seemed able to eat or drink any more, and Peg was beginning to look decidedly sleepy. Outside the sun was still shining brightly, but the shadows were becoming longer.

'Just ten minutes to see round the garden and have a

look at the ducks and hens – you'd like to see those,
wouldn't you?' asked Mrs Wildgoose, 'and then I think
the two little ones ought to go to bed.'

'I don't go to bed same time as Peg!' protested Jo.
'She's only a baby; not even in the Hospital I didn't.'

'But just tonight, my dear,' replied Mrs Wildgoose, 'for
you've come a long way you know – besides, everyone
goes to bed earlier in the country than they do in the

town – you know that, don't you?' No, Jo didn't. '*Everyone?*' he demanded. 'You, and Mr Wildgoose, and Elsie-
as-helps-me?' Mrs Wildgoose nodded and said yes,
everyone. And to Kate's surprise – for she had expected
protests – Jo said no more. Truth to tell, he too was sleepy
– not to say extremely tired, though nothing would have
induced him to admit such a thing.

The garden at the Dew Drop Inn was not large but after the back yard at One End Street it seemed spacious indeed. At one side of the little path Kate had noticed from the window was a small lawn bordered with flower-beds gay with tulips, lupins, and many other flowers whose names she did not know but which she told herself she would soon find out. On the lawn itself were two very old gnarled and twisted apple trees leaning crazily but confidingly towards each other as if about to impart some secret, while beyond the flower-beds stretched a neat – oh-so-neat – vegetable garden. Rows of cabbages, leeks, early carrots; a big patch of onions; another of potatoes; lines of mysterious little seedlings under wire-netting, and some thing evidently very precious indeed sheltered beneath curious-looking glass bells. Farther on there were currant and gooseberry bushes; raspberry canes and, in one corner, what appeared to be – and was – straw!

'Strawberries!' cried Peg, who had been identifying both fruit and vegetables to herself in a loud whisper, pointing triumphantly and smiling up at Mrs Wildgoose. '*Straw-berries!*' and Mrs Wildgoose said yes, strawberries it was.

At the end of the tiled path was a little wooden gate leading into a small orchard where in one corner, in a wire-netted enclosure, stood a hen-house, and crowded together and pressed close against the wire, smooth, white, beady-eyed ducks, and brown, white, and what Jo called mixed-coloured hens, all announcing with a great deal of noise that they were extremely hungry and their meal, for some reason, disgracefully late this evening!

At this moment the smiling Elsie came down the path with two large buckets of scraps and the noise grew even louder. Kate begged to be allowed to carry one of the buckets and help with the feeding, but Mrs Wildgoose shook her head. 'Not in those nice school clothes as you've got on' she said, 'I wouldn't; tomorrow, now – there'll be lots of tomorrows – the poultry won't run away – though it's true we do have a job to keep the ducks in sometimes.' So Kate, like Jo, said no more, for her school clothes *were* very special and, as Mrs Wildgoose said, there would be lots of tomorrows. She began counting them up; forty, forty-one, forty-*two* if you counted the morning of the day they would have to go home. . . . And while they watched the clamorous, gobbling ducks, and the clucking, impatient hens, pushing and scrambling for their food, she was busy planning in her mind. . . . She must make a list of all the things she most wanted to see and learn about. . . . Perhaps Mr Wildgoose who was such 'a one for information' might help her? He would be busy in the bar till supper they had said at tea . . . in the meantime, as soon as Peg and Jo were in bed, well, she might anyway start some exploring. . . .

But alas for plans! By the time she had helped Mrs Wildgoose unpack all their things, wash and undress Jo and Peg and get them into bed, she began to feel almost too tired to think – and it was still quite a long time to supper. She was not hungry after her good tea and although it was only half past seven she wished very much she, too, could go to bed, but if you were twelve-and-nearly-nine-weeks it was next to impossible to suggest such a thing at such an hour. Fortunately Mrs Wildgoose seemed to be one of those noticing sort of people who knew exactly how one felt. Supper wouldn't be ready for quite a while yet she said; how about some cocoa and biscuits and an early bed tonight? Adding that anyone – even a grown-up – would be tired after a journey and looking after two small children – not to mention all the worry of the malt-and-oil and the lost train – she knew *she* would! This made things much easier and Kate was able to say with no loss of dignity that yes, she *was* rather sleepy, and, in good imitation of Mrs Ruggles, 'small children fair wear you out' – and perhaps it would be best.

'Sure you won't be lonely now?' asked Mrs Wildgoose when the cocoa and biscuits had been disposed of. 'I sleep in the room just below – you can tap on the floor or call out of the window if you wants anything and I'll hear at once – I'm a very light sleeper. And you just stay in your bed till I come along tomorrow morning,' she added, 'you want all the sleep you can get I can see – been working too hard at school I shouldn't be surprised. . . . Come, give me a kiss now and then off you go.' And Kate, blushing rather, because she was not much in the habit of kissing – particularly strangers – said, 'Thank you, Mrs Wildgoose, I'll be quite all right,' and then, in a sudden burst of confidence that surprised even herself, 'I just *love* the Dew Drop and I think you're ever so kind, and . . . and I can't tell you how glad I am, because till we got here this afternoon I thought nothing was never going to go right again, and now I sort of feel that everything's going to be all right for ever and ever!'

'That's a very rash thing to say!' replied Mrs Wildgoose kissing her, 'but all's well as ends well – off you go now, and sweet dreams.'

The light was beginning to fade and in another five minutes, thought Kate, the passages would be full of horribly creepy shadows. She remembered the way perfectly, however, and hurrying along was soon past the stepping-stone mats and up the stairs to the top landing. The door of the larger room was ajar and, almost lost in the big bed, Peg and Jo were sleeping soundly, Buttonhook between them, his unblinking boot-button eyes staring straight ahead. She tiptoed across the red carpet to her

own little room and switched on the light. Oo! how tired
she was! Really she felt almost too sleepy to take off her
clothes; as for washing – which meant going to the bathroom next door – she couldn't even consider it!

She kicked off her shoes, undid her suspenders, and
peeled off her stockings by the simple method of running
her right foot down her left leg and vice versa; wriggled
out of the rest of her clothes, slipped her nightie over her
head, and seizing the hair-brush, gave her wispy locks a
perfunctory brush. In less than three minutes she was
ready for the night!

Kate put out the light and got into bed. It wasn't
properly dark yet. Lying down she could see the honeysuckle sprays and the thick ridge of thatch that fringed
the window. A great deal of subdued rustling and twitter-
ing seemed to be going on there. Swallows! *Could* it be?
How perfect to have a swallow's nest almost *in* your bedroom! Oh, this was Real Country all right; where she had
always wanted to be; where she felt, somehow, she
belonged. As for the Dew Drop Inn, it was everything she
had imagined – and more – and Mrs Wildgoose was a
dear! Tomorrow she would write home and tell Mum so.
And, she supposed, about the malt-and-oil (which wasn't
going to be so easy) and about the size of the kitchen . . .
and the garden . . . and the big tea they'd eaten . . . and
the ducks and hens . . . and Elsie-as-helps-me, and . . . and
. . . (The bedroom to oneself and the bathroom she would
reserve specially, she decided, for a letter to Lily Rose.)

In the sky stars now began to show faintly and some
owls in what looked like a wood a little way off started
calling softly to each other. From far away came the plaintive whistle of a railway engine. It was all very peaceful.
She lay for a while thinking how quiet it all was, when

suddenly, from a near-by field, a cow began to moo, and moo – and moo again! Loudly, forlornly, piteously! Oh dear, what *could* be the matter with it? Oh, there it went again – and again! It must be ill or lost or both. Ought she to tell someone? She lay for some time listening to the heart-rending sounds. The soft calls of the owls had developed into screeches now, and the rustlings in the thatch grew suddenly noisier. Lily Rose, were she here, would have no cause to complain of the quietness of the countryside, she thought. And all at once she found herself wishing desperately that Lily Rose was there! It was awfully lonely, after all, in a room all by oneself. . . . And quite suddenly Kate felt homesick for the big bed, the trellised wall-paper with the pink and yellow roses, and all the familiar things of One End Street. Tears came into her eyes and trickled slowly down her nose; she sniffed miserably. How queer life could be! Here she was where she wanted to be more than anywhere, and as mournful as the cow outside! Poor thing! Would it never stop? She had no idea a cow could moo so frantically. Thinking of it she forgot her own troubles. She had just decided she could bear it no longer and must get up and find someone to go to its help, when the mooing abruptly ceased. She lay still, listening. Not a sound. Someone must have gone to comfort it. All the same, she would tell Mrs Wildgoose in the morning. *No* cow ought to go on like that, she felt quite sure!

She lay for a little watching the stars multiply and brighten. Presently the owls stopped calling; the rustlings in the thatch subsided. She wondered if Lily Rose were asleep yet . . . if . . . if . . . She was asleep herself!

She awoke suddenly, about an hour later, in the middle of a dream about ducks. There was a noisy opening of

doors, and the sound of tramping feet on the gravel outside. Men's voices sounded in the darkness. ''Night, Bill;
'night, Charlie; 'night, Mr Wildgoose; 'night, all.' She lay
for a moment, drowsy, wondering. Oh, of course! *Closing
Time!* So unlike its counterpart, the Brewers' Arms at the
bottom of One End Street, was the Dew Drop Inn, it was
difficult to remember it was, after all, a public house!

She blinked up at the stars for a moment, then rolled
over on her side and was soon fast asleep again.

CHAPTER SIX

Country Days and Ways

(i) Exploring

KATE was awakened next morning by the sun shining full
on her face. She lay for a moment dazzled by the brightness; then stretched herself luxuriously. The next minute
she was up and leaning out of the window.

It was a perfect morning and oh, how different a view
from the bedroom at One End Street! Except for a row of
yellow-coloured cottages a little to the left on the other
side of the road, fields, trees, and woods – as far as you could
see; a curly, twisting little river, and on the far horizon
gently sloping, bare, but rather exciting-looking hills.
True, there were all these things around Otwell but you
had to walk to find them, and usually, by the time you
arrived among them, it was time to come home again.
And how lovely and dewy everything looked! She pulled
a spray of the roses climbing up to the thatch towards her
and buried her nose in one of the creamy-pink flowers.
Oo-oo . . . the smell! . . . the smell! . . . How could you
describe it? . . . *How?* . . . It was . . . it was the smell of

creamy-pinkness its very self, she decided. . . . She wondered what the time was and, almost in answer, a church
clock somewhere not very far away behind the Inn,
struck seven. Seven! She'd like to get up and rush out, but
Mrs Wildgoose had said particularly to 'stay put'. Kate
peeped round the door to see if Peg and Jo were awake
but they were still sleeping soundly. She was glad of this
for there would be no peace once they woke and if she
couldn't go out she wanted to enjoy her little room in
quietness. She got back into bed and sat, her hands
clasped round her knees, listening to the twitterings and
rustlings in the thatch (she was afraid it was only sparrows

after all!) and watching the strange, changing patterns
made by the sunlight shining through the leaves outside,
on the bare whitewashed bedroom wall. How fascinating
they were! You could imagine anything out of them. Now
it was a lake with trees all round it; now a rough sea and
lots of little islands; now a range of terrific mountains with
jagged, snowy tops. It was like watching some mysterious
hand drawing on a huge sheet of clean white paper. She
sat watching, entranced. Now came a procession of
animals. A horse – two horses, a polar bear . . . then some-

thing that looked rather like a cow without horns. . . . Oh! that reminded her! How was the poor cow that had mooed so last night? The thought had hardly entered her head when, Moo-oo! Moo-oo-oo! sounded almost under the window and looking out she saw a large shaggy, red-and-white beast walking towards the gate in a field nearly opposite, raising its head in anguish to Heaven at intervals as it came. Moo-oo! Moo-oo-oo!

At that moment Mrs Wildgoose tapped gently and then put her head round the door.

'Wide awake! Well I never! Good morning, my dear, and did you have a good sleep? The two little 'uns is still fast as fast!' Yes, thank you, answered Kate, she had, 'but oh, Mrs Wildgoose', she cried, 'that cow! Does no one know about it? It must be terribly ill or something! Can't we do anything for it? The poor thing! It was going on like that last night; I nearly came to tell you and then it stopped. I just can't bear to hear it.' And Kate looked nearly ready to burst into tears.

'Bless your heart!' cried Mrs Wildgoose glancing out of the window 'that's Mr Plodder's old cow – she's all right; it's only they've took her calf away a day or so ago, poor thing, and she's not got over it yet. Don't you fret yourself about her!'

'Took her calf away!' repeated Kate indignantly, 'But how cruel! Who has – and where to? Can't we get it back for her? I just hate to hear her so miserable!' Mrs Wildgoose was just about to explain the necessity for this sad state of affairs, when Peg and Jo awoke simultaneously. Both apparently in the highest spirits; leaping out of bed and rushing straight for their clothes, without so much as the thought of a wash!

Mrs Wildgoose was a *little* shocked. 'Soap and water, first, *please*!' she cried. And Kate, who believed in morning

if not evening ablutions, and jealous for the family honour
in respect of cleanliness, jumped from her bed, and catching Jo by the arm, dragged him into the bathroom, where
she was soon scrubbing his ears with a thoroughness that
would have done credit to Lily Rose who, as has been
stated elsewhere,* was an expert in this matter in regard
to her younger brothers and sisters. Mr Plodder's cow was
forgotten, and it was not until later in the morning, when
she had set forth on the exploring expedition she had been
too tired to suggest the previous evening, that Kate remembered it again.

The day was a Saturday – always a busy one for Mrs
Wildgoose for, as she said, she didn't 'hold' with work of
a Sunday. A day of rest it were supposed to be, and a day
of rest she tried to keep it. Elsie 'stayed home' that day;
the house was closed for drinks except in the bar in the
evening, and if there were a service in the morning she
liked to go to church. All the same, Sunday or not, one
had to *eat* and Mr Wildgoose liked a good dinner that day.
Most of Sunday's cooking therefore had to be done on
Saturday, and with three extra she and Elsie would have
their hands especially full that morning. She suggested
Peg and Jo should play about in the sun on the lawn
where she could keep an eye on them from the kitchen
window, and perhaps Kate wouldn't mind going round
to the shop for one or two things that had been forgotten –
she might care to have a look round the village at the same
time? 'Won't take you long, that won't!' added Mrs
Wildgoose laughing 'and if you think you're likely to get
lost, you ask Mr Wildgoose to draw you one of his little
maps – you ask him anyway – just loves doin' them he does,
bless him' she added affectionately.

* *The Family from One End Street.*

Kate's eyes sparkled. What a lovely idea! She was quite sure she wouldn't – couldn't – possibly get lost in a place like Upper Cassington but it was far more exciting to feel she *might* and have the fun of consulting a map as to her whereabouts! She went off in search of Mr Wildgoose while Mrs Wildgoose wrote out her shopping list, and Elsie spread a large waterproof rug on the grass for Peg and Jo, for, as Mrs Wildgoose reminded them, it *was* still only May for all it looked so warm and dry.

Kate found Mr Wildgoose in the bar busily polishing glasses, and whistling to himself as he polished. They had already become quite friendly at breakfast when she had overcome her first shyness towards him in asking to be told about the yellow cottages. Mr Wildgoose was always pleased and proud to impart information about his native village – yes, he had been born at the Dew Drop, and his Father before him, and *his* Father before *him*, he told Kate, and he was as pleased to be asked to make a map as she was to have one. In fact he became so absorbed in the elaboration of various details that Kate began to feel she would never start! The clock striking ten recalled Mr Wildgoose to earth.

'Bless my soul!' he exclaimed, 'ten o'clock, opening time in half an hour – the glasses not done and me fooling about with maps! There,' adding one more touch, 'that completes it – take it away – and if you get lost for even *five minutes*, I shall never hold up my head again!' And his face assumed such a serious expression that Kate looked quite alarmed.

'Don't you take no notice of his teasin', my dear,' said Mrs Wildgoose, coming in at that moment with her shopping list. 'You won't get lost and if you do, bless me, you've only got to ask anyone, man, woman or child, for the Dew Drop. Here's what I wants now,' she went on, 'a half-dozen of matches; bar of cookin' salt; a packet of postcards, and two pounds of sweet biscuits. That last's something you like, I don't doubt – you choose what sort you fancies. Mrs Megson (that's the lady as keeps the shop) has got several nice kinds she'll show you; and here's my old purse with the money inside, and a basket to put everything in. There! Now give her the map, Charlie,' she said turning to her husband, 'and let her get off.'

'Right you are, missis!' replied Mr Wildgoose, and he stopped looking serious, and twinkled his eyes at Kate behind his glasses. 'All have to do as she says, you know' he said, handing over the map. 'Keeps us all in order, does Mrs Wildgoose!'

'Go on with you!' replied his wife, giving his shoulder a little shake, and then bending down she kissed the top of his head. 'Just like Mum and Dad!' said Kate to herself as she stepped out into the sunshine, holding the map in one hand and the basket in the other, and feeling almost a country girl already.

'When you come out of the Dew Drop,' Mr Wildgoose had said, 'you're on the main road. Face left, and then look at the map.' Kate obeyed. 'Post Office Lane', 'Church Street', 'Church End', 'Parsley Lane', 'Hare's Corner', she read. These thoroughfares, it appeared, were the chief – in fact the only – roads of Upper Cassington, though there were two or three little squiggles that appeared to end in fields and which she decided must be footpaths. One of these was marked 'Pond Passage' and at the end Mr Wildgoose had drawn a tiny house, and what looked like two little men, one of whom was labelled 'S' and the other 'M', while a short, dotted line where Church End and Parsley Lane appeared to join each other, was marked what at first she read as 'The Narrow Way' (but later discovered was The Marrow-Way) 'Digweeds' Farm only'. Here Mr Wildgoose had put a rather crooked sort of house; a queer-looking round tower with a roof like a witch's hat, and several triangles with whiskers that looked as if they might be meant to represent haystacks. 'Digweeds' Farm Only' must certainly be inspected. (Mr Digweed, Kate remembered, was the owner of the strange-coloured cows.) The church and churchyard were indicated by a tower and a lot of little crosses; there were various fields with odd-sounding names 'Tithe Meadow', 'The Ten Acre', 'Long Pasture'; several stiff-looking little trees; while a thick, snake-like line labelled '*The* Stream', wriggled right across the map presenting neither end nor beginning!

Where he had written 'Main Road' and indicated the door of the Inn, Mr Wildgoose had drawn two arrows. One, pointing to the left, said, 'To the station', the other, pointing right, 'To the Green, Lower Cassington, and Beyond'.

Well, she was now *on* the main road, said Kate to herself, and facing left, so first turn *on* left must be Post Office Lane, and there on one side of the road marked with an 'X' was the Post Office itself, as you might expect, and on the other side, almost opposite, Mrs Megson's shop, marked with a large exclamation mark, which you would certainly *not* expect – anyway on a map!

Folding up the map carefully and putting it in her pocket, she set forth, but before 'turning left' she crossed the road to look in the field opposite and see what had happened to Mr Plodder's cow. It was still there, but over at the far end, eating away after the absorbed manner of cows and apparently perfectly content. Well, that was a relief! Kate went happily on her way. Passing the row of orangy-coloured cottages, she was conscious of being observed by some of the inhabitants half-hidden behind their

window curtains and pots of geraniums, but except for a
woman sweeping a door-step who smiled and remarked it
was 'a lovely day'; some very small children who looked at
her with round, inquiring eyes; and a black dog lying in
the sun, there seemed no one about. She turned into Post
Office Lane and quickly arrived at Mrs Megson's shop.

And what a dear little shop it was! A short flight of stone
steps, with a railing on one side to help yourself up, led to
the door, and this door was no ordinary one but the kind
more usually seen in stables, divided in two across the

middle so that the top half could be opened like a case-ment window, while the bottom half remained shut. On one side of the steps grew a fine laburnum tree, now just past the zenith of its flowering, its golden flower-sprays spilling their petals thickly over the steps and roadway. On the other side was the window of the shop, a tiny, three-sided affair, filled with bottles of alluring-looking sweets, oranges, blocks of writing-paper, picture post-cards, and an assortment of small tin and celluloid toys. After a long look in the window, Kate went up the worn, petal-strewn steps and pushed open the queer half-door.

The shop was low-ceilinged and dark and seemed even darker than it was by contrast with the brightness outside. From thick oak beams across the ceiling hung pieces of bacon, strings of onions, tin kettles, and blue wrapping-paper. The counter took up most of the floor space, and behind it, surrounded by tins and jars of every description, boxes of oranges, scrubbing-brushes, balls of string, fly-papers, tooth-brushes, and the hundred and one things that go to make up the stock of a village stores, seated on a high stool and knitting as if her life depended upon it, was Mrs Megson herself.

In front of her lay an enormous ball of wool the colour of a newly-painted pillar-box; further reinforcements were parked on tins and boxes near at hand, while, on one side of the counter, a framed notice in poker-work letters on a buff ground, proclaimed for the benefit of those who might possibly be tempted to linger over their shopping:

If you've nothing to do, don't do it here!

Life was evidently very real and earnest indeed at the Upper Cassington village stores!

Among the local inhabitants it was said that Mrs Meg-son's red knitting – which never seemed any nearer

completion – indeed there were some who insisted that as
soon as it was finished she unravelled it and began again –
was a sort of danger signal – like the traffic lights at the
crossroads – a warning as to the mood in which one
might expect to find the proprietress of the village stores.
When the knitting was absent, they affirmed, Mrs Megson
was kindly and polite, charitable concerning her neighbours, and pleasant to strangers. But when the red balls
loomed large about the counter, then beware!

Kate, of course, knew nothing of these matters though
she was very quickly made aware of the mood of Mrs
Megson, who, continuing to knit furiously, regarded her
customer with a cold and hostile stare. Kate put her
basket down on the counter and, feeling a little intimi-
dated by her reception, explained rather nervously that
she had come for some goods for Mrs Wildgoose.

'Humph! One of her slum children, I suppose!' said
Mrs Megson rising from her stool, laying down her knitting, and thrusting the needles into the ball of pillar-box-
coloured wool with such force that Kate was surprised
they remained unbroken. 'Well, you just wipe your shoes
when you come into my shop – there – on the mat in the
corner; bringing in dirt and them dratted laburnum
flowers. I'd have you know I've spent near twenty minutes
already this very morning sweeping the floor clear of
petals!'

Kate felt very abashed. She looked round for the mat
and discovered an object some ten inches square on which
she obediently wiped her almost clean shoes to which a
few golden petals were clinging. How could anyone
possibly mind them? She had thought how lovely they
looked scattered all about as she came down the road . . .
if *she* ever had a house she wouldn't mind petals *everywhere*
. . . and 'slum child' indeed! She went pink with indig-

nation, and putting up both her hands settled her hat more firmly on her head, hoping thereby to draw Mrs Megson's attention to the school band and crest so proudly displayed. She then advanced to the counter once more, and enumerated Mrs Wildgoose's requirements, adding she had been told she might choose the sweet biscuits herself.

'Oh, you have, have you!' said Mrs Megson, slapping down the bar of salt and the matches on the counter, and then rattling open a drawer for the postcards. 'Well let me tell you there's no choosing about it; the traveller's not called and until he do there's only one tin of sweet biscuits in the shop – Sandwich Creams – so it's those or none at all. Do you want them or no? Sharp now! I've no time to waste with little bits of orders like this!' And she slammed-to the drawer and stood with the packet of postcards in one hand, the other poised over a biscuit-tin.

'Oh, yes, I do want them, *please*,' said Kate very fervently, for not only did she feel she must at all costs bring back what Mrs Wildgoose had asked for, but she adored Sandwich Creams! She watched Mrs Megson bang open the tin and shake the biscuits into the scales, trying to summon up enough courage for a request of her own. This was the purchase of a picture postcard of the Dew Drop Inn which she had noticed in the window. Other postcards were displayed in the shop but this particular one was not among them and she wanted it very specially. The matter of the six pennies rejected at the station by George had been troubling her a little. 'Keep them for sweeties' he had said, but Kate hadn't felt they were exactly her pennies – her very own – to keep. They still really belonged to Mrs Ruggles. She had decided to compromise in the matter by buying a postcard for her with them and what could be a happier choice than a picture of the Dew Drop Inn? Already, in imagination, she had marked her bedroom window, and that of Peg and Jo, with two large X's. . . . But Mrs Megson made short work of the request when at last she managed to make it.

'I'm takin' nothing out of the window' she announced, 'Understand? Nothing! If you wants a picture postcard there's plenty to choose from here; plenty! Disturbing my window! The idea!' And then as Kate lingered, uncertain what to do next in the circumstances, Mrs Megson bundled her purchases into her basket; pushed it towards her, and picking up the red knitting with one hand, with the other she waved majestically towards the poker-work-lettered notice.

'You see what it says: "If you've nothing to do, don't do it here!"'

And Kate, feeling more certain than of anything in life that if she *had* nothing to do, the last place she would choose to do it would be Upper Cassington village stores, seized her basket, and making for the door, almost jumped the flight of little stone steps in her pleasure at quitting the premises! After her, from the half-doorway floated the reproving tones of Mrs Megson.

'You should say "good morning", little girl,' she called. 'You should say "good morning".'

Kate walked a few steps down the road, then stopped, took off her hat and fanned her face, hot and burning with hurry and indignation. *Little girl*', *Slum child*', *Bits of orders*'! Did you *ever*! Mrs Megson was just another *Mrs 'Nosey-Parker' Smith – her very first cousin*! She understood now, oh, perfectly, why Mr Wildgoose had put an exclamation mark at that particular spot on his map; had he put half a dozen she would not have considered them too many.

But it was a pity about the postcard. She wanted it very

much! Perhaps the Post Office would have one; but would they be horrid in there too? She walked across the road with the idea of looking in the window, anyway.

Upper Cassington Post Office was a small orange-coloured cottage with a low-lintelled door, three windows not much larger than the old pillar-box marked 'V.R.' let into the wall by the gate, and one a little larger in which some stationery and a few bottles of sweets were displayed. Kate had never seen a 'V.R.' pillar-box before and she stood regarding it with interest and a little awe.

Miss Midgley, assisted by her mother – an old lady half-paralysed as the result of an accident some years ago – kept the Upper Cassington Post Office; Miss Midgley was serving behind the counter, while through a door in the shop opening directly into the living-room, Mrs Midgley was to be seen, dressed in black with a lilac shawl about her shoulders, seated in a wheel-chair, surrounded by papers and ledgers intent on important Government business. On fine days the wheel-chair would be in the little strip of garden that looked on to the road, and Mrs Midgley in it – a rug over her knees, an umbrella tilted to one side to keep off the glare of the sun, doing the Post Office accounts. She was there now, a small table covered with official looking forms beside her, busily adding up figures.

'Did you want something, my dear?' she inquired, pausing for a moment and looking up and noticing Kate hovering near the gate. Her manner was kindly and like balm to Kate's present ruffled feelings. Encouraged, she pushed open the gate and came up the path. 'I was looking for a postcard of the Dew Drop Inn' she exclaimed, 'do you know if they sell them in the Post Office, please?'

'Why yes, we did have some,' replied Mrs Midgley. 'You go inside and ask my daughter, Minnie – she'll tell

you. Stayin' with Mrs Wildgoose are you, my dear?'
Kate nodded. 'Ah, I thought you might be! And enjoyin'
it I'll be bound?' Kate nodded again, too interested in
Mrs Midgley and her wheel-chair and the whys and
wherefores of her being in it to answer politely. Then
suddenly aware that she was staring rather, and Mrs
Midgley in the middle of some work, she smiled and said,
a little confusedly, that the Dew Drop was just lovely,
thank you, and went into the shop.

No black looks here! She was greeted with a very
friendly smile by the plump lady behind the counter,
while on the counter itself, instead of a horrible poker-
work notice, a white cat was curled up; a snow-white cat,
with long silky hair, a delicate shell-pink nose, and eyes
the colour of ripening green gooseberries.

'Oh!' gasped Kate, all thoughts of her postcard driven
out of her head by this piece of animal perfection, '*Oh*,
isn't he lovely! Please may I stroke him?'

'Yes, he's lovely all right' replied the plump postmis-
tress, 'and well he knows it – don't you, Thomas, old man?
You stroke him as much as you like – he won't object.'

'His *fur*!' exclaimed Kate, burying her hand in it, 'and
his dear little pink nose ... and his funny, greeny eyes!
... Thomas ... oh, Thomas! ... Oh, I think he's the
loveliest cat I ever saw!'

'Well you'll go a long way to find his equal,' said
Thomas's owner complacently, 'That's certain. He's everything a cat ought to be – that's what Thomas is; everything a cat ought to be' she repeated, 'and you can't say
more than that!' No indeed; but where – how – did one
get a cat like that? How often had she begged Mrs Ruggles
to keep a cat ... and always the same answer! 'Cats need
milk, and milk costs money; you'll have to wait awhile.'
... Well, she *had* waited – ages; but suppose ... suppose

she could find a white cat like Thomas . . . or better still, a
little, *tiny* kitten . . . and arrive home *with* it . . . a little
baby kitten wouldn't drink *much* milk . . . and Mum
couldn't just turn it out into the street . . . no one
could. . . . Suppose . . .

'What was it you were wanting?' inquired Miss
Midgley and recalled to the present Kate explained what
she had come for.

'A postcard of the Dew Drop Inn?' repeated Miss
Midgley. 'Yes, we did have some – there's a few left put
away in a box somewheres. . . . But you're staying along
of Mrs Wildgoose aren't you?' (How *did* everybody know
that!) 'You've no call to buy one – she's got plenty; keeps
them special for her visitors – she'll give you one if you
ask her. You keep your pennies for something else, my
dear – you'll need them for sure!'

Really, thought Kate, as she left the shop – after a
lingering farewell to Thomas (and remembering a polite
'good morning' to Miss Midgley) there was some fate
about those pennies!

She stopped at the gate, intending to say 'good morning' to Mrs Midgley too, but she was busy adding up a
column of figures and held up a warning finger not to be
interrupted.

How dreadful to have all that adding up to do! thought
Kate who detested arithmetic in any form or shape. Poor
Mrs Midgley! A sort of cripple *and* doing sums all day!
She felt quite sad as she opened the gate and started off
down Post Office Lane. But not for long. There was too
much to see and to think about. Her head was full of white
kittens and further exploring, and Post Office Lane looked
particularly inviting. She stopped for a moment and,
putting the white kitten ideas away at the back of her
mind for the present, pulled Mr Wildgoose's map out of

her pocket and studied it carefully. Nothing further of
interest was marked until one turned into Church Street
so she folded it up again and walked on. On past yellow-
coloured cottages of varying degrees of orange, some
thatched, some tiled, and other more usual-looking little
dwellings; past gardens in which iris and lupins, tulips
and peonies and all the riot of late spring flowers mingled
with fast-fading forget-me-nots and hyacinths; past others
not so flowery but from which warm, intoxicating scents

floated out; flowering currant, wallflower, bergamot; on
under the shade of three tall chestnuts growing close
together in a very friendly kind of way beside a high brick
wall; a wall in which was a mysterious-looking little door,
its once green paint now almost blue, blistered and flaking
with sun and time; on to where the wall ended and became a tangly hedge, the road turned sharply to the right,
and, almost before you knew it, you were round a corner
and into Church Street. Here she stopped and consulted
the map again, for it was somewhere in Church Street Mr
Wildgoose had put the squiggle marked Pond Passage.

This name excited her curiosity – why, she couldn't tell. She only knew she wanted to explore it very specially. Yes, there it was, marked about half-way up on the left.

Church Street was rather different in character from Post Office Lane. To begin with, except for the school just opposite the church, there were houses on one side only and these had no front gardens but were bordered by a high footpath. On the other side of the road was a kind of mud and plaster wall with something Kate had certainly never seen before – a little roof of thatch to protect it from the weather! It varied somewhat in height and in most places she was unable to see over it, even standing on tiptoe. Where she could, however, she identified some of the fields with peculiar names Mr Wildgoose had marked, and 'The Stream' winding across them, a curving, twisting line, now blue, now silver. All at once there was a gap in the thatched wall, and a narrow, well-trodden little path led away into a green leafy tunnel formed by high tangled hedges and the intertwined overhanging branches of trees. This must be Pond Passage and, feeling rather excited, Kate plunged into it.

The hedges were so high and so thick the sunlight was almost shut out, but the little path went turning and twisting in a delightfully mysterious way, and then, just when you expected it was going on for ever, ended abruptly in a precarious-looking one-plank bridge with a rickety hand-rail, spanning a swiftly-running stream which a little farther on widened into a small willow-fringed pond. On the other side of the stream was a strip of green, then a low brick wall with iron palings, and a gate leading into the garden of a tiny cottage. This cottage was divided into two, each half having a door and two windows, one upstairs, one down; across the front was painted 'Pond

Cottages 1847', while on the doors, numbers '1' and '2' in brass shone so dazzlingly bright that one suspected the inhabitants must hold a daily polishing competition.

In the garden of the nearer of the two cottages an old man was sitting in the sun. All around were currant and gooseberry bushes covered with old lace curtains to keep off the birds, and, in case this was insufficient to curb their activities, to each bush was attached a long piece of string. At intervals on this string, tin lids and cans were tied. The ends of the strings were gathered together in one of the old man's hands, and every now and then he would jerk his arm and the tin cans would clang and rattle a warning. A robber thrush, unimpressed, perched on a lilac bush behind him.

Dividing his garden from that of his neighbour were several old iron bedheads which served as a fence, while the path to the door was bordered by a neat row of up-ended half-buried green bottles placed side by side.

'And what might you be wanting, my dear?' he called, looking up and seeing Kate hesitating with one foot on the little bridge. 'You come over if you want – the bridge is safe enough.' Reassured that this was so, for she was longing to walk across it, Kate needed no further telling.

'I'm not really *wanting* anything,' she explained when she was safely on the strip of grass on the other side, 'I'm just exploring. That *was* Pond Passage, wasn't it?' she added, pointing over her shoulder.

'Aye, that's Pond Passage right enough,' replied the old man, 'and who might you be, my dear? Ah, drat you – !' as a large blackbird alighted on one of the currant bushes. And he gave the string of tins a vigorous jerk.

'My name's Kate – Kate Ruggles, and I'm staying at the Dew Drop Inn with Mrs Wildgoose,' replied Kate. But unlike Mrs Megson at the shop, or the ladies at the Post Office, the old man seemed neither to know nor be interested in this last piece of information.

'Ruggles?' he repeated, 'Ruggles? Ah. That's not a name as we gets hereabouts; no more nor mine come to that. I likes on-common names myself,' he added, 'and just as well, seein' I've got one. *Ah! You there! . . .*' to some sparrows. And he rattled the tins noisily.

'What *is* your name, please?' asked Kate remembering the mysterious 'S' and 'M' on Mr Wildgoose's map. The old man chuckled.

'Well you'll never guess'un,' he said. 'Never; so I might as well tell 'ee. I be Mr Shakespeare – Mr William Shakespeare! Never thought to meet *him* now, did you!' and he chuckled again.

'And what's more,' he went on, as Kate stood regarding him in round-eyed astonishment, 'what's more, I lives next door to Mr Milton. "Poets' Corner" they calls us! You've heard tell of Mr Milton? You've not!' – as Kate shook her head. 'Dear, dear; what's they learn you to school these days! Never heard of *Paradise Lost*? Well, well! Mr Milton'll be upset to hear that – very upset he'll be!'

Kate put her basket (which for some time had been growing a little heavy) on the strip of wall beneath the palings and regarded Mr Shakespeare gravely – surprised beyond measure. William Shakespeare! She had never thought anyone *could* be called that somehow; at least not a real alive person, though there was no reason why not if you thought properly about it. . . . But did the old man imagine she thought he was the *real* William Shakespeare! She hastened to assure him she did not!

There was silence for a minute (except for a faint jingling of the tin cans). Kate regarded Mr Shakespeare a little anxiously. She hoped he was not offended. Suddenly he chuckled again.

'They says,' he remarked, nodding his head as he spoke, the better to emphasize his words, 'they says as old birds ain't caught with chaff. No, nor young 'uns either seemingly today! But jokes apart,' he went on, ''tis right what I tells you, my dear. I were christened William Shakespeare well and truly – same's my friend next door were christened John Milton. I can't tell you truer nor that! And here he comes – here comes Mr Milton; but you must speak up loud to him, my dear, for he's very hard o' hearing.'

Kate looked towards the other half of the cottage. Emerging from the door was a very old man indeed, with a long white beard. On his head was a battered straw hat, and over his trousers he wore a dark blue apron with a pocket in front like the pouch of a kangaroo. Peeping from it was the tip of a trowel and several odds and ends of raffia. Over his shoulder he carried a large garden fork. 'Comin' to dig his potatoes for dinner,' explained Mr Shakespeare.

At first sight Mr Milton's garden appeared to consist almost entirely of potatoes, but if you looked carefully you could see a patch of newly-sown peas and beans. From sticks firmly planted among these, cats' heads cut out of black tin, with glittering green marbles for eyes, hung suspended by strings to keep off the birds, while the path to the gate instead of being bordered by bottles, was neatly edged with old scallop shells.

Kate was introduced as 'a young lady from foreign parts come to visit us' which made her feel very grown-up and pleasantly important. But Mr Milton appeared quite unimpressed. He regarded her stolidly and remarked it were a fine day – very.

'She's never heard tell of *Paradise Lost*!' shouted Mr Shakespeare, 'there's schoolin' for you!'

Mr Milton put his hand to his ear. 'What's that you say – it's going to rain?' Mr Shakespeare repeated his information.

'What's that – the goat's loose again?'

'It's no good. It's one of his bad days – he's deafer some days nor others,' explained Mr Shakespeare. And though Kate was sorry for Mr Milton's affliction, she couldn't help feeling if he was going to be upset by her lack of 'schoolin' perhaps it was a good thing it *was* one of those days!

But Mr Shakespeare seemed almost to *want* to upset his friend!

'You'm late with your taters, John!' he shouted, 'never have they cooked by dinner-time you won't – 'tis long gone the quarter!' Whether Mr Milton heard or not he said nothing but, turning his back on them both, lifted the fork from his shoulder and set about his digging.

But Kate was aghast! 'Long gone the quarter' – *already*! 'Be sure and be back by a quarter to twelve sharp, my dear,' Mrs Wildgoose had said, 'because dinner'll be early today.'

'Oh, how long past the quarter has it gone please, Mr Shakespeare?' she cried. 'I've got to be back at the Dew Drop at a quarter to twelve, *special*!'

Mr Shakespeare drew a watch the size of a small saucer from his pocket and consulted it in a leisurely manner.

'Twenty-eight – and – three-quarter-minutes-past-the-hour,' he announced. 'Easy does it . . . easy does it!' he cried as Kate seized her basket and the bag of biscuits fell out, part of its contents spilling over the grass – some of them perilously near the stream. 'Easy does it!' he repeated ''Tis only ten minutes walk to the Dew Drop – not that!'

'But I want to go back by Church End and Parsley Lane and Hare's Corner, not up Post Office Lane,' explained Kate, feeling like an inhabitant of twenty years' standing at least as she glibly named these thoroughfares.

'Bless you, they be all of a lump together – just round the corner!' replied Mr Shakespeare, 'Pond Passage be the very middle of the village – 'tis the same distance to the Dew Drop whichever way you goes – as I ought to know, fetching me beer these thirty years! Don't you go a-hurryin' or you'll be dropping all they things in the water!'

'I'll be very careful, Mr Shakespeare,' said Kate, picking up the biscuits and settling the bag more firmly in the basket, 'and I *have* liked meeting you! Isn't it funny, I felt all the time there was going to be something specially

interesting about Pond Passage! I do *hope*,' she went on,
'you won't mind if I ask, but do – do you think you might
be a *relaytive* of the *real* Shakespeare – a sort of cousin or
something? You see, we're going to *do* him at school next
term and if I could tell the girls I'd met one of his relaytives they *would* be thrilled! ... And ... oh – I've just
thought of something! If I brought my Book of Celebrities
along, would you write your name in it? You see Shakespeare was such a really *terrifically* great man that an auto-
graph of someone who was even only *perhaps* a relaytive
would be marvellous to have! I've only got the mayor of
Otwell so far,' she concluded a little sadly.

Mr Shakespeare chuckled once again. 'Well,' he said
slowly, 'I've never heard tell, so far as I knows on, as I
were a relaytive, but come to that I've never heard tell as
I *weren't*; and at this time o'day I don't see who's to sort it
out. No. You tell 'em that, my dear. I can't say fairer.
And bring yer book along! "Celebrity"! ... Old William
Shakespeare of Pond Cottages! ... You tell that to
Charlie Wildgoose when you gets back to the Dew Drop –
he'll enjoy that, Charlie will! ... and happen next time
you comes Mr Milton'll be better. ... Yes, maybe he
will!' And uncertain whether to be pleased or dismayed
at this prospect, Kate said good-bye.

It was true; they were 'all of a lump together'. Church
End was just the end of Church Street and Hare's Corner
(*why* Hare's corner? – she longed to know!) the end of
Parsley Lane. There was only time for a glance at 'The
Marrow Way – Digweed's Farm Only', but it was con-
soling to see it was definitely unapproachable without
gum-boots. (How lucky Mrs Ruggles had insisted on
packing a pair, even though they were old ones of Lily
Rose's and quite three sizes too big. 'Big they may be, but
better big than none, and better still than wet feet and

colds,' she had said when Kate had raised objections to
them.)

Parsley Lane was well named. The high banks on either
side were covered with a creamy foam of cow-parsley,
delicate as lace – a bridal veil of loveliness. ('You should
see it by moonlight,' said Mr Wildgoose when Kate
mentioned it later in the day. ''Tis a rare sight by moonlight!') And when you reached the end of Parsley Lane,
there was the main road again; a cottage or two; some
little girls who stared, and whispered, and then giggled;
The Red Lion – a public house as different-looking from
the Dew Drop as was the Brewers' Arms in One End
Street – the now familiar row of orangy-coloured cottages;
and, last of all, the field with Mr Plodder's cow. Kate
spared a precious moment to look over the gate and see
how it was getting on, but the field was empty. Perhaps
they had taken it back to its calf? She hoped very much
this was so. She hurried across the road to the Dew Drop
Inn and as she opened the kitchen door the church clock
chimed a quarter to twelve!

'Well, *there's* a good, reliable, girl!' cried Mrs Wildgoose as Kate put her basket down on the table with a
small sigh of satisfaction.

(ii) An Invitation

Dinner was over and all Kate's adventures related – those
concerning Mrs Megson with some indignation.

'I should have warned you,' said Mrs Wildgoose.
'Must have been one of her bad days – was there some
red knitting about, did you notice? There was? Ah, that
was it then! She don't mean half she says – very kind she
is really – specially if anyone's in trouble.' Kate looked

incredulous but Mrs Wildgoose nodded. Then she decreed a short rest on their beds for her visitors. 'Just today, my dears, anyway,' she urged, 'because you see yesterday you all came a journey, and today – well, Kate's seen more of Upper Cassington in an hour than I do in a twelvemonth – and where Peg and Jo have been I *don't* know!'

'Why, we've only been in the garden – and most of the time on a *mat*!' protested Jo who rather resented the waterproof rug.

'Well, I heard all kinds of adventures going on,' replied Mrs Wildgoose, 'shipwrecks, and robbers, and bears-coming-out-of-a-forest – Elsie and I got quite frightened!'

'*I* got frightened too,' observed Peg. 'I don't like bears, I don't. Only Buttonhook. Can I have him now, please?' And she pointed across the room to the chair to which he had been banished during the meal. Mrs Wildgoose handed him over, and Jo regarded her out of the corners of his eyes, uncertain whether she was laughing at them or not. Only in a nice way he decided, while Kate protested she was not 'one atom' tired.

'No my dear, I dare say not, not now,' replied Mrs Wildgoose, 'but you will be by tonight. Now you all go up and have a nice rest on your beds for an hour – there's some story-books on the shelf in the sitting-room – you take some of those with you, and at two o'clock I'll give you a call, and we'll all go out together; up you go now, and remember, *shoes off* before you gets on the beds! And now Elsie and I must get on with the washing-up.'

There was no resisting story-books for Kate, and when she had chosen one for herself and another she considered suitable for Peg and Jo, they all went upstairs, obediently took off their shoes, and curled up on their beds though it all seemed very strange at one o'clock in the afternoon, and something they had most certainly *never* done at home! Kate was soon lost in her book but Peg and Jo were sleepy after their long morning in the sun and good, hot dinner and, after ten minutes or so, Peg's 'What's *that*?' and the rustling noise of pages turning over stopped and there was silence from the big feather-bed. It certainly did not seem as if an hour had gone by when they heard Mrs Wildgoose calling.

But when they arrived downstairs, a disappointment awaited them. Someone had called on business connected with the Inn; Mr and Mrs Wildgoose were with him in the sitting-room, and Mrs Wildgoose would not be able to come out with them after all, she told them, putting her head round the door for a minute. She was sorry; it *would* just happen today, but Elsie would tell them what had been arranged, and they must be good and mind what she said, and tea would be all ready when they got back.

It seemed they were to have gone with Mrs Wildgoose to Lower Cassington, to take a basket of eggs for a friend and customer of hers. These eggs were specially needed before tomorrow, and another basketful had to be taken to Mrs Megson's shop. Unluckily Elsie had to leave early today as a sister from London was coming to spend the night; there would be no time for her to go to both places and so, thinking Kate might not want to meet Mrs Megson again just yet, Mrs Wildgoose had suggested she should take the eggs intended for Lower Cassington while Elsie with Peg and Jo took the ones for the shop, coming along as far as possible, in the time, to meet Kate on her return journey.

Peg and Jo looked pleased, for they had already formed a great affection for Elsie-as-helps-me as Jo would persist in calling her, while Kate, though she would have liked Mrs Wildgoose's company, was pleased at the idea of further exploring by herself. How did she get to Lower Cassington, she asked?

Well, said Elsie, you couldn't miss the way. You just turned right when you came out of the Inn and, almost straight ahead of you, you saw some big, wide-open gates. These gates, it seemed, guarded the entrance to a drive that was the property of a very grand lady – Mrs Ayredale-Eskdale, who lived in the big house called The Priory that you could see as you went over the bridge which formed part of the drive.

'But don't you go along the bit of drive that leads to the house itself, whatever you do!' said Elsie, 'and keep careful to the gravel all the way, for if Mrs Ayredale-Eskdale or one of her gardeners catch you as much as an inch off it, there'll be trouble! You just walk straight on after the bridge,' she continued, 'and then you'll see another lot of gates. Go through them, and you're right *in* Lower Cassington. There *is* a proper road, of course,' she added, 'but 'tis much further that way and old Colonel Ayredale-Eskdale, as died a few years back, he always let people use his drive; but Mrs Ayredale-Eskdale – she's a haughty one she is – they say as she don't like it and would stop it if she could, but her daughter – Miss Alison – *very* nice young lady she is – all thinks she persuades her mother to allow it. . . . But mind and keep to the gravel like as I said. Here's the eggs now – they're for Mrs Paddle at Hazel Cottage – you can't miss it – it's the first you come to – the name's on the gate – and we'll come and meet you soon's we done at the shop. You'll like to come along of Elsie, won't you, ducks?' she asked, smiling at Peg and Jo. They both smiled back, partly with pleasure, and partly at the unfamiliar term of endearment, and Peg immediately began whispering into the ragged ear of Buttonhook.

'What's it you're tellin' him so special, my pet?' asked

Elsie, who had decided she would like a little boy and girl of her own one day like Peg and Jo. 'Tell Elsie!'

For a moment Peg looked undecided whether to reveal her secret or not. Then, 'It's some moneys we've got to spend – Buttonhook and me,' she announced. 'It's nuffing to do with Kate and Jo,' she added, 'It's my moneys!'

Kate and Jo looked a little surprised.

'What do you mean "your moneys" – you haven't got any money?' said Kate. 'Mum gave all our pocket-money to me to keep.'

'I *has*!' replied Peg, and she nodded her head vigorously. 'I has! I got moneys of my own! Dad give it me – day afore we come away,' and she turned her back on Kate and after much fumbling in the pocket of her frock, produced a very small, very crumpled, paper bag. Out of it, slowly and with great solemnity, she shook four farthings.

'Those makes a penny!' she announced with awe. '*One whole penny!*' Jo stared – a little impressed, but Kate tossed her head and said in a superior voice, 'Oh! – *farthings!*'

A very stormy look indeed appeared on Peg's face and Elsie, fearing tears, said well, farthings was farthings and four *did* make a penny, and for that, in Mrs Megson's shop there were oh, *ever* so many things to choose from! Harmony was restored, and a few minutes later they all set forth.

Kate quickly found the big gates and walked briskly along the drive which sloped gently downhill between fields where root and other crops were planted. All along one side grew vast elm trees but gradually these gave place to fencing and the fields to water-meadows. Very

soon the bridge came in sight, and a little way beyond it
she could see The Priory, an immense grey stone building
with a battlemented roof, and what she called 'church'
windows – narrow, pointed, small-paned windows, set
deep into the stone. What an *enormous* house! As soon as
she reached the bridge, Kate put down the basket of eggs
and, leaning her elbows on the low, stone parapet, stood
regarding it with amazement. How *old* it looked! And
fancy living in a house that size – just Mrs – what was
her name – Mrs Ayredale? – Surely that was a sort of
dog? and Kate giggled a little to herself – Mrs Ayredale,
and Miss – Miss Alison – wasn't it? Elsie had called her.

She had sounded nice. . . . However many rooms could
there be? . . . and what would it be like to wake up in one
of them in the morning? . . . How would . . .

'Little girl!' said a deep voice behind her, 'Little girl!
What are you doing, loitering on this bridge? Are you
aware this is Private Property?'

Kate gave a start, and turning round and nearly
knocking over the egg-basket found herself confronted by
a tall stately lady who regarded her very coldly through

a pair of tortoiseshell-rimmed lorgnettes. Mrs Ayredale – her very self!

'If I have to complain *once* more about Cassington children,' continued this alarming personage, 'I shall . . .' But at this moment, from somewhere beside the bridge, another, very much younger lady appeared. She wore no hat; she had shining grey eyes, and in her arms she carried a very tiny, snow-white kitten – a kitten who was, without doubt, a near relative to Thomas at the Post Office!

'I don't think, Mother,' she said, glancing at Kate and addressing the older lady, 'I don't think this *is* a Cassington child.'

'Well, Alison,' replied the stately lady, 'you ought to know – with your Guides and your Clubs and your Sunday Schools; but really it makes no difference *where* she comes from. I will not,' and here she tapped her daughter on the arm with her lorgnettes, narrowly missing the white kitten's nose – 'I will *not* have children – or anyone else – loitering here. This drive is not a Right-of-Way, it is *A Concession*! Off you go, little girl,' – turning to Kate, 'at once! And don't let me find you leaning over my bridge again! Now you see, Alison – what I am always saying. You give them an inch and they take an ell! Run along little girl – quickly now – Do you hear me!'

Kate heard – only too well! With flaming cheeks she picked up her basket and scuttled off; but she thought she detected a look of sympathy on the face of the Ayredale lady's daughter. Oh, if only she could have met *her* – alone – and asked where she got that white kitten!

Half-walking, half-running, fearful of dropping the eggs out of the basket, Kate reached the end of the drive, went through the gates, and very quickly discovered Hazel Cottage. Rather breathlessly she delivered the eggs, and slowly started to walk back towards the drive. At the gates

she paused. Would Mrs Ayredale be on the bridge still –
or *anywhere* about? She just hated the idea of meeting her
again! . . . But Elsie would be waiting, and she had promised to be quick; there was nothing to be done but go on
and hope for the best. . . . She looked anxiously ahead,
however, as she turned in at the gates. At first the bridge
was hidden by a group of limes but once she had passed
these it came into sight, and oh, thank goodness – there
was no one there! No one about at all! But yes, yes there
was! Away beside the house stood Mrs Ayredale – but –
she had her back to the drive and was apparently in earnest
conversation with a man with a wheel-barrow. Kate went
swiftly on her way, never pausing until she was out of
sight of the house and half-way to Upper Cassington; then
she stopped.

Phew! how hot she was! All that rushing, and *worry*!
Off the gravel or not, she must have a rest if it was only
for two minutes. And she crossed the strip of long, lush
grass that bordered the drive and sat down, leaning her
back against the bole of one of the big elm trees.

How lovely it was sitting there! Looking up, the glossy
spring-fresh leaves made dazzling patterns against the
sky, and the long cool grass all around was somehow rest-
ful and soothing. She went off into what Mrs Ruggles
called 'one of her dreams' and it was nearer five minutes
than two before she remembered time again. She jumped
to her feet, and as she did so she saw someone coming
towards her. This someone was singing; she was without
a hat; and as she drew nearer it was seen that she had
shining grey eyes, and was carrying a very little, snow-
white kitten! With a hop, skip, and a jump, Kate was on
the gravel again, but before she had time to think what to
do next, the owner of the white kitten was speaking.

'I see you've delivered your eggs safely!' she said. 'I'm

so glad; I was afraid you might drop them – having to hurry so. You're staying at Upper Cassington, I expect?' she went on, 'with Mrs Wildgoose, perhaps? She told me last week she was expecting some visitors. Now I wonder if that is so, how long you'll be there because soon we shall be having our hay-party; Mrs Wildgoose always comes, and I expect you'd like to come too, wouldn't you?'

For a moment Kate was too surprised to speak at all! No cross looks! No reproofs! No orderings-about! Instead, an invitation to a party – a hay-party – whatever that was – though she was sure any party given by the lady with the shining eyes (as she now privately christened 'Miss Alison') would be no ordinary one! At last, however, she managed to stammer out that she *was* staying with Mrs Wildgoose – for a whole six weeks – and oh, yes, she *would* like to come to a party, thank you! And then, rather shyly, and please could her little brother and sister come too? The lady with the shining eyes smiled and said, yes, of course – how old were they and what were their names? And was very soon being informed not only of these facts, but about measles, and railway journeys and many details of family life at One End Street. There was no doubt she was a sympathetic listener – certainly Kate had never felt less shy so quickly with anyone, she told herself later. 'And oh, Miss!' she added when at last she came to the end of her travels and family history, '*could* you tell me where I could find a little white kitten same as the one you've got? I do want one so!'

'Well actually he's not mine,' replied Miss Ayredale-Eskdale (to give her her correct name). 'He really belongs to my mother. She has a pair of white cats and every now and then they present her with a little family. This one – we've christened him Samuel – has two sisters and a brother. He's *very* young,' she went on, 'not quite three weeks old, but he's not been very well and I thought a little sunshine might do him good.' Kate's face fell somewhat. Oh why, *why* must the white kittens belong to the Ayredale lady of all people!

'Do you think, Miss?' she asked after a little hesitation, 'do you think Mrs — your mother – would *sell* me one – if, if *you* asked her?' she added hastily. 'I've got 2s. 6d. pocket money,' she went on, ' 1s. Mum gave me, and 1s. 6d. I've saved up for – oh – *ever* so long; and perhaps I could earn some more while I'm here – I don't quite know how, but I could *try*! Would a little kitten like that cost a *fearful* lot? I *would* so love to have one!'

Miss Ayredale-Eskdale smiled a little and said she was afraid her mother never sold her kittens. Sometimes she gave one away to a friend, or someone she was interested in – there was one at the Post Office – a big cat he was now – perhaps Kate had seen him?

Oh, thought Kate sadly, that settled it! The Ayredale lady's interest in her she was quite, quite sure would never be of a kind to warrant the gift of a white kitten!

Miss Ayredale-Eskdale noticed the look of distress on her face. 'Don't worry,' she said kindly, 'and I'll see what can be done. Why, you've only just come and you say you're going to be here six weeks; no end of things can happen in that time you know! . . . But listen! I believe I hear someone calling . . . yes, look! There's Mrs Wildgoose's Elsie waving to you.'

Oh dear, so it was!

'I'm coming! I'm coming!' called Kate. 'Good-bye, Miss, and thank you *ever* so! I'm just longing for the party – please, what sort did you say it was – a *hay*-party?'

'Yes! You ask Mrs Wildgoose what that is – you little town-mouse! Good-bye now, don't keep Elsie waiting.'

And not quite sure if she liked being called a town-mouse at all (much less a little one) Kate said good-bye again and ran off up the drive.

'Well, you're a one, you are!' exclaimed Elsie as Kate reached her. 'Calling and calling I've been and you standing there talking away to Miss Alison as if I'd never a train to go and meet!'

'I'm sorry, Elsie,' said Kate, 'I forgot; I really did! You see the lady with – Miss Alison I mean – asked me to a party – all of us – and it was so exciting, and oh, Elsie, what *do* you think? She's got a little white kitten like Thomas like as I told you of!' she added, forgetting her grammar badly in her excitement, 'and – why –' she broke off, 'What's the matter with Peg?' For Peg was giving little whimpers and sniffs, and looked as if she had not long ago cried *very* hard.

'It's all over now,' said Elsie, 'so don't say no more about it,' and she gave Kate a very meaning look. 'Mrs Megson upset her,' she added in a whisper. 'Wouldn't change them farthings – in one of her moods – oh she *was* and no mistake! But we're going to the Post Office on Monday, aren't we, duck?' she said aloud, looking down at Peg, 'And they won't say "no" to farthings *there*; but we just hadn't time today. I offered her a penny of my own,' she added turning again to Kate, 'but she wouldn't have it; must be those farthings she spent or nothing.'

Kate was just about to say, 'Well, how silly,' but Elsie held up a warning finger and hastily changed the subject.

But Peg remained subdued, even through the lovely tea Mrs Wildgoose had ready for them when they got back; and all the rest of the day, right up to bed-time, she kept whispering, whispering, in the ear of Buttonhook – what, no one could guess, though Jo privately decided it must be a plan to murder Mrs Megson; and he observed his small sister with interest.

(iii) Four Farthings

On Sunday at the Dew Drop Inn everyone got up much later, and there were sizzling brown sausages for breakfast.

'And today,' said Mrs Wildgoose when her visitors had done full justice to these, 'the service at the church is in the morning, so we'll all go along.'

'But isn't there always one on Sunday morning?' asked Kate in a surprised voice. 'At our church at Otwell there's one in the morning, and one in the evening – and one for children in the afternoon – besides some sort of extras,' she added.

'Ah, but I expect you've got a clergyman all to yourselves,' said Mrs Wildgoose. 'I mean,' she went on, as they all looked rather astonished, 'I mean a clergyman with only one church to attend to. It's different here in Upper Cassington. Mr Wilson – he's the Vicar – has another church over to Hadden – that's four mile away – so we have to share him, as you might say, with the Hadden folk. It's one Sunday Morning service here and Evening there, and the next the other way about.'

This was something quite new to the Ruggles children and Kate couldn't help wondering how Mr Theobald, the very energetic vicar of St Mary's at Otwell would care about being 'shared'!

'No Sunday School, then?' asked Jo hopefully. For though he normally enjoyed this and was, in fact, rather a shining light in his class, it was, after all, a sort of lessons and they *were* supposed to be having a holiday!

Mrs Wildgoose replied there was a Sunday School right enough – at two o'clock in the Church Room if Jo wanted to go – but there was no children's service – only once a month – they all came to the ordinary one, and did Kate think Peg would manage to sit quiet for an hour – it was never much more? Perhaps, she went on, regarding her smallest guest a little doubtfully, Peg would rather stay at home with Mr Wildgoose who would not be coming because someone must mind the house? But before Kate had time to reply Peg protested so strongly against this that Mr Wildgoose looked quite hurt. He said he was afraid Peg didn't like him very much!

'I do!' protested Peg, 'I *do* like you! But I wants to go to church. I wants to go *special*!'

'Well that's something new!' said Kate. 'I expect it's because she thinks it's grand to go to a grown-up service,' she said by way of explanation to Mrs Wildgoose. 'She makes no end of a fuss about going at home!'

Peg gave Kate a very black look and Jo, remembering the whisperings of the evening before, became suddenly interested.

'Will Mrs Megson be there?' he inquired. Mrs Wildgoose laughed, and Kate looked a little concerned. She had half-forgotten about Mrs Megson.

'Maybe,' replied Mrs Wildgoose, 'but she don't always come. We shan't be sitting near her anyway, so don't you worry. And now, if Kate'll give me a hand, I'll clear away – I don't wash up Sundays – and then we'll all go and get ready. And mind!' she called as Peg and Jo prepared to follow Mr Wildgoose into the garden, 'no going near the ducks and hens in your nice Sunday clothes!'

The approach to Upper Cassington church was very pretty. Through an iron gate of beautiful design, made by a blacksmith in a neighbouring parish 'in the days when they did such things' explained Mrs Wildgoose, a path of cobblestones, laid in patterns and bordered by little polled lime trees, led to an immensely thick oak door, with massive iron hinges, set in a porch of lichen-grey stone, worn and weathered by the storms and sunshine of nearly seven centuries. Mrs Wildgoose, holding Peg by the hand, led the way up the cobblestone path, Kate following and Jo bringing up the rear. But however beautiful the iron gate might be; however intriguing the cobblestone patterns; however interesting the big oak door and the old stone porch, for Kate, Peg, and Jo they did not exist! They were conscious only of eyes – dozens of pairs of eyes! Inquisitive, inquiring eyes! The eyes – or so it seemed – of all the children in Upper and, probably, Lower Cassington! There they stood, beneath the polled limes and grouped about the stone porch, children of every sort, shape, and size; and one and all staring with all their might at Mrs Wildgoose's three visitors!

It was as bad as the first day at her new school, thought Kate – worse – for there at least you knew some of the people by sight if not by name. However many were there! It looked like *hundreds*! (In reality it was only about twenty-five – the combined Sunday Schools of Upper and Lower Cassington.)

She was glad she was wearing her school blazer over her Sunday dress. Like her hat with its striped band and crest it somehow helped to give her confidence, and, she hoped fervently, might impress her present audience. Mrs Wildgoose nodded at some of the children as she led the way through the porch and into the cool, dim church. At a pew about half-way up in the middle she paused, told Kate to go first so that Peg might sit between them and followed after, settling herself with Jo on her other side.

There were not very many people in the church thought Kate when after sitting quietly for a few minutes she began to look about her, and of Mrs Megson there seemed no sign. But away, up in the very front pew of all sat – yes – there was no doubt of it – the Ayredale lady, very resplendent indeed in a long grey silky sort of coat, and a hat covered with roses and velvet. Beside her was her daughter in a soft green dress with a green straw hat to match.

Presently the organ began to play, and all at once there was a tramping and shuffling of feet and in came the 'combined' Sunday Schools. Jo looked round for a minute but encountered such a battery of eyes he was effectively cured of doing so again! The next minute the curtains of the vestry were pulled back and the choir, two very old men, one very young one, and four little boys – one not much bigger than Jo himself – all with rather muddy boots showing beneath their cassocks, came up the aisle.

Kate looked curiously at the 'shared' vicar who followed them – a tall, thin, elderly man with a kindly face. He looked nice, she thought, and his voice, when he began to read, was delightful.

Until the time for the first lesson, Peg's behaviour, except for a little fidgeting, was perfect. But now, as they prepared to sit down, she turned suddenly to Kate.

'When do we put our moneys in the bag?' she demanded in a loud whisper, and pointed hopefully at the penny provided by Mrs Wildgoose for the collection lying on the book-board in front of her.

'Hush!' said Kate in a shocked whisper.

'But when *do* we?' persisted Peg, even more loudly.

'Oh not for ages yet – be *quiet*!' whispered Kate with an anxious look at the Vicar who was preparing to read, 'and listen to the story.'

Peg subsided and Kate hoped the lesson might indeed

be a story and one which her small sister could understand. Daniel in the Lion's Den, or about Joseph and his dreams perhaps. . . . But alas! as so often happened if one went to a grown-up service, it seemed one had come in in the middle of something – at least that's how she would feel if it were the cinema, she thought. . . . And although she listened very carefully, try as she would she could not understand what it was all about. . . . If only it could be explained before the reading began what had happened earlier – like the serial stories in 'comics' – and, for that matter, perhaps something of what you might expect to hear if you came next week? . . .

In the prayers and singing that followed, Peg became very fidgety indeed, demanding at frequent intervals when 'bag-time' would be, and it was a relief when the time for the sermon arrived.

'The *next* hymn after this will be the bag one,' whispered Kate as the one they were singing came to an end and the Vicar climbed into the pulpit and they all sat down.

Mrs Wildgoose put an arm about Peg hoping she would remain quiet, but Peg wriggled and pulled away. Well, she had not behaved badly on the whole, thought Mrs Wildgoose . . . as for Jo, he was a real little angel, singing away lovely! . . . Fortunately Mr Wilson never preached long. . . .

Today he was even briefer than usual and less than five minutes later Mrs Wildgoose rose thankfully to her feet.

As the final hymn was announced, from a pew near the front where he had been hidden from them by a pillar, an old man emerged with a collection bag. *Mr Shakespeare!!*

In her surprise Kate nearly dropped the penny she was holding in readiness.

As he approached their pew he gave her a kind but-I-
don't-smile-in-church sort of look, and Kate tried hard to
give him the same kind back when – good gracious!
Whatever was happening! What *was* Peg trying to do? For
no sooner had the bag been passed to Mrs Wildgoose, who
prepared to hold it while Kate, Peg, and Jo put in their
pennies, than Peg snatched it from her and, turning
round, proceeded to empty its entire contents – two half-
crowns, a sixpence, and several pennies, on to the seat!
And before Mrs Wildgoose or Kate – much less Mr Shakespeare – had grasped what was happening, pulled four
farthings from her pocket, replaced them with a penny
from the contents of the bag and, adding her 'collection'
penny, bundled back the remaining money. Finally, with
a small sigh of satisfaction, as of one who has completed a
good day's work and is proud of it, she handed the bag to
Mrs Wildgoose.

'Can we go home now, please?' she asked – in a very
loud whisper indeed!

'But why didn't you ask me to give you a penny for your
farthings, my dear?' asked Mrs Wildgoose as they stood
in the churchyard a few minutes later discussing Peg's
curious behaviour.

'Whyever couldn't you have waited till tomorrow, and
changed them at the Post Office – like Elsie said you
could?' demanded Kate rather crossly.

'Be-cos,' said Peg, slowly, and replying carefully to
each question in turn, 'Be-cos *you*' – pointing at Mrs Wildgoose, 'might say "no"; and be-cos the people in the Post
Office might say "no" too – like Mrs Megson. In church,'
and she nodded her head emphatically, 'in church, *no one*
can't say "no"!'

CHAPTER SEVEN

A Day of Disasters

I

HOW quickly the days went by – and yet how long and packed with things to do each one seemed! At the end of a week Peg and Jo began to feel they had lived in the country for years and years, while Kate used up her ten fingers twice over counting up all the agricultural lore she had acquired since she arrived, from why calves had to be taken from their mothers, to the reasons for rolling winter-sown wheat or 'spreading muck'. Before ten days had gone by, 'though I say it myself', said Mrs Wildgoose, 'no one wouldn't know them for the same children – so much better they all look!' And she wrote glowing accounts to Mrs Ruggles, which were sometimes supplemented by Kate, and, once, by Jo – Peg adding very large 'X's' at the bottom of each letter.

As time went on they came to know many more people in the village though Kate's first friends, the inhabitants of Pond Cottages and the ladies at the Post Office, remained her favourites to the end. Her autograph-book was duly signed by Mr Shakespeare with a great flourish and splutter of his pen, but though she shouted herself hoarse she never really succeeded in making Mr Milton hear a word she said! They all visited the Post Office frequently, Peg and Jo inventing every possible excuse to go inside in order to stroke Thomas, and once they were invited to tea, Thomas sitting up at the table in his own special chair and lapping delicately from a saucer as white as himself. As to possessing a kitten even remotely resembling him, much less one of his august relatives at The Priory, Kate had sadly abandoned the idea for ever. Miss Alison they met often, 'Busy as twenty bees' as Mr Wildgoose said; and the 'shared' vicar, Mr Wilson, who had always a kindly word, toffees in his pocket, and something *almost* resembling a wink for Peg! Digweed's Farm was duly visited, for they made great friends with a farm-hand, Willie Sims, who lived in one of the yellow cottages opposite the Inn. Willie Sims was a perfect mine of information on country matters – and – what was almost better – never minded answering questions. He introduced them to Mr Digweed himself who showed them all over his farm, listened with the utmost seriousness to Kate's agricultural ambitions, and said he only wished his own little girls felt the same. His little girls, who were her own age, were kind and friendly, but they couldn't understand how any girl could *possibly* want to farm! Oh, they loved the country and the animals they assured her, but it was *dull*! They wanted something exciting and they had both, they confided to her, made up their minds, to be what they called 'Secre-*taries*'.

They made other friends among the children – and one or two enemies, notably Johnnie Sears, of whom you shall hear presently; and a very superior young woman, Angela Smallpiece, who, hearing of Kate's ambitions from the Miss Digweeds, informed her (on the authority of her father, Mrs Ayredale-Eskdale's head gardener) that 'no one who hadn't been "born and bred on the land", would ever be any good on it'.

Kate was so upset by this statement that she summoned up all her courage and consulted Mr Digweed about it.

Mr Digweed settled the matter swiftly, in two words, 'Arrant nonsense', and dismissed Miss Smallpiece as an

'ignoramus', a lovely and comforting word which Kate
lost no time in repeating to her.

Mrs Megson remained a trial, for the shop had frequently to be visited, but, towards the end of their second
week, she was suddenly taken ill and whisked away to
hospital. A married daughter came to mind the shop and,
though everyone was sorry for Mrs Megson, there was no
denying shopping in Upper Cassington became a pleasanter and less alarming experience!

What an amount there would be to tell when they went
home, thought Kate one day, and remember! And not
only people and animals, but places and *things*. She would
remember, she was sure, all her life, the walk Mr Wildgoose had taken them one Sunday afternoon to the little
wood on the hill which she saw from her bedroom window.
The way lay across fields beside the river; rather boggy in
places. Big yellow iris grew there – 'flaggers' Mr Wildgoose called them, and the low banks of the river itself
were fringed with blue forget-me-nots. Between the fields
the hedges were beginning to be pink with dog-roses
following on the now-fading May; the sweet, sweet-
smelling May with its little red-stamened flowers that
somehow reminded her so much of Mrs Wildgoose's
nutmeg-sprinkled junkets! In the wood itself, where they
had tea from a thermos, and big, sugar-covered buns,
there were rabbits and squirrels to watch, some early-
ripened wild strawberries to pick, while in a nettle-bed –
surely a strange place to choose for a home! – they had
found a nest, hardly bigger than the palm of one's hand,
made, it seemed, entirely of grasses and horse-hair and a
fluffy feather or two. Inside, five goggle-eyed little fledg-
lings that Mr Wildgoose said were whitethroats, sat
huddled together, their tiny wings spilling over the sides,
their bills gaping open, all clamouring for food.

They had stayed until the shadows grew longer and longer, and a strange hush fell upon the little wood, and outside, in the fields, a milky mist began to rise.

They had arrived home very late for supper with wet feet, scratched faces, and nettle-stung legs, carrying armfuls of the 'flaggers' and their hats decorated with wild roses. Their noses were burnt scarlet from the sun, and her own face more than ever like a turkey's egg for freckles. A perfect, an unforgettable walk!

And now it was the last week of all! The-day-after-the-day-after-tomorrow would be Mrs Ayredale-Eskdale's party, and after that there would be only *two more days*!

'Oh!' said Kate to Mrs Wildgoose, 'I just can't bear to think of it!' and she looked almost ready to cry.

'Bless me!' exclaimed Mrs Wildgoose, 'if you go on like that you won't enjoy the days as *is* left! And, who knows, perhaps you'll all come again next year?'

But Kate shook her head. 'You have to be ill to have a holiday,' she said sadly. 'I know I wasn't – not really; it were just Mrs Beaseley's doing for me, but that couldn't ever happen again!' and she shook her head again, very mournfully.

'Don't you be so sure what'll happen,' said Mrs Wildgoose. 'You knows the old proverb, "Nothing happens but the unforeseen."'

Was that true? Kate wondered. But later, after the party and the days that followed it, thinking things over, she inclined very much to agree that it *was*!

Very early on the morning of Mrs Ayredale-Eskdale's party the sun was shining brightly, but by six o'clock, when Kate woke up, its brightness was beginning to fade. Leaning out of the window and looking anxiously towards what she had learnt from Mr Wildgoose to call 'the rainy quarter', she saw dark clouds gathering on the horizon; the bare hills stood out sharply, and it looked very, very like rain!

It mustn't, oh, it *mustn't* rain! 'Oh, God,' she prayed, 'do let it stay fine, *please*!' But was it any use asking? Only yesterday Willie Sims had said *he* was praying for rain for his roots – and probably Willie Sims's roots were far more important because they were necessary sort of things and Mrs Ayredale-Eskdale's party was just fun. . . . But couldn't the roots wait till tomorrow? One day couldn't matter *much*. . . . It looked as if they could not! By half past six a shivery little wind had sprung up, and a few rain-drops begun to patter down on to the honeysuckle leaves. Quicker, and quicker, and quicker they came; before seven it was pouring in good earnest!

'Dear, dear, *dear*!' exclaimed Mrs Wildgoose coming in to the bedroom just as the clock struck the hour, 'and so lovely it looked round about five o'clock too! I made sure we was in for a fine day! But don't you fret yourself, my dear,' she went on, noticing the expression of acute despair on Kate's face, 'you know the old saying, "Rain afore seven, fine afore eleven". There's plenty of time yet.' Kate tried to feel comforted, but the rain continued to pour steadily down and by ten-thirty it was still what Elsie described as 'teeming'. Anyway the hay would be spoilt, and how could you have a hay-party without hay? To this all-important question Mrs Wildgoose had to say she didn't know, but added she was sure Miss Alison would arrange *something*.

'Cheer up! cheer up!' cried Mr Wildgoose coming in for a moment before the bar opened. 'It's going to clear all right, tho' I don't say it won't be showery.'

'Oh, Mr Wildgoose, how *do* you know?' asked Kate. 'The sky's just grey as grey!'

'Have you looked at the hens – and the cows? You've not? Dear, dear! I thought we'd made more of a country girl of you by this time!'

Kate hung her head. How stupid she was not to have remembered! She felt very annoyed with herself as she recalled Mr Wildgoose's information – given the very first wet day after they arrived. Always to notice cows and hens, how hens ran in for a shower, but stayed out for a down-pour – 'not feeling it worth while getting their feathers wet for a short spell'; and how cows usually, 'I don't say *always*, mind you,' Mr Wildgoose had said, stood up and went on grazing if it was only a shower, but would lie down and so keep themselves at least one dry patch if it appeared to be 'setting in'.

'The cows are standing up!' cried Jo running to one window, 'and the hens are all out,' he announced dashing across the room to another from which the hen run was visible. 'And, oh, *look*!' he cried a moment later, 'Look! there's a *tiny* little bit of blue sky, away behind the hill with the wood on it!' Everyone crowded to look. Yes, so there was!

'Is it enough to make a sailor's trousers?' asked Mrs Wildgoose passing the open door on her way to the kitchen. 'What! never heard that?' she laughed as the children all looked puzzled. They stood gazing at the little patch. . . . It was hard to decide . . . perhaps . . . well, perhaps enough for a very *small* sailor. . . . But soon the patch spread – and spread – and spread again; before the kitchen clock chimed a quarter to eleven the rain really did seem to be coming down less violently. Very soon the blue patch was enough for a whole boat-load of sailors! In another five minutes the rain was quite definitely stopping and, almost on the stroke of eleven, the sun burst suddenly through a bank of cloud making the

puddles on the ground shining mirrors of silver, and
the drops of water on the leaves and thatch sparkle like
diamonds.

Kate pressed her hands tightly together, and gave an
enormous sigh! It was a miracle! An answer to her prayer
– and Willie Sims's! It only remained now for the sun to go
on shining, really hot, for the next three or four hours for
all to be well. But in regard to the latter Mrs Wildgoose
was doubtful. 'Ground'll be very wet a while yet,' she
observed, 'and mind, gum-boots on, all, please, if you're
going out.'

'But we can't go to the *party* in gum-boots!' protested
Kate, aghast.

'I'm not sayin' for the party, I'm talking about now,'
replied Mrs Wildgoose, 'and that reminds me, Kate,
you'd best put the clothes you're all going to wear this
afternoon out ready so's there won't be a rush getting
dressed and you all arrive late.'

'Oh, Mrs Wildgoose, I've done it!' cried Kate, '*I*
thought of that too!' she added, proudly, 'and there was
nothing to do while it was raining so I've been upstairs
and put them all ready. My blue Sunday dress with the
white spots, and my best stockings; Peg's Sunday frock
and her new pink socks; and Jo's tidiest jersey and his
Sunday trousers – I can't find any very clean socks for him
though,' she added, 'they're all rather dirty, but they're
brown so the dirt won't show much.'

'Good gracious!' exclaimed Mrs Wildgoose, 'you
don't want to go to a hay-party in your Sunday clothes!
Nice state you'll get them in!'

'But, but . . . Mrs Wildgoose!' stammered Kate, 'Mrs
Ayredale-Eskdale's such a frightfully grand sort of lady I
thought we *must* – I'm sure *she'll* wear a silk dress and a, a –
hat all over roses!'

'Maybe she will,' replied Mrs Wildgoose, 'but remember, Mrs Ayredale-Eskdale's – I was going to say an old lady – tho' I don't suppose she'd like that – and anyway it's not true for she's not really old though of course she's not exactly young. But anyway she won't be scrambling and rolling about in the hay – why, whatever's the matter? For Kate, overcome at the idea of Mrs Ayredale-Eskdale rolling about in hay, was suddenly convulsed with a fit of the giggles. 'Go on with you!' admonished Mrs Wildgoose, laughing herself. 'And now run upstairs and put those Sunday clothes away – all of them – do you hear? All you need is a clean cotton frock each – you and Peg – and a tidy jersey for Jo; his everyday trousers are quite good enough – I'll give 'em a good brush afore he goes. . . . A clean handkerchief *each*, mind – don't forget that; and coats for all, for I'm not hopeful there won't be more rain afore evening.'

Kate went slowly upstairs and regarded rather sadly the finery she had laid out on the bed. She *did* want to wear her spotted frock – what *would* Miss Alison think – much less Mrs Ayredale-Eskdale. . . . And – had Mrs Wildgoose forgotten – she had only two 'cottons' – the one she had on, and another, *very* faded. It was clean but it hadn't at all recovered from being packed in the suitcase and was dreadfully squashed-looking. Perhaps Elsie would find time to iron it, though ironing at the Dew Drop Inn seemed rather an event – not like at home where you just ran into the kitchen and Mum did it in a jiffy along with the customers' things. Sighing, she put the best dresses away again, selected a cotton frock for Peg and a jersey for Jo, socks for both of them and her own best stockings, which only had darns in the toes and a *tiny* ladder in one leg that didn't show much if you were careful to wear it facing inwards. Her school hat and blazer

she was determined to wear, whatever Mrs Wildgoose
said. Even Mrs Ayredale-Eskdale ought to be impressed
with those! By the time she came downstairs again carrying the cotton frock for Elsie to iron it was after twelve
o'clock.

'Where's Peg and Jo?' asked Elsie as she came into the
kitchen, 'I thought they was up along of you – it's time
they had a wash for it's close on dinner-time.'

'I haven't seen them,' replied Kate. 'I expect they're
over in the Buttercup Field – I'll look and see if their gum-
boots are gone,' and she went out to the passage behind
the kitchen where everyone's Wellingtons were kept. The
two smallest pairs were missing.

'Their boots are gone, Elsie,' she called. 'They're over
there for sure – I'll go and call them in,' and she ran off
singing.

'The Buttercup Field', so christened by Peg and Jo,
was the field immediately opposite the Inn, where Mr
Plodder's cow, now happily reconciled to the loss of her
calf, contentedly passed her days. It was golden-yellow
with the shiny faces of millions of buttercups – buttercups
which at first – much to Mr Plodder's scorn – all the
Ruggles children had been convinced were responsible
for the extremely yellow-creamy milk his cow produced
in such quantity.

'A buttercup-eating cow – I'd like to see it!' he snorted.
'You town children, you got a lot to learn you have! You
don't believe me?' – regarding their incredulous faces.
'Well you *watch*; and if you sees my cow eat a buttercup
I'll – I'll – well I'll give you sixpence apiece! Yes, you can
come in the field – much as you likes, and pick all the
flowers you please, and welcome,' he went on. 'But one
thing; don't you go a-touchin' of the cow. She's quiet
enough – no cow's quieter – but she's got her ways – same's

we all has, and she can't abide being touched by strangers.'

'Sixpence apiece' was worth earning, apart from anything else, and for some time Kate, Peg and Jo watched Mr Plodder's cow intently while she fed. Kate at last decided Mr Plodder must be right about the buttercups but Peg and Jo remained unconvinced and for a long while followed the cow about, hoping against hope.

After the Dew Drop Inn garden the Buttercup Field became their favourite playing place. They seemed never to tire of picking the shining buttercups or hunting among them for the big white moon-daisies now just coming into flower. As for touching 'Sairey' as they later discovered the cow to be called, they were far too frightened. But, as the old proverb tells us, 'Familiarity breeds contempt.' Every day they began to be less and less in awe of her. Cows of all sorts were now encountered daily; they were rapidly becoming as familiar as lamp-posts in Otwell. And one afternoon, peeping in at the sheds at milking-time, Jo had actually been invited in by one of Mr Digweed's men to hold the tail of a specially restless one! This was such a marvellous thing to have done, that the doing of it had astonished even Jo himself! He boasted about it to his sisters, and even Kate was impressed. He also, unfortunately, boasted about it to Johnny Sears.

Johnny Sears was a boy who, looking through the gate into the Buttercup Field one day, and seeing Jo keeping his due distance from 'Sairey', had taunted him with being 'feared' of cows.

Contrary to Jo's expectations, however, Johnny Sears appeared totally unimpressed with his prowess in the milking-shed. *He* had held cows' tails since he were three years old, he scoffed! . . . There was nothing he couldn't do with cows. . . . He had even ridden one! He dared Jo to do the same – tho' of course (with biting scorn) a town kid like him never *would*!

The 'kid' more than the 'town' angered Jo. He'd show Johnny Sears, he told him; he'd show him! Only let him wait a bit – that was all! And saying nothing to anyone but Peg, and watching very closely all Sairey's habits, Jo had bided his time.

Kate stopped singing as she came out of the porch and looked up at the sky. Lovely! The sun was *blazing* away . . . the hay must be drying beautifully! She was just about to call, 'Peg! Jo! *Dinner*!' when out of the gate opposite ran Peg, scattering buttercups in every direction, and screaming loudly, 'Kate! Kate! Mrs Wildgoose! Elsie! *Somebody!!*'

'Whatever's the matter?' cried Kate running towards her, and then, seeing she was apparently unhurt. 'Where's Jo?'

'The cow! The *cow*!' screamed Peg, clutching Kate round the knees and butting her with her head, 'The cow! The *cow*!'

'Let go – let *go*! What do you mean, "the cow"?' and pushing her sister aside Kate ran across the road and into the field.

Mr Plodder's cow was standing near the gate. There was a strange look in her eye and she was lashing angrily with her tail. Of Jo there was no sign at all!

Kate looked wildly round. Away in the middle of the field was something blue among the buttercups – a little blue heap that, as she ran towards it, resolved itself into Jo. He was lying on his back; his face was very white, and his eyes were shut. For one horrible moment Kate thought he was dead. 'Jo! Jo!' she cried wildly, 'What's happened, what's *happened*?' and she tried to lift him up. Jo's eyes opened slowly; he looked about him in a dazed sort of way, then shut them again. Her heart pounding against her ribs, Kate laid him down and stood torn with anxiety as to whether to stay with him or run for help. But before she could decide, there was a sound of running feet, and the next minute Elsie came flying across the field followed more slowly by Mrs Wildgoose, while Peg stood at the gate, afraid to come further, and still wailing, 'The cow! the cow!' A minute later Mr Wildgoose came running, and the next, appearing through a gap in the hedge, Mr Plodder himself, armed with a large fork.

'Ah! I *told* 'em not to touch her!' he cried. 'I told 'em how it 'ud be! And what do I see? Cartin' muck I were, and I look up, and there's my cow bein' rid – *rid* I tell you – by a brat of a boy! Settin' there a-holdin' on to her horns! And next thing I see – boy flyin' thro' the air! . . . Aye, reckon he *is* hurt. . . . Well, I told 'un!'

And now people were coming from the yellow cottages;

men home for the dinner-hour; children home from
school. . . . But Mr Wildgoose took command. First Mr
Plodder was to lead his cow right out of the field. . . . Then,
taking off his coat, Mr Wildgoose made a sort of cushion
of it under Jo's head; lifted him – oh, so gently, and saying
sternly to the crowd collected at the gate, 'Let me through,
please – quickly!' carried him over to the Inn, up the
stairs, along the twisting passages, right up to the top
room, to the big feather-bed.

Kate and Peg sat alone in the kitchen. Everyone was
upstairs with Jo. The clock chimed half past twelve;
saucepans were boiling over, and something was burning
in the oven. But nothing mattered – nothing; except about
Jo.

'*What* did you say you did?' asked Kate for at least the
fifth time, '*Rode* Mr Plodder's cow?' Peg, large tears still
rolling down her cheeks, shook her head. 'Not me didn't;
I've *tolded* you! It were Jo as did! He's said he would,' she
went on, 'lots of times; ever since Johnny Sears dared him
to he has!'

So that was it! It was a 'dare'! Well, thought Kate, she
hoped Johnny Sears knew what had happened.

And what *had* happened? Oh, would they never come
downstairs? She'd promised not to go up. . . . It was like
when Jo was at the hospital all over again! She sat
imagining every possible horror; writing a letter in her
mind to Mrs Ruggles to say Jo had broken his leg – both
legs . . . his arms . . . his arms and legs. . . .

Suddenly there were footsteps. Mr Wildgoose came
whistling along the passage.

'Cheer up! cheer up!' he cried coming into the kitchen,
'All's well – no bones broken. He's – I was going to say
sitting up and smiling – well, he's not quite that – but he's

all right. And it's a lot more than he deserves – it's a wonder he hasn't broken his neck! Ridin' on a cow! How he got *on* it beats me!'

'We was sittin' on the gate, and she was a-side it, and he just sort of moved over on to her,' explained Peg. 'She didn't seem to mind a-cept when she began to move and Jo held on to her horns. She didn't like that; she kicked and sort of shook about; and then, all of a sudden, she give a kind of jump – right up in the air – and Jo fell off,' she concluded sadly.

'I expect Mr Plodder's *awfully* cross!' said Kate. Now she knew Jo was all right there was time to think a bit.

'I shouldn't be surprised if he were,' replied Mr Wildgoose severely. 'Milking cows aren't meant to be ridden – nor any other cows, come to that!'

'Mr Plodder *said* not touch her!' said Peg sniffing mournfully.

'Quite so,' said Mr Wildgoose. 'Now perhaps you see what happens when you don't do what you're told. Well, Jo won't be able to go to the party this afternoon so perhaps that'll learn him to be obedient.'

Kate stole a look at Mr Wildgoose. She had never heard him speak so sternly. Perhaps he, too, had been frightened. Of course, she reflected, it would have been awful for him if Jo had been killed – or even badly hurt – sort of in his care. . . . *Now* what was the matter? For Peg had burst into loud sobs. 'Not go to party? Jo not go to party? Oh, oh, oh!' she howled.

'Of course he can't go!' said Mr Wildgoose, 'Now be quiet – we've had enough worry for one day!' And so surprised at his sharp tone was Peg, that she stopped crying at once and, retreating to a far corner of the room, took refuge beside her beloved Buttonhook. Mr Wildgoose busied himself with the boiled-over saucepans and the something-very-burnt in the oven, and a minute later in came Mrs Wildgoose.

'Goodness, gracious me!' she exclaimed. 'Look at the time – nearly one o'clock! Well, my dear,' turning to Kate, 'Jo's all right. Real nasty fall he's had, but there's no bones broke so don't you worry. He's feelin' a bit sick-like so he's best where he is for the present and keepin' quite quiet. We've put him in my bed for the time being,' she went on, 'so's he can have a nice sleep and not be disturbed when you and Peg goes to get dressed. You'll keep very quiet ,won't you? Elsie's stayin' with him now till he goes to sleep. My word, what a turn it's give me! Nice thing if I'd had to write and tell your mum as he'd broke a leg or an arm! Ridin' on a cow! Whatever put that idea in his head!'

'Johnny Sears did!' said Kate furiously, 'it was "a dare" – Peg says he kept saying Jo wouldn't never do it.'

'I'll "dare" him,' said Mr Wildgoose – 'young Johnny Sears. He'd best keep out of my way for a day or two or he'll get what for!'

'*I* shall speak to his mother,' said Mrs Wildgoose. 'And now we must all have dinner – that is if there's any dinner left! From the smell I should think my nice meat pie I left in the oven's burnt black! And just look what those wicked saucepans have done to my clean stove! Dear, dear, dear!'

2

The sun was not shining quite so brightly when, just before three o'clock, Kate and Peg set forth alone for the party. There were storm clouds over 'the rainy quarter' again – and there were storm clouds on Peg's face too! There had been a sharp tussle of wills in the top bedroom

not many minutes earlier. Leaving Peg dressed and ready
all but her socks and shoes, Kate had run down to the
kitchen to fetch her dress which Elsie had somehow
managed to find time to iron. When she returned, Peg's
socks and shoes were on, and in addition she was struggling
into a not-very-tidy-looking jersey on top of her clean
cotton frock.

'What ever are you doing of?' exclaimed Kate as Peg's
face, scarlet with exertion, emerged through the neck of
the jersey while her arms waved wildly, half in and half
out of the flapping sleeves. 'You don't want a jersey on a
day like this – it's much too hot – and I've put your coat
ready for coming home in case it rains. Take if off – quick
– or we'll be late! Come here, and I'll "skin" you out of
it,' and Kate made a grab at her sister. But Peg dodged
away and ran over to the other side of the room.

'I'm not *going* to take it off!' she cried defiantly, and
there was a glitter of angry tears in her eyes. 'I wants to
wear it!'

'But what ever *for*?' cried Kate, slipping her newly-
ironed frock over her head. 'You'll be much too hot – and
it isn't even properly clean; you can't go to a grand party
in a jersey like that! Come here at once and let me take it
off.'

But Peg refused to move. 'I wants to wear it *special*,'
she announced.

'When you want something "special",' said Kate
angrily, thinking of the matter of the farthings, 'it's always something naughty. If we'd got more time,' she went
on, seizing her belt and buckling it, 'I'd *make* you take it
off; but we're late now. Here, let me get your arms into
the sleeves if you *must* wear it!' And seizing Peg's arms –
rather roughly it must be owned – with a push here and a
tug there – she soon had the offending garment on. 'There!

Now we'll have to go. You *do* look a little sight! Put on your hat and bring your coat and don't you dare say *one* word going downstairs or you'll wake Jo up!'

'Good-bye, my dears!' called Mrs Wildgoose softly from the kitchen as they tip-toed by. 'Have a lovely time and enjoy yourselves. I only wish I were coming too but I'd not be happy leaving Jo. He's sleeping lovely, so go quietly as you can down the road. There's no need to hurry – you're well in time.'

But all the same, hurry they did! There were no children about so everyone *must* be there already, said Kate, and she walked as quickly as she possibly could, Peg running and panting like a little dog to keep up. So intent was she on speed, that it was only when they were more than half-way to The Priory that she noticed Peg was not carrying her coat.

'You little silly – I *told* you to bring it – now what'll you do if it rains! We can't go back for it possibly,' she cried.

But Peg said nothing, only scuffed with her toes at the gravel as she walked, thereby earning a further reproof.

'You're in a real naughty mood today!' went on Kate, repeating one of her mother's favourite rebukes, 'but you'd best behave properly at the party,' she continued, 'or Mrs Ayredale-Eskdale'll have something to say to you, my word she will!'

Peg still said nothing, but glancing sideways at her Kate thought she looked impressed; she sincerely hoped this was so. The possibility of being disgraced in any way before Mrs Ayredale-Eskdale simply did not bear thinking about!

It looked as if they were the last to arrive. As they crossed the bridge and turned down the part of the drive that led to The Priory itself, they could see a large crowd of people grouped about the great stone porch. Kate felt suddenly very small and shy and if Peg had not already been silent she would most certainly have become so! It was a tremendous relief when Miss Alison detached herself from the group of people and came forward to meet them.

'But where are Mrs Wildgoose and Jo?' she asked when they had, rather shyly, shaken hands.

The sad tale was told. Miss Alison looked most distressed, especially when Kate explained, as they walked towards the house, it was all the result of a 'dare'.

'Oh, they are the stupidest things!' she cried.- 'Poor little Jo! I do hope he'll soon be all right; I know how he'll hate missing the party! Everything seems going wrong this year! First the weather – really, this morning I thought the haycocks would soon be floating! And several people haven't been able to come! Somebody with bad toothache; and a family down at Lower Cassington because their Grannie has died, over at Hadham, and the funeral's arranged for today. And then, just about an hour ago, Mrs Sears sent a message to say two of her little girls have got measles – you'll know how *they* feel, poor dears – so none of that family can come! I know you've all had it,' she went on, 'or I'd have sent to tell Mrs Wildgoose and suggested you should stay away.'

'But *I* haven't,' said Kate, 'it's only Peg and Jo – and Lily Rose – my other sister – as did!'

Miss Alison stopped and turned towards her, looking rather concerned.

'Yes,' she said slowly, 'I remember now; you did tell me. . . . I'm afraid I forgot. Oh dear! . . . Anyway,' she went on after a pause, 'I think if you didn't catch it when you all had it at home you're not likely to now. . . . As to the hay,' she continued, as they walked on, 'it's still very,

very wet and I'm afraid it's quite impossible to play in it; but we've arranged something else,' she ended as they reached the group near the house.

'*You've* met my mother,' she said, with a ghost of a smile at Kate, 'but I don't think Peg has? Mother, this is Kate, and this Peg Ruggles, who are staying with Mrs Wildgoose; their poor little brother has had an accident riding on a cow and can't come, so she's staying behind to look after him.'

Mrs Ayredale-Eskdale, dressed just as Kate had expected, in a silk dress and a hat covered with roses, bent forward graciously and shook hands, but if she remembered Kate loitering on her bridge she showed no sign of it.

'Poor little boy,' she said kindly, in reference to Jo, 'It was not a bad accident, I hope? *What* did you say he was doing? *Riding a cow* – I trust not one of *mine*?'

'Oh *no*!' said Kate, a little breathlessly. 'It was Mr Plodder's – a gentleman as lives near the Dew Drop – a gentleman who. . . .'

But Mrs Ayredale-Eskdale seemed to have lost interest and had turned away to speak to another guest.

Kate pulled Peg by the hand and retreated thankfully and as far as possible from her hostess.

It was a disappointment to learn Johnny Sears would not be at the party; she had promised herself to tell him just exactly what she thought about his silly 'dare' and its dreadful result. And while she was really sorry his sisters had measles she couldn't help feeling that she wouldn't mind in the very least if she heard Johnny himself had got them – though not, of course, terribly badly!

And now Miss Alison was calling all the children together. . . . Everyone, she said, seemed to have arrived so she would explain what they meant to do. . . . It was very, very, sad but it was really too wet for tea and games in the hay. Some of the haycocks, however, had been kept dry by covering them up overnight.

'There's a "cock" each,' she went on, 'and under each one, a ball. I'm going to blow a whistle and then off you all go, and whoever gets back with their ball first here,' – and she indicated a large round flower-bed filled with flaming red salvias – 'gets a prize. One prize for the "under sevens" and one prize for the "overs". Then we're going to have tea in the Big Barn, and after that some games and competitions. It's just too bad about the weather but it's no good getting colds in damp hay or beginning tea or games outside and then having to rush indoors. As it is,' and she glanced upwards, 'I think we'd better start the ball hunt quickly, because the sky looks very black and I'm afraid it may begin to rain again any minute!'

And she was right! They had hardly lined up in two groups – the 'under sevens' on one side of the salvia bed and the 'overs' on the other, before the sun disappeared behind large dark clouds; and as the whistle blew and they rushed across the lawn, through a gap where the railings had been taken down, to the hayfield, large drops of rain were beginning to fall.

Although Miss Alison had said there was a haycock each it seemed terribly difficult to find one in which somebody else was not burrowing, and Kate became quite desperate running from one to another! At last she found one to herself, quickly discovered the ball – a good, strong, high-bouncing looking rubber one – and clutching it tightly rushed headlong for the salvia bed. But although she overtook several competitors on the way, others had already arrived, and she was sorry to learn that the winner was the detestable Miss Smallpiece (who later received her prize – a lovely, fat-looking book – just what she would have liked herself, thought Kate rather enviously – with a very smug smile and a superior toss of her curls).

Last of all the competitors – very much last – came Peg! And though the rain was now beginning to come down in earnest, she was making no effort whatever to run but ambling along at a sort of slow jog-trot. Only when she emerged from the hayfield was it seen she was carrying not one ball but two! For, as she presently tried to explain to Miss Alison, when everybody had gone, she had found *another* hay-cock, and had looked 'inside' in case there was *another* ball – 'to take home to Jo'.

Kate was very shocked, and about to apologize for such behaviour, but Miss Alison only laughed and said it must have been the hay-cock and ball really meant for Jo, and of course Peg could take the ball home for him. Peg looked very pleased with herself but Kate, painfully aware that Mrs Ayredale-Eskdale was regarding them both through a pair of lorgnettes, her eyebrows raised very high indeed, felt anything but happy.

But once they arrived inside the Big Barn for tea she forgot her worries. The Big Barn was big indeed – as big as a small church, and rather like one she thought, with its lofty great rafters and tremendous oak beams. At one end, on trestle tables covered with dazzling white cloths, and decorated with gleaming cut-glass bowls full of the loveliest garden flowers, was the tea. And what a tea! There was white, brown, and currant bread and butter; scones and buns; Swiss rolls, jam tarts, and macaroons; jams of every description in little glass dishes; while at intervals down each table there were at least half a dozen large iced cakes! Coffee and chocolate, pale green, pale lemon, and beautiful lilac and rose-coloured ones; some decorated with sugar fruits or flowers, others with little silver balls! And last, but certainly by no means least, there were plates of chocolate biscuits – every sort and shape and size.

As Peg was led away to sit with some of the smaller children, Kate fully expected protests but to her surprise she trotted off, holding the hand of a complete stranger and smiling happily.

It was only when the sumptuous meal was over, and they had all gathered at the other end of the barn for games that she began to be difficult.

'Hunt-the-slipper' had been suggested to start off the games, but Peg, climbing on to a chair, resolutely refused to play. In turn Kate coaxed, cajoled, and commanded, but in vain; Peg remained sitting stolidly on her chair, her hands crossed firmly across her tummy, refusing not only to move but to speak.

'What is it, lovey?' asked a kindly parlourmaid who was standing near. 'Perhaps she's not feeling well?' she added, turning to Kate. 'I noticed as she didn't eat much tea. I shouldn't force her if she doesn't want to play' – as Kate made one more effort. 'You skip off and enjoy your-self – I'll stay beside her.'

Kate hesitated; the game was about to start.

'You skip off,' repeated the parlourmaid whose name was Emily. 'I won't leave her.' And thus encouraged, though still with some misgivings, Kate ran off.

From time to time she glanced anxiously in Peg's direction but receiving reassuring nods from the kindly Emily, and in the noise and excitement that followed as game succeeded game, she presently forgot her small sister.

But all parties come to an end some time and presently the mothers of some of the younger children began to collect hats and coats and announce it was time to go home

Kate glanced towards Peg. There she sat, still clasping
her tummy and looking the picture of misery. The kindly
Emily still stood beside her but now she had been joined
by the august Mrs Ayredale-Eskdale herself.

'I'm afraid,' she announced as Kate came running up,
'I'm afraid this child is not well. A child that doesn't want
to play and sits clasping its stomach like that can't possibly be well! You had better get her home as soon as

possible – did I hear you say it was raining, Emily?' she
asked, turning to the parlourmaid.

'Yes, madam – coming down terrible heavy it was
when I looked out five minutes or so ago.'

'Well I suppose they've brought coats – No?' As Kate
timidly attempted to explain matters – 'What ever was
Mrs Wildgoose thinking of – I thought she had more
sense!'

'I've got My School Blazer,' said Kate proudly, 'and
that jersey Peg's got on will keep her dry.'

'Nonsense!' said Mrs Ayredale Eskdale – so sharply
that Kate almost jumped. 'Nonsense!' she repeated, 'The

child would be wet through in five minutes! Run up to my bedroom, Emily, and fetch that short waterproof cape I keep for the garden – and an old umbrella from the hall stand – they can return them tomorrow. . . . That child looks to me suspiciously as if she were sickening for something!'

Oh dear! thought Kate. Could Mrs Ayredale-Eskdale be right – and what could it be? Not measles, anyway. Scarlet fever, perhaps? or influenza? or – or – What else was there? – she could think of no more complaints. . . .

'Stand up now, little girl,' commanded Mrs Ayredale-Eskdale turning to Peg, 'you're going home.'

'Yes, stand up, Peg,' echoed Kate, and she held out an encouraging hand.

Very slowly, ignoring the hand, her own two still clasped firmly across her tummy, Peg slid slowly down from her chair. Kate waited in an agony of suspense. Suppose Peg were sick? – sometimes, if you felt like that and *moved*, it was fatal. . . .

But once on the ground Peg stood squarely on her sturdy legs. She doesn't *look* ill, reflected Kate, only . . . only sort of rather *frightened*-looking. . . .

A moment or two later Emily reappeared carrying the waterproof cape and a large umbrella.

'Wrap the cape well round her, Emily,' directed Mrs Ayredale-Eskdale.

'Put your hands through the slits in the sides, lovey – see,' coaxed Emily holding up the strange-looking garment.

'Unclasp your hands, Peg,' said Kate impatiently, 'so's she can put it on you! Oh!' as Peg made no effort whatever to move, 'you *are* a little silly!' and darting forward she seized her sister's tightly clasped hands and pulled them apart.

Good gracious – what was that! Down on to the floor
fell something with a soft bump. . . . *A bun!!* . . . then
came another, followed by a cake and a jam tart; then
another cake – and yet another – and finally a perfect
cascade of chocolate biscuits! One after the other they came
tumbling out from beneath Peg's jersey, the jam tart
rolling gaily along the floor and coming to anchor right at
Mrs Ayredale-Eskdale's elegant patent-leather-shod feet!

For a moment there was a terrible, deathly silence!
Kate, scarlet to the roots of her hair with mingled shame
and anger, stole a look at her hostess. But Mrs Ayredale-
Eskdale's face was quite expressionless. The next moment
Peg burst into noisy sobs and tears. Mothers putting coats
and hats on their offspring stopped and stared; older
children drew silently near to see what it was all about.
Over the whole gay and chattering assembly spread an
awed hush, broken only by Peg's wailing.

Then suddenly, clear above the din, rang out the icy
tones of Mrs Ayredale-Eskdale.

'Pick up those buns and cakes, Emily,' she commanded,
stepping sideways to avoid the jam tart, 'and remove them.
I hoped,' she went on, addressing the company in general,
'I *hoped* all our guests had been offered as much as they
could possibly require. Evidently not!' And without so
much as another look at Kate and Peg she stalked majestically away!

'Be *quiet*, Peg!' cried Kate furiously, almost crying
herself with despair as Peg, seeing Emily about to bear
away in her apron the scattered cakes and buns, redoubled her yells.

'Why, what ever *is* the matter!' exclaimed Miss Alison
returning at this moment from seeing some friends off at
the front door. 'What is it? Oh, I was afraid Peg wasn't
feeling very well!'

'She's not ill at all!' cried Kate, 'only just frightfully naughty! Oh, Miss Alison I – I don't know what to say to you, truly I don't! She's – she's been *stealing* . . . ! Be *quiet*, Peg,' as the yells became even louder, 'BE QUIET!' And unable to bear it any longer, Kate seized her sister and shook her violently.

'Stop! Stop!' cried Miss Alison pushing her aside. 'You mustn't do that! Now, Peg, stop making that horrible noise – do you hear – *stop*! and tell me what it's all about. Come, we'll sit over here.' And picking Peg up in her arms she carried her to a far corner of the barn, Kate following.

Perched on Miss Alison's knees, Peg gradually stopped crying. 'I didn't steal nuffing – *nuffing*!' she said between sniffs; and she gave an angry glance at Kate. 'It were all give me to eat my own self and I put it under my jersey for Jo 'cos he couldn't come to the party! There was some things fell on the floor and I took those too 'cos they said they didn't want them. I've not stole *nuffing*! And I've only ate some bread and butter and one bun – and I'm *very* hungry!' she ended with a very plaintive sniff indeed.

By now people had begun crowding round.

''Tis true,' said one old lady, grandmother of two little boys who had sat at the same table, and who was standing near; ''tis true what she says – as she didn't eat nothing – I noticed it pertikeler. And there *were* a plate of cakes upset as they said didn't matter and to leave 'em be as they'd a-gone on the floor and there was plenty more. P'or l'il mite – *she* didn't mean no harm – she's naught but a baby yet, onyway!'

'She's *five*!' interrupted Kate indignantly, 'and she knows *quite* well not to take things. She's – '

'Let's get this clear,' said Miss Alison. 'You took the things for Jo, Peg, because he couldn't come, and you

didn't have any yourself so that he could have your share
– that was it, wasn't it?'

'*Yes*,' said Peg, nodding her head earnestly, '*yes*. And I
didn't steal *any*-thing! and now *she*' – pointing to Emily
who was disappearing out of a door at the end of the barn,
'has took them all away!' And once more tears began to
gather in her eyes and roll down her cheeks.

'Never mind about that,' said Miss Alison, 'You shall
have some others – you wouldn't really like those now
they've been on the dusty floor, would you? You let Kate
put the cape round you, and while you're getting ready I'll
find you some other cakes for Jo.'

'Oh, Miss Alison,' cried Kate, 'you *didn't* ought to
bother – she shouldn't have done it!' But Peg smiled
seraphically and, nodding at Miss Alison, said, '*And*
choc'late bikkits. Don't forget the choc'late bikkits!'

'Well, *really*! . . .' began Kate, but Miss Alison laughed
and said, 'Yes, chocolate biscuits too – I won't forget!'

They were only just ready, Peg looking a strange little
object in Mrs Ayredale-Eskdale's cape, when she was
back carrying a small basket covered with a white cloth.
'To keep everything dry,' she explained, though she was
glad to say it was not raining nearly so heavily. All the
same they had better get off in case it got worse again.
'Don't undo the basket, Peg,' she added, for Peg had lifted
a corner of the cloth and was peeping inside, 'leave it as it
is for a surprise for Jo, and I hope he's quite well again.
You've got his ball, haven't you?' Kate showed it her.
'And the umbrella?' Yes. 'Nothing else?' No, nothing
else. 'Come along then. . . .' But oh dear, at the door
stood Mrs Ayredale-Eskdale.

'You'll take care of my cape and umbrella, little girls,
and remember to *return* them?' she said.

'Oh *yes*, Mrs Ayredale-Eskdale,' said Kate. 'I'll bring

them back the very first thing tomorrow morning – and
the basket,' she added. And then in a rather trembling
voice, 'and thank you ever so much for the lovely party.
Peg, say "good-bye" to Mrs Ayredale-Eskdale and
"thank you" for the lovely party.'

There was a pause and Mrs Ayredale-Eskdale smiled
faintly. Peg scuffled with her toes on the door-step. 'Say
it!' said Kate in a loud whisper, nudging her, '*say* it!'

Peg looked up from under her eyelashes at Mrs Ayredale-Eskdale. 'I'll say "good-bye",' she said at last, 'but
I won't say, "thank-you-for-the-lovely-party". It hasn't
been a lovely party – it's been *horrid*!'

'That child,' said Mrs Ayredale-Eskdale, turning with
rather a grim smile to her daughter, as Kate, putting up
the umbrella, bundled her erring little sister out into the
rain, both, she was convinced, disgraced for ever in the
eyes of their hostess, 'that child should go far!'

They arrived back to find Jo in the kitchen making
toffee with Mrs Wildgoose. He looked a little pale but
otherwise seemed to have recovered completely, and his
very first question, as they came in at the door was, had
Johnnie Sears been at the party? And though delighted
with the ball and proudly-presented basket of cakes,
greatly to the disappointment of Kate and Peg appeared
far more interested in the fate of his enemy, and in the
results of the toffee-making, than in any of their adventures at the party!

As early as possible next morning Kate set off to return
the cape and umbrella. It was a perfect day – sunny with
just a joyful little breeze and every growing thing looked
pleased with itself. Why, oh why, she thought, couldn't
it have been like this yesterday?

She walked quickly, hoping against hope Mrs Ayredale-

Eskdale might still be in bed or at least breakfasting late after yesterday's festivities; but as she turned into the drive leading to the house she saw Miss Alison coming across the lawn towards her. It was a surprise – and relief – to learn that Mrs Ayredale-Eskdale had gone away by the early train to London and would not be back for a week or ten days.

'But she's left a letter for you,' said Miss Alison 'and a – a parcel!'

Kate looked up – astonished beyond measure. A letter! From Mrs Ayredale-Eskdale! For *her*? And a *parcel*! And before she had time even to try and guess what it could all mean, Miss Alison had taken the cape and umbrella from her, run into the house, and returned carrying a small hamper.

'Look inside,' she said, smiling. 'I'll hold it.'

Her heart beating fast and her fingers trembling with excitement, Kate lifted the lid.

To one side was an envelope addressed 'Miss Kate Ruggles' and in the middle, curled up and half asleep, was a snow-white kitten!!

For a few moments Kate was unable to speak at all. 'Oh!' she murmured at last, '*Oh*!'

'It's for all of you,' said Miss Alison, 'You, and Peg, and Jo, and the other children at home. Do you think they'll like him?'

'*Like him!*' repeated Kate, 'Oh, Miss Alison!' And, for some inexplicable and ridiculous reason, she felt her eyes filling with tears! Fervently hoping Miss Alison had not seen she winked them back and taking the letter from the hamper tore it open. It was not really a letter; just a sheet of notepaper on which was written, 'For all the Ruggles children, with best wishes from Adelaide Ayredale-Eskdale.' Pinned to the letter was a one pound note. This

Miss Alison explained, was to pay for the kitten's food 'for he'll want lots of milk for a long time yet, and we don't want your mother to have any expense over him. What do you think you'll call him?' she went on. 'We've not given him a name so you must think of one.'

Kate clasped her hands together and stood thinking deeply. Suddenly overhead a bird swept by. They both stared upwards, following its flight.

'Cuckoo! . . . Cuckoo! . . . Cuck-*cuck*-coo!'

It was like an answer!

'Cuckoo – no – cuckoo-*coo* – the "coo" for short – let's call him that, Miss Alison!'

And though Miss Alison said it was a strange name for a cat, the white kitten had been christened. . . .

But why, why had he been given them? Kate couldn't understand it at all.

'I – I thought your mother didn't like me very much, Miss Alison,' she said, 'and Peg's been most *awfully* naughty! It's, it's . . .'

'A big surprise!' finished Miss Alison for her. 'Well, it was meant to be! As a matter of fact my mother thought you were a very nice little girl; and I think she was just a *little* bit amused by Peg – she is only a baby after all you know . . .'

Really, thought Kate as she walked back up the drive, carrying the precious hamper and stopping and murmuring endearments to Cuckoo-Coo every few minutes, grown-ups were extraordinary! And what was it Mrs Wildgoose had said the other day? . . . 'Nothing . . . nothing happens but the unforeseen' . . .

It certainly seemed like it! And looking down at Cuckoo-Coo, now beginning to get a little restive in his hamper, she stopped once again and kissed his small pink nose. He felt the same, she was sure.

CHAPTER EIGHT

The Wedding of Uncle Albert

I

MEANWHILE, at No. 1 One End Street, life was going on much as usual.

'You'd *think*,' said Mrs Ruggles to her husband one morning, 'you'd *think* – wouldn't you – with three of 'em away things 'ud be a bit quieter!' But Mr Ruggles said no, he wouldn't, for it were the wrong three as were away. It were the twins and William as were the noisy ones – though Lily Rose, he added as his eldest daughter came clattering downstairs singing 'The Lambeth Walk', wildly out of tune, 'ran 'em pretty close'!

Lily Rose was singing to keep up her spirits – though it could not be said with truth that these were noticeably low. She missed Kate more than she had expected, however, and while she had no desire to be in the country herself, in spite of letters full of glowing descriptions of the Dew Drop Inn and its surroundings, she did wish *something* – something really exciting could happen to her! After all, it was she and not Kate who had been ill. Surely when a girl was almost fourteen, the eldest of seven, and had had measles – however slightly – *something* was due to her! But, she told herself, it never was the least bit of good expecting things to happen – especially nice and exciting things. It never worked; the very fact of expecting seemed to put them clean off! This time, however, Lily Rose was wrong. Something really exciting was about to happen quite soon. It began, in fact, the very next day!

'Well I never!' exclaimed Mrs Ruggles as she stood beside the breakfast table reading a letter the postman had just brought, 'well I never *did*!'

'Wot you never did?' demanded Mr Ruggles, his mouth full of bread-and-fried-bacon-fat. But Mrs Ruggles took no more notice of him than if he had been a fly on the ceiling. 'Well I never did!' she repeated and turned over a page of the letter.

Mr Ruggles felt faintly aggrieved. Few letters came to No. 1 One End Street and those that did were considered more or less common property. He finished the bread-and-bacon-fat, took a gulp of strong tea, and turned his attention to some bread and margarine. Mrs Ruggles continued reading. It seemed a very long letter. Perhaps it were A Complaint, thought Mr Ruggles. Not that many customers *did* complain – on the contrary – they were usually more than satisfied with Mrs Ruggles's efforts. Even so, they never dreamed of writing to express their approval – whereas a button missing or a handkerchief short ... Well, if it *were* a complaint, it were a pretty long one, he decided!

He finished his breakfast, stood up, pushed back his chair and, wiping his mouth with the back of his hand (a practice his wife usually resented bitterly), began putting on his coat. At the same moment Mrs Ruggles's letter appeared to come to an end.

'Well I never!' she exclaimed once more. 'If that don't beat all! Just fancy, Jo – it's a letter from Albert – *Albert* – after all this long time!' There was a short silence.

'And what's Albert done now?' inquired Mr Ruggles a little aggressively it must be owned but he was still feeling rather ill-used at being kept out of the secret so long.

'What do you mean, "done now"?' retorted Mrs Ruggles indignantly. 'Albert's all right these days.

Everybody makes mistakes sometimes – and it were only
Fourteen Days, anyway. Albert's doin' well for himself,
that's what he's doin' – *and* he's gettin' married – yes,
married!' and she gaily waved several sheets of note-paper,
covered with her brother's large sprawling handwriting.

'Is *that* all!' said Mr Ruggles disappointedly. 'Looks to
me rather more like as he *were* married from the length of
that!' he added, eyeing the letter rather sourly.

'It looks to *me*, Jo Ruggles,' said his wife, 'as *you* got out
of bed wrong side this morning! Now just listen. Albert's
goin' to be married; he's havin' a real posh wedding and
he wants us to come along, and, what's more, he wants
our Lily Rose to be a bridesmaid! There! What do you
think of *that*? Here's what he says:

Dear Sis,

Seems a long time since you heard from me I dare say but
here's hoping this finds you and Jo and the kids as it leaves me –
that is Feeling Fine. After my little Holiday I've kep away feeling
as I might not be welcome but hope now as you'll let bygones be
bygones because am doing well for myself now and am part-
owner in a Petrol Station over Horsham way and am getting
married this Whitsun Bank Holiday. My young lady is a real
knock out and is doing well in the dress-makery. I met her on the
Dodgems at a Fun Fair last August. Her name is Winnie Whiffen
and her folks are in the grocery and general line and got a tidy
little business just outside of Horsham. Her old man is giving us
a real posh wedding with Recep. and all after, so you and Jo
must come along and wish us luck. There's a bus from Otwell
every two hours. Two of Winnie's sisters and a niece is actin'
bridesmaids and we wants to have one of your kids for 4th. All is
round about 12 or 13 so how about your eldest what must be
about that by now? Winnie is making her own dress and others
and says if you'll send measures she'll make your kid's too so be
sports and come along. I am sending you a Swank Invite separate.

Your loving brother, Albert.

PS. — Winnie says to tell you as the bridesmaids' dresses is to be
Turquoise Satin Picture Dresses. This means Old Fashioned-Like
in frills to their Toes. She hopes this will suit your Lily Rose. You
see I ain't forgot her name!   A.
PS. again. Winnie don't know nothing of my troubles so hope you
nor Jo won't say nothing. I shall tell her at end of Honeymoon
which I think is only fair.   A.

'As if we should!' said Mrs Ruggles putting the letter
down on the kitchen table and pouring herself out a cup
of tea. 'Well,' as her husband made no reply, 'aren't you
pleased? You looks about as cheerful as a wet week-end –
anyone 'ud think as you'd been asked to a funeral 'stead
of a weddin'!' And then, as Mr Ruggles still made no
reply, 'Say *something*, do!'

There was a long pause. 'Well, Rosie,' said Mr Ruggles
slowly. 'Well – all I can say is I hopes – I *hopes*, as nobody'll
forbid the banns.'

Mrs Ruggles, tea-pot in one hand, cup in the other,
faced him angrily. 'Really, Jo Ruggles!' she exclaimed,
'you makes me tired! Here's your brother-in-law doing
well for himself, and invitin' you to a real slap-up weddin',
with your kid asked to be bridesmaid in turquoise satin, and
all you can find to say is as you hopes no one'll forbid the
banns!... Perhaps you'd like to forbid 'em yourself?' and
she banged down the tea-pot on the table.

'No,' replied Mr Ruggles slowly. 'No. I wouldn't go
as far as that; but you knows well enough, Rosie, as Albert
and me was never the best of pals – even afore his spot of
trouble, and I only hopes, as I says, as everything's all
right. And it's all very well,' he went on, as his wife made
no reply, 'it's all very well his writin' as there's buses to
Horsham every two hours. So there may be; but he don't
offer to pay the fares, do he? Horsham's a tidy step from
here. I dare say return fares for three don't mean nothing

to him these days, with his Petrol Station and all, but they does to me. Just you remember, Rosie, as there's no Pig Money now to fall back on. And you'd best say nothin' about bridesmaids and turquoise satin and suchlike nonsense to Lily Rose,' he added as the sound of a door being opened above was heard, 'for she's going to be disappointed if you do!'

For a moment Mrs Ruggles was speechless. She put down her cup of tea and, her arms folded in defiance, faced her husband.

'Now just listen to me, Jo Ruggles!' she cried furiously. 'Lily Rose is goin' to that wedding! She's had an Invite and a dress promised, and she's a *right*! She's goin', I tell you – and I'm goin' too! If you don't want to come you can stay home – and a nice bit of talk it'll cause! As to no Pig Money – maybe there isn't – but there's still overtime to be worked, I suppose? And beer not to be drunk? And pipes not to be smoked? And if there *isn't*, Jo Ruggles, then there's *the Pawn Shop* – though I never,' and here Mrs Ruggles dabbed away an angry tear with the corner of her apron, and gave a little sniff, 'I certainly never thought to go to my own brother's wedding on pawn-tickets as you might say!'

'*And* you won't!' retorted Mr Ruggles, angry now in his turn. '*Pawn-tickets! The idea!*'

At this moment Lily Rose burst into the room, closely followed by the twins.

'Oo! a letter, Mum! Is it from Kate?' she cried catching sight of the envelope on the table. Then, noticing the angry faces of her parents, 'Not – not *A Complaint?*'

'No,' replied Mrs Ruggles, turning away for a moment to recover her composure, 'No, it's not. It's something pleasant for a change! A lovely surprise – just like you're always wanting – that's what it is! Stop jumping about now' – as Lily Rose began skipping up and down with excitement – 'and sit down proper and get on with your breakfast and let your Dad get off to his work, and then I'll tell you.'

Mr Ruggles took his cap from the door. 'I've warned yer, Rosie,' he said quietly, putting it on. And without another word he went out, shutting the door firmly behind him.

'I just can't believe it, Mum!' exclaimed Lily Rose, bouncing about in her chair when Mrs Ruggles had finished telling the joyful news, 'I just can't! When is it – Whit Monday? . . . That's – that's two weeks the day before the day before yesterday! Coo! – not much more than ten days! Oh, Mum, do you think Uncle Albert's Young Lady can possibly make the dress – a dress like that – all frills – so quick? Oughtn't we to send the measures at once – almost this minute? And oh, Mum, can I read Uncle Albert's letter? I want to *see* my Invite all written!'

'You'll see your Invite in good time,' replied her mother. 'Your uncle says he's sendin' a special one separate. This here's just a letter to me and your Dad and there's nothing in it to interest you. And for goodness sake stop fussin' and bouncing about like that,' she went on, 'of course your new auntie can make a dress in ten days – leastways I should hope so, seein' she's in that line of business. It's William *I'm* worrying about,' she continued, 'we can't take *him* to a weddin', and I couldn't possibly leave him nearly a whole day with no one but the twins to mind him.' (Here John and Jim looked at each other thankfully. 'Minding' William at any time was an occupation they detested beyond all others. The thought of William for nearly a whole day . . . !)

'How about leaving him with Mrs Mullett, Mum?'

suggested Lily Rose. 'He knows her – so he mightn't scream *very* much,' she added hopefully.

'Well that's an idea, that is,' said Mrs Ruggles. 'There's not many I'd trust William to it's true, but if there's one I would it's Mrs Mullett. I'll try and pop round some time and see what she says. And then there's you two to be considered,' she went on, regarding her sons thoughtfully. 'Goodness knows what *you'll* be up to left alone for an hour, much less nearly a whole day – and of course it would be a day there's no school! . . . Perhaps if I put you up your dinners, Mrs Mullett 'ud let you eat 'em along of her, and play in her yard.'

There were vigorous protests from both twins. Had Mum forgotten? Whit Monday the circus was coming! *The circus!* Sam Bates was going and Sid Morley, and they . . .

'Now listen to me,' said Mrs Ruggles, 'You're not going near that circus. I said "no" when it were first spoke of and when I says "no" I means "no". There's mumps about and we've had more than enough with measles. And it's a poor sort of a circus anyway,' she went on, 'just a lot of silly women jumping through hoops, and some unfortunate animals in cages. And if there's one thing I don't hold with,' she added, 'and never have done, it's *dumb animals behind bars*.'

'But Mum!' cried Jim, 'it's all *settled*!'

'And you can't have *talking* animals, Mum,' objected John, 'leastways only parrots and such, and they're not proper animals!'

Mrs Ruggles looked at them both sharply.

'That's enough,' she said. '*You're not going*, so stop about it. And you, John, give over being cheeky and get on with your breakfast.'

The twins subsided, but they looked very sulky, and

there was silence, except for the scraping of knives and forks, for a little.

'I think Uncle Albert might have asked *us* to his wedding too,' said Jim presently in an aggrieved voice.

'Pooh!' cried Lily Rose, still very elated and finishing her third slice of bread and margarine, 'nobody wants boys at weddings – nice nuisance you'd be! It's different about me; I'm asked to be a bridesmaid and *help*.'

'And perhaps,' said Mrs Ruggles, 'it hasn't occurred to you as it costs quite a lot of money to take people all the way to near Horsham from here? Even as it is,' she turned to Lily Rose, 'your Dad's by no means particular set on *us* going.'

'Oh, *Mum*!' cried Lily Rose, aghast, 'he *hasn't* said we can't, has he – he *couldn't*! Oh, I should just die! You *won't* let him say no, *will* you?'

'You needn't worry,' replied her mother, 'we're *going* – somehow. But you'd best say nothing about it dinner-time,' she continued. 'And if the proper Invite should come by the next post, I'm going to answer it straight away and say we're coming; and soon as you gets back from school this afternoon I'll take your measures for the dress and send them off too. And talking of school – My goodness – just look at the clock! It's high time you was all off! Hurry now! Sharp!'

Yes, thought Mrs Ruggles, that's what she'd do. If the Invite came, answer it, and post the letter straight away. Then she'd slip into the bus office on the way back from her shopping later and find out exactly what those fares really *would* cost, and perhaps, if there was time, call in for a minute at Mrs Mullett's and ask about William and the twins.

It was a lovely morning, the sun was shining brilliantly,

and after putting William in his playpen in the back yard,
she set briskly about her housework. Goodness, how quickly the minutes went! It seemed no time before the town
clock was striking eleven. Any moment now the postman
would be knocking his way up the street. She made herself a cup of cocoa and stood drinking it at the kitchen
window watching for him. Ah, there he was! . . . Letters
for the Smiths – they always seemed to get a lot. . . . Letters for the Hares next door but one. . . . Nothing for next
door. . . . Something – yes – no? – *yes* – *Some*thing for No.
1! And, her heart beating, she picked up a silver-bordered
envelope that fell through the slit in the door which served
as a letter-box. On it 'Mr, Mrs, and Miss Ruggles' and
the address were scrawled in Albert's large, untidy
writing. It was the Invite all right!

Mrs Ruggles took a knife and slit open the envelope
very carefully. Inside was a silver-bordered card, and on
it, also in silver – except for the names, which had been
written in ink, she read as follows:

Mr and Mrs Amos Whiffen
Request the Pleasure of the Company
of
Mr, Mrs, and Miss Ruggles
At the marriage of their daughter
Winifred Violet
with
Mr Albert Moss
At St John's Church, Wideway
At 2.30 p.m. Whit Monday, 1938, and
afterwards at 'The Willows', Wideway.
R.S.V.P.

Albert had written truly; it was indeed a swank Invite!
She stood for a moment or two gazing at it. 'R.S.V.P.' –
what did that mean? She'd been told once but she'd

forgot. Some foreign stuff – reply quick or some such. . . .
Well, she was going to – none quicker! And taking the
bottle of ink off the dresser, and a sheet of her best professional note-paper, she wrote that Mr, Mrs, and Miss Lily
Rose Ruggles would have much pleasure in accepting Mr
and Mrs Whiffen's kind Invite. She had just sealed up the
envelope and was putting back the ink on the dresser when
a terrible thought occurred to her and she almost dropped
the bottle. Albert, to say nothing of his young lady, would
expect a wedding present! How, in the name of fortune,
with no money, were they to provide one?

Really, she thought, as a few minutes later she set off for
her shopping with William in his push-chair, and dropped
the letter in the box round the corner of One End Street,
no sooner did you dispose of one worry than up came
another, bigger one!

She was so absorbed in her thoughts that turning into
the High Street she almost bumped William into another
push-chair approaching from the opposite direction. . . .
Why, Mrs Mullett and her Muriel! Well that *was* a bit of
luck! . . .

It was not long before Mrs Mullett had heard the whole
story. Like most women she was stirred by the thought of a
wedding and the possibility of her friend being prevented
from attending one by anything short of death filled her
with deep indignation. If she could help in any way she
most certainly would! She would *gladly* look after William
– and the twins, too, as far as their dinner was concerned,
though she couldn't guarantee to keep them out of mischief. But Mrs Ruggles could go to the wedding – and go
she *must* – with a quiet mind as far as William was concerned.

'Like to spend a day with Auntie Mullett, wouldn't
you, my pet?' she cooed ingratiatingly, to him. But Wil-

liam who, as has been said elsewhere,* had been slow in getting his teeth, was proving even more backward in learning to talk, and at twenty-two months his vocabulary was still sadly limited. Every now and then, however, he would suddenly acquire a new word, using it with persistent zeal, day in, day out, and bestowing it impartially on the most wildly inappropriate objects. Thanks to a large tabby-cat which had recently taken up its abode next door, 'Pussy-cat' – a word the Ruggles family were beginning to know only too well – was his latest achievement.

He made no reply to Mrs Mullett's endearments, merely gurgled and blew bubbles on to the head of a stuffed dog clasped in his arms, while he gazed unblinkingly at Miss Muriel Mullett drawn up in her push-chair alongside him.

'It's not as if he didn't *know* you,' said Mrs Ruggles a little hesitantly, 'I'm sure he'll be all right, and I *hopes* he'll be good, and I'll be that grateful to you, Mrs Mullett, indeed I will. After all it's not every day one gets an Invite like this . . . and Albert's always been my favourite brother. . . . Well, I must get on . . . say "bye-bye" to Auntie Mullett, William – say "bye-bye".'

William removed his gaze from Miss Mullett and transferred it to her mother.

'Say "bye-bye",' repeated Mrs Ruggles. '*Say* it!'

There was a pause.

'Puss-y-cat!' said William, and looked delighted with himself. '*Puss-y*-cat!'

Mrs Ruggles finished her shopping and was just entering the bus office when whom should she meet coming out of it but her husband. Mr Ruggles was looking

* *The Family from One End Street.*

pleased but he seemed a little self-conscious on encountering his wife.

'Why, Jo!' she exclaimed, 'What's you doin' here?'

'Might ask the same of you, Rosie!' he replied.

'It's never gone twelve, surely!' said Mrs Ruggles, ignoring the last remark.

'It's just about to go a quarter past!' answered Mr Ruggles, and even as he spoke the town clock began to chime.

They stood for a moment looking at each other. Then, suddenly, they laughed. Comic – that's what it was! And what was the use of quarrelling anyway. . . . But the time . . . the time! Writing that letter and chatting with Mrs Mullett – that's where it 'ud gone, said Mrs Ruggles to herself; aloud she only said, 'My goodness me! My potatoes'll be all boiled dry!'

'Then unless you've business here, Rosie,' said Mr Ruggles slowly – and he gave her the faintest suspicion of a wink – 'we'd best be gettin' home.'

Something's come over him, thought Mrs Ruggles, as without another word she turned William's push-chair about and they all set off in the direction of One End Street.

They went on their way in silence for a little. Presently Mr Ruggles cleared his throat.

'Rosie,' he said slowly, 'Things is better than what I expected; quite a lot better. It seems there's special *facilities*' – he brought out the word with some pride – 'special *facilities* to Horsham and those parts, Bank Holidays. They're runnin' extra buses, and children of fourteen-and-up-to is allowed half-fares. I think as we might be able to manage it, somehow, after all.'

'And it's just as well, Jo,' said Mrs Ruggles a little tartly, for pleased – and surprised – as she was, she had not

entirely got over her husband's behaviour at breakfast.
'Yes, it's just as well,' she repeated, 'for the special Invite
Albert mentioned come after you'd gone and I answered
it saying as we'll all three be coming, and the letter's in
the post!'

'Oh it is, is it!' said Mr Ruggles, but he did not sound
angry. His wife stole a look at him. He appeared quite
unruffled. Better tell him about the wedding present,
quick, while the goin' was good. . . . But before she could
begin, Mr Ruggles, most surprisingly, plunged into the
subject himself!

'I've been thinkin', Rosie,' he said, slowly, as they
turned out of the High Street. 'All morning I've been
thinkin'. It's like this; cheap fares or no, we can't go to a
slap-up weddin' like it seems this one's to be – without we
takes a present – let alone Albert being your brother – for
all his queer ways.' Mrs Ruggles darted an angry glance
at him but Mr Ruggles took no notice.

'If we goes,' he went on, 'we goes proper, if you gets
me. Albert may own Half a Petrol Station, his young lady
be in the Dress-Makery, and her folks have their own
business, and no doubt all of them think Dustmen's no
cop. Well, we've got to *show* 'em, Rosie!'

And he went on to say that he had talked the matter
over with his mate, Mr Bird, 'two heads – men's heads, of
course', he added, 'being better than one'.

Mr Bird, it seemed, had had a brilliant idea. 'We
decided afterwards it must be on account of his name,'
went on Mr Ruggles, 'put it into his head like.'

'What ever *do* you mean?' exclaimed Mrs Ruggles, half
her mind on the important question of the wedding present and the other half divided between the thought of her
potatoes and trying to steer William's push-chair along
the crowded pavement, 'What put *what* into his head?'

'I'm trying to tell you,' replied Mr Ruggles sighing patiently. 'Listen. You know I said as I thought that biggest brown hen was a-goin' broody again? Well, she's gone – definite. I'd happened to mention the matter earlier to Bird, and after he'd been thinkin' a bit it sort of come back at him. "What about that hen you mentioned?" he says. "How about *that* for a present? You say as she don't lay all that regular and's for ever goin' broody. You don't want for to keep a hen like that. Make a handsome present, though – 'long of a nice settin' of eggs." "Well that's an idea that is," I ses – not but what I'd miss the old girl; and I thinks it over, careful, and – well, livestock, Rosie, is livestock. It's – *it's important*; it'll show 'em Jo Ruggles isn't doin' so bad either! Keeps poultry . . . oh, just a little 'obby like. . . . Been negotiatin' about a Pig, recent . . . thinkin' about a little farm one day. . . .'

'Go on with you!' said Mrs Ruggles with a laugh. But she was impressed all the same. Not half a bad idea it weren't really! and even though she felt such an Invite demanded something . . . well, perhaps more *showy* than a broody hen and a sitting of eggs – still, with no money you couldn't be too choosey. And Jo was right. Livestock, there was no denying it, *was*, as he said, 'important'.

'But what about the eggs?' she asked. That, too, it appeared, was arranged for. A friend of Bird's sold sittings. He could get one cheap from him, and he had agreed to be paid back in instalments. Everything was settled.

They turned into One End Street smiling happily.

Lily Rose had laid the table – she had also saved the potatoes! Dinner, in every respect, was a pleasanter meal than Mrs Ruggles had anticipated. And that evening, after tea, she took Lily Rose's measurements for the brides-maid's dress, remarking as she sealed up the envelope containing them, that the new auntie was going to get something of a shock when she learnt the amount of turquoise-blue satin it would take to cover her new niece!

For the next ten days or so, conversation at No. 1 One End Street was centred almost entirely on weddings – the conversation of Mrs Ruggles and Lily Rose that is, Mr Ruggles and the twins being heartily sick of the subject after the first half-hour. They would look at each other in silent sympathy, casting their eyes up to the ceiling, as the duties of bridesmaids were interminably discussed, and the the glories of turquoise blue satin expatiated on for at least the hundred-and-fiftieth time!

If only the wretched garment would arrive! Then perhaps they could all talk of something sensible again.

But the days went by and there was no sign of the expected parcel. Time was getting on. Lily Rose's excitement started to give way to attacks of nerves and she began to imagine every possible calamity, and at school was constantly in trouble for being inattentive.

When the Thursday before Bank Holiday had come and gone, however, and no parcel had arrived, even Mrs Ruggles began to feel a little apprehensive; and when Friday passed, with still no sign of it, she was even more so; with the wedding Monday it didn't leave much time if any alterations were needed.

On Saturday, Lily Rose, with not even school to distract her, was in a fever of anxiety, and finally took up a stand at the corner of One End Street, in order to catch the very first glimpse of the postman. Not, however, until after four o'clock, by the last post – later for some reason than ever before – was she rewarded, and even then the postman refused to allow her to take the parcel, insisting on delivering it himself though she assured him her Mum was out and her Dad busy in the back yard!

The parcel, a large cardboard box, was addressed to
Mrs Ruggles, and though her fingers fairly itched to untie
the string so that she might just peep inside, Lily Rose was
far too afraid of the consequences to do so. She carried
the box very carefully upstairs to her mother's room and
awaited her return in an agony of impatience. Oh, why
was she so long? She'd only gone to the Vicarage with
some laundry! Ten minutes that seemed like ten hours
went by, however, before she appeared, pushing William
in his pram; and then – could you believe it? – not until
tea was not only over, but washed up, and Dad provided
with his carpet slippers and the local paper, and cajoled
into 'minding' William, would she consent to come
upstairs and undo the box!

Mr Ruggles sat in the wicker armchair, his feet on the
fender, the newspaper in his lap, puffing contentedly at
his pipe and casting an occasional glance at William who
crawled happily about in his playpen. It was not often he
got his own kitchen to himself, he reflected, and could have
a nice quiet read in peace. He opened the *Otwell Gazette*,
glanced at the headlines, and decided it looked like being
a good twopennyworth this week. There were so many
excitements it was hard to know which to choose but
finally he selected a column headed, 'Body in River
Ouse: Coroner's comments,' and settled down to enjoy
himself.

Upstairs, Mrs Ruggles had undone the parcel and was
removing layer after layer of smooth tissue paper while
Lily Rose stood by, her hands clasped in ecstasy, her eyes
nearly popping out of her head with excitement as folds
of bright blue satin began to be revealed.

'Coo!' she exclaimed when at last Mrs Ruggles removed the final piece of tissue paper and lifted the dress

from the box, reverently shaking out its many frills, '*Coo!*
ain't it a treat!'

'It's made beautiful!' said Mrs Ruggles, her voice
faint with admiration. 'Your new auntie's a clever
woman; sensible too, for I see she's put in a bit of the stuff
case it don't fit, though I took the measures careful enough
I'm sure. Don't you dare touch it!' – as Lily Rose put out
a finger to stroke the gleaming folds that shone with the

curious metallic lustre that only 'art' satin can achieve –
'your hands is none too clean. Just slip down to the
kitchen and give 'em a thorough scrub and then we'll have
a try-on.'

Lily Rose needed no second bidding. She flew from the
room and in less than five minutes was back, wriggling out
of her jumper as she came, her hands scarlet from hot water
and scrubbing soap.

Mrs Ruggles stood reading a note which she had discovered accompanying a small parcel at the bottom of the
box. She was frowning and not looking too pleased.
Beside the dress, now lying on the bed, was a wreath of
white artificial daisies with very bright pink centres and
tied together with some pink ribbon.

'That there,' she said indicating it with her elbow, 'is
for your head; and this here,' pointing to the note, 'is to
say as you've to wear white shoes and stockings if you
please – though actually there's no "please" about it. All
it says is, "Wreath for head. White shoes and stockings to
be worn".'

'Oh, *Mum*!' exclaimed Lily Rose, '*whatever* shall we do?
I've only got my sandals and my lace Sunday shoes, and
they're both brown! And white stockings! Why, I've
never had any, ever!'

'Goodness knows!' said Mrs Ruggles irritably, 'a
cheek, I calls it! But before we bother about anything
else, you'd best slip the dress on and see how it fits. *Careful*
now!' – as Lily Rose made a dart towards the bed – 'Are
your hands *really* clean?' They were held out for approval;
her neck also was inspected, and, both being satisfactory,
the dress was slipped on.

The length was perfect – just the toes of her well-worn
brown sandals showing and nothing more. But how *queer*
a long dress felt! She did hope she wouldn't trip over it!
How dreadful if she were to slip going up the aisle, for
instance! But, on the other hand, what a comfort to know
her fat legs were so well hidden beneath its many folds
that no unkind comments could be made!

'Stand still, do,' commanded Mrs Ruggles struggling
to do up the hooks at the waist. 'My word, it won't meet
by *inches*! You must have got fatter – I can't have been all
that out in my measures! There – now there's a hook come

off – not very good sewing, that isn't. . . . Let's try the back. Stand straight and put your shoulders back . . . no, it won't meet there neither – no, not no how, it won't! Turn round . . . yes . . . it's cooping bad across the chest too . . . I'm afraid to force it for fear the satin'll split. . . .'

Lily Rose was almost in tears. 'Oh, Mum!' she cried, 'I can't go in a dress as doesn't do up at the back – just think how it'll show! I *can't* have got all that fatter in only just ten days! Whatever can we do? And about the shoes and stockings, too! I can't look all different from the other girls!'

'It's my belief she's read the measures wrong,' said Mrs Ruggles. 'The only thing I can see to do's to let in a bit at the back and waist with the snippets – for that's all they are – she's sent. A nice nuisance! How I'm to manage it I don't know – as if I hadn't got enough to do!'

But Mrs Ruggles managed it somehow. And she managed the white stockings too, for she suddenly re-membered Kate's white gym socks. They'd be too small in the foot but that was a minor matter – and with the turn-overs pulled up, under a long dress they'd pass for stockings easy!

As for the white shoes, it was Mr Ruggles who solved that problem! His 'quiet read' had been of short duration. It was getting near William's bed-time and it was not long before he began to whine and whimper, and very soon, driven to desperation, his father carried him upstairs.

The sight of the bridesmaid's dress knocked Mr Ruggles 'all of a heap' as he expressed it. Such grandeur could certainly not be marred by the wrong-coloured shoes!

'You give me them sandals you've got on, my girl,' he said to the now very tearful Lily Rose. 'You just give 'em me and tomorrow you won't recognize 'em. I've got the very ticket! What? Ah, you wait and see!'

And, sure enough, next morning Lily Rose did hardly know her sandals. Mr Ruggles had painted them with what he called 'a spot' of white paint left over from a small decorating job last year. Just, and only just, enough there'd been too!

'Careful now!' he warned, 'they're still a bit tacky; by tomorrow they'll be dry as dry – and if the Whiffens don't like 'em – well they can do t'other thing!'

After that it really did seem as though everything was happily settled – in fact Mrs Ruggles was almost on the point of saying so when there was a sudden furious knocking on the door! On the step, hatless, breathless, and agitated beyond description, stood the husband of Mrs Mullett.

'I've come to say,' he gasped, 'to say – as my wife's just been took to Hospital – appendicitis the doctor thinks it is. . . . She wanted me to tell you as you won't be able to leave your baby Monday like you'd arranged, nor yet the two boys. . . . She's ever so sorry – it's fretted her a lot, but I said you'd understand; I must go – I've left our Muriel alone in the house. . . .' And the next minute, gone he was.

The Ruggles looked at each other in silence (and only the faces of John and Jim showed any sign of approval). There was nothing for it, said Mrs Ruggles at last, but to take William with them. As to the twins, she'd cut them sandwiches and trust them – she eyed them both sternly – *trust* them to behave proper.

Mr Ruggles and Lily Rose sighed deeply. The prospect of William as a wedding guest did not very much appeal to either of them.

2

On the morning of Uncle Albert's wedding the 'rain spreading from the West' so cheerfully prophesied in the evening weather report had definitely spread, but the leaden-looking sky seemed to hold out little hope of the 'bright intervals' promised for later in the day.

' "Wet Monday" – that's what my old mother always called it,' said Mr Ruggles struggling rather sulkily into his best black suit, 'and as usual she weren't far wrong!'

'You and your mother!' cried Mrs Ruggles, feverishly undoing the dozens of tight little plaits into which she had forced her hair overnight. 'What about last year? Perfect day it were – from start to finish – couldn't have had a better. It's a wet season, that's what it is – everything's late. Last Whit Monday you'll mind you had a Whitsun Boss for your buttonhole – this year they're hardly showing for bloom. . . . Oh, Jo,' she faced him anxiously, 'whatever *are* you wearin' by the way – I'd forgot all about it!'

'Don't fret, Rosie,' replied her husband, '*I* ain't forgot. I'm wearin' a carnation,' he added impressively. 'Proper thing for a weddin'.'

'A carnation!' exclaimed Mrs Ruggles. Mr Ruggles nodded proudly. 'I told you we'd show 'em, Rosie, and we will! Bird give it me,' he went on. 'His friend as sold the eggs grows 'em; *shillings* they cost, but this one were broke off short and he were give it. He'd had it two days in water, but it's fresh as fresh. I've got it out in the tool shed. When it's pinned in no one won't know it's got no stalk. It's a beauty I can tell you!'

It certainly was, and when they all set forth, William in his best woollies; Mr Ruggles in his black suit, greeny-black bowler hat and well-polished brown boots, carnation and all; Lily Rose in her Sunday dress and coat – even if a little short and tight, and herself in her last year's Bank Holiday outfit, Mrs Ruggles decided Albert need have no call to be anything but proud of his relatives.

But the rain! It had lessened a little before it was time to start for the bus but was still coming down quite heavily enough. In one respect it was a good thing, for there was no one waiting and they were able to secure front seats which, apart from the advantage of the best view, made it easier to accommodate the hamper with the hen, the box of eggs, and the suitcase with the bridesmaid's dress – to say nothing of more space for William.

William was behaving very nicely. For the first part of the journey he sat on Mrs Ruggles' lap, gazing out of the window, and occasionally pointing out something with a fat finger, and gurgling appreciatively. After half an hour or so he began to be drowsy, and was soon happily asleep. It was only when they were nearing their destination that he awoke and began to be fidgety.

'Nearly there, my lovey,' said Mrs Ruggles outwardly cheerful though inwardly she had misgivings. What would the Whiffen family say to an uninvited guest – and a baby at that? Well, no one could help it – she'd done her best. 'Nearly there!' she repeated. 'Look, *there's* a pretty cow!' But William's eyes were fixed on his father.

'Dad-Dad!' he gurgled, 'Dad, Dad!'

'Want your Dad to hold you for a little, do you?' asked Mrs Ruggles. 'Very well. Jo, he wants to come to you.' And she stood up preparing to hand him over. But William gave a sharp cry of displeasure.

'Dad, *Dad*,' he repeated, 'Dad, *Dad*,' and he leant forward in her arms, struggling and pointing to Mr Ruggles's hand.

'He wants the bus tickets!' said Lily Rose, '*that*'s what he wants.'

Greatly relieved at not having to nurse his son, Mr Ruggles, smiling, and with alacrity handed over the three bright pink return tickets he had absent-mindedly been holding ever since the conductor clipped them just after leaving Otwell.

'He'll drop them,' said Mrs Ruggles, but she was wrong. William clasped the tickets tightly, cooed with delight and, regarding them with deep interest, changed them from hand to hand, hand to hand, quiet and absorbed until the bus stopped suddenly with a jerk.

'Wideway!' called the conductor, 'Wideway – you there in the front – here's where you get out.'

Goodness! they had arrived. . . . The next minute a head poked through the door and a voice cried, 'Hallo, Rosie!' And there, resplendent in a new blue serge suit, hair well oiled, and in his buttonhole a carnation rivalling Mr Ruggles', was Uncle Albert!

What a surprise! They had certainly never expected to be met! They bundled out.

Uncle Albert gave his sister a resounding kiss, seized Mr Ruggles' free hand and shook it vigorously, and expressed astonishment (to the point of a pretended faint) at the growth of Lily Rose. He was then introduced to William who promptly turned his back, burying his face in his mother's shoulder. Explanations and apologies for his presence followed, but Uncle Albert, deeply thankful at not being expected to kiss his nephew, said gaily, no matter – the more the merrier! His Winnie's Grandma was staying in the house, she wouldn't be coming to the church along of her bad legs, and would look after him fine. And now they must all come along and have a bite of food, and how about a hand with all these boxes and parcels? And he seized the hamper Mr Ruggles had put down for a moment.

'Whatever's in here!' he cried. 'My goodness' – peeping inside – 'My goodness, if it ain't a *hen*! You turned farmer since I saw you last, Jo?'

'Not yet, Albert,' replied Mr Ruggles sedately, 'not yet I haven't, though I'm thinking of. . . .' But Uncle Albert was not listening.

'What's in *there*?' he interrupted, pointing to the egg-box. 'A *cock*?'

'They're your weddin' presents, Albert, dear,' said Mrs Ruggles a little shyly.

'It's one of our own hens – and a *very* special settin' of eggs,' explained Mr Ruggles as impressively as he could. 'She's broody,' he added. 'All you've got to do is to set her.'

'Well I never!' exclaimed Uncle Albert, too astonished even to say "thank you", '*A broody hen!*' And he remained for several seconds staring at the hamper as if unable to believe his own eyesight. 'Well – I – never!' he repeated.

The rain had stopped but a dank grey mist, no doubt hoping to be mistaken for one of the promised bright intervals, seemed to pervade everything. The country was flatter than around Otwell, there were large trees which dripped by the roadside in a rather melancholy way, and the road itself was full of puddles. Fortunately it was only a short distance to 'The Willows', the Whiffens' house.

Uncle Albert carrying the hamper led the way, while Mr Ruggles with the egg-box, Lily Rose with the suitcase, and Mrs Ruggles with William, all picking their way carefully to avoid getting their shoes dirty, followed after.

Judged by some standards 'The Willows' was not large, but to the Ruggles, used to the cramped accommodation at One End Street, it seemed a commodious residence indeed. Built of very red brick it stood alone in a small patch of garden; no willows of any kind were visible, but there were two grave-like flower-beds flanking the yellow gravel path leading to the front door. On either side of the small entrance hall was a door; at the far end were others, while up the white-painted, red-carpeted stairs, opening on to a small landing, were still more.

From a room on the left as they entered came a buzz of conversation, and from upstairs giggles and occasional squeals of merriment, and all the Ruggles felt suddenly very shy indeed!

'Come along, come along in!' cried Uncle Albert leading the way, and he ushered them into a small, warm, and very crowded apartment.

'Here we all are,' he announced. 'Where's my Winnie – upstairs? Well, let me introduce my relaytives. My sister, Mrs Rosie Ruggles; her husband, Mr Josiah Ruggles; their daughter, Miss Lily Rose Ruggles; and last, but I'm sure not least, Master William Ruggles!'

A deathly hush seemed to descend upon the company and then from among the assembled Uncles, Aunts, and Cousins, the parents of the bride detached themselves and came forward. Mrs Whiffen, very short and fat, wearing a puce-coloured dress with large green spots; Mr Whiffen, also short but thin; rather bald, very bent at the knees, and with feet that seemed to be fixed permanently in the position of a clock pointing at just after a quarter to three. They shook hands in a rather dispirited sort of way and murmured they were pleased to meet Albert's relaytives. The Ruggles murmured the same sentiment, and offered apologies and explanations for the presence of William.

They were then introduced to an old lady seated in an armchair by the window, a rug over her knees, and a stout stick leaning against either side of her chair. This was Grandma Whiffen, who Uncle Albert had so confidently assured them would look after William while the wedding ceremony took place. He now made the suggestion to Grandma herself.

'H'oh!' said the old lady who apparently had some difficulty with her aitches, 'H'oh! So that's the h'idea, h'is it!' And she regarded the entire Ruggles family with all too obvious distaste.

'Well, h'in for a penny, h'in for a pound,' she continued, sighing. 'You needn't worry,' – she turned to Mrs Ruggles – 'Used to little boys, I h'am. Should be; H'ive brought up thirteen children – yes,' nodding her head, 'thirteen! H'eight of 'em boys, too – and only six not lived to grow h'up. Oh 'e'll be h'all right along of me!'

There was a rather strained silence. Mrs Ruggles clutched William more tightly, and William himself stared at Grandma with round, unblinking eyes.

To create a diversion Uncle Albert slipped out to the hall and returned carrying the hamper and box of eggs.

'See here, ladies and gentlemen!' he cried gaily, holding the hamper aloft. 'I'll bet you've none of you seen a wedding-present like this one afore! I'll give you three guesses each what's inside!'

The company brightened up a little but before anyone had time to hazard a guess, Grandma Whiffen tapped sharply on the floor with one of her sticks and with the other pointed to the box of eggs.

'Before you starts h'any silly games, young man,' she announced, 'look at that box! There's something a-h'oozing h'out of it h'all h'over my son's good carpet!'

All eyes were turned on the egg-box from which, alas, a thin stream of yellow liquid was trickling! Uncle Albert hastily put down the hamper and producing a very gay silk handkerchief mopped up the worst of the mess, while one of the guests, with great presence of mind, produced a newspaper from his pocket which together they wrapped round the box.

But it was all too much for the broody hen! Perfectly quiet till this moment, she now began to cluck wildly, scuffling around in the hamper and doing her best to prise up the lid. The guests looked somewhat taken aback and Grandma Whiffen after remarking tartly, 'Oh, so it's an *'en* is it!' went on to demand what 'our Winnie' was going to do with such a 'h'extraordinary present!'

'She'll set it on the eggs, Grandma,' said Uncle Albert brightly, trying to make the best of the situation, 'leastways, I will (if there's any of 'em left)', he muttered under his breath. 'It's broody, see? They're very *special* eggs,' he added impressively, 'Pedigree.'

But Grandma Whiffen refused to be impressed.

'Special mess they've made of the carpet,' she said. 'H'egg stain's not a h'easy thing to get h'out. Not at h'all it h'aint.'

Mrs Whiffen now came forward and suggested Uncle Albert should remove both box and hamper to the kitchen, and, the hen still clucking madly, he picked them up and gratefully followed her from the room, leaving his relatives scarlet with confusion and eyed very much askance by the other guests.

It was a relief when a voice was heard calling from upstairs, and Mrs Whiffen returned to say her daughter was asking for Miss Ruggles to go up and change into her bridesmaid's dress. And Lily Rose, swelling with pride at being addressed as 'Miss Ruggles', followed by Mrs

Ruggles and William, hurried thankfully from the room, while Mr Ruggles put as much space as possible between himself and Grandma Whiffen's armchair.

Upstairs, things went better than Mrs Ruggles had dared expect.

The bride, who was short and inclined to be fat like her mother, but very pretty, and who was being assisted to dress by two female friends, greeted them kindly, and bestowing a kiss on the top of William's woolly cap, remarked that he was 'a sweet'.

William, in fact, was an instantaneous success all round! Both the female friends, and all three bridesmaids sitting primly in their turquoise blue satin dresses on the edge of the bed, expressed a desire to hold and pet him. William offered no resistance. He was singularly quiet, sucking a thoughtful thumb and regarding everything about him with wide, solemn eyes. Had Mrs Ruggles not been so agitated over the hen incident and less concerned with the dressing of Lily Rose, she might have noticed that he looked a trifle pale. But for once William was not her chief care. For the time being it was Lily Rose; the question whether the pieces put in the back and waist of her dress were going to 'hold'; and to prevent, if possible, anyone from seeing her shoes were painted, and socks instead of stockings being worn. Fortunately everyone was so engrossed with William that matters were easier than she had hoped and, retreating to a far corner of the room, she and Lily Rose set about the business of dressing unwatched and undisturbed.

Lily Rose pulled up the socks as far as they would go; put on the sandals (which shone like the best patent-leather and which no one except at the very closest quarters could possibly suspect of being anything else), and slipped on the dress. The pieces 'held' but even so it was a very tight fit.

'For goodness sake don't go taking deep breaths, nor get a fit of the giggles,' whispered Mrs Ruggles. 'It's only *just* met and the stuff splits terrible easy . . . I'll have to tell your Auntie as I let it out. . . . Are you all ready now? Oh – the wreath! . . . you'd best let her put that on so as to be sure it's like the other children's. . . . There, you

looks very nice,' she added encouragingly, for Lily Rose was fairly shaking with nervousness, 'Very nice indeed.'

Lily Rose really did look nice! The bright blue of the dress suited her and the length and many frills seemed, strangely enough, to take away from her bulk, while her fat legs were completely concealed.

Miss Whiffen made no comment about the alterations beyond saying she was sure she had followed the measures 'exact'. But she smiled kindly at Lily Rose and said she was a big girl, my word she was, and would make two of her (the bride's) sisters and niece! Lily Rose began to feel better; her nervousness vanished, and presently she was so overcome at the sight of what she called her 'Book – aye' – a bunch of mixed flowers tied with pink satin ribbon, and the bridegroom's gift of a pink pearl necklace, that she could think of nothing else at all!

It was now almost two o'clock, and everyone, except the bride, who remained upstairs with her two friends, gathered in the small front room where light refreshments in the form of cups of soup and paste sandwiches were handed round on trays.

The entry of the bridesmaids caused a considerable diversion; the hen incident appeared forgotten and the party seemed warming up. Before long, chivvied by Mr Whiffen, Uncle Albert and his best man departed for the church and presently it was announced it was time for all to leave.

Doing her best to appear calm, but inwardly filled with many misgivings, Mrs Ruggles handed William over to the care of Grandma Whiffen, and was hustled into a taxi in company with Mr Ruggles and two or three other guests while Lily Rose was hustled into another with Mrs Whiffen and the other bridesmaids. The remainder of the guests following in a third.

The church was quite near and they were at the gate almost before they knew they had started, so quickly did the taxis cover the short distance.

It was still misty but a pale gleam on the horizon gave a heartening promise that perhaps, after all, the sun might shine upon the bride.

Seats were reserved for the bridegroom's relatives on the right and the Ruggles were pleasantly flattered at being shown into the very front pew until presently, glancing round, they saw they were the only people on that side of the church at all!

Uncle Albert and his best man in their blue serge suits, their heads glistening with hair-oil, and the backs of their necks unnaturally red and scrubbed-looking, stood whispering together by the chancel steps while the organist played what was later described in the local paper as 'a tasteful voluntary'.

Presently there was a commotion in the porch; everyone turned round and the organist burst into a torrent of chords and trills. The bride had arrived!

A few moments later, in gleaming white satin, veil and orange blossoms complete, leaning on the arm of the splay-footed Mr Whiffen, and followed by her four satin-clad bridesmaids, she passed up the aisle; the Vicar stepped forward, and the service began.

At the words demanding whether anyone had any objections to the marriage, and if so 'let him now speak or else hereafter for ever hold his peace', Mrs Ruggles held *her* breath while Mr Ruggles shifted nervously from foot to foot.

There was a short pause; the proverbial pin could have been heard to drop and an acute observer might have noticed Uncle Albert's neck turn an even deeper red.

The Vicar glanced slowly round the church, waited another moment, then resumed his reading, and Mr and Mrs Ruggles looked at each other with unutterable relief.

The service proceeded smoothly, and though the replies of Uncle Albert and Miss Whiffen could hardly be heard, the firm tones of little Mr Whiffen, as he gave his daughter away, were audible even outside in the church-yard!

And now those in the front pews could hear the instructions to produce the ring. There followed some whispering

between Uncle Albert and his best man, and then, so
quiet was the congregation, so tense and expectant the
atmosphere, that the sound of its tinkle as between them
they dropped it on the paved floor could be heard over
the whole church!

'Oh dear!' sighed Mrs Ruggles. Oh dear! To drop the
ring was most unlucky – *most* unlucky! . . .

And *now* what was happening! . . . for the best man was
down on his hands and knees. . . . Uncle Albert was on his
hands and knees . . . and yes . . . the Vicar himself! . . . All
of them grovelling for the ring! . . . The bridesmaids
bent sideways (and she trembled for Lily Rose's dress)!
Only the bride, with admirable composure, remained
upright!

A whisper ran round the waiting guests. The ring! . . .
They had dropped the ring! . . . The ring was lost! . . .

The Vicar stood up. He beckoned to a choir-boy;
hastily whispered some instructions, and the boy disappeared through a side-door.

It was true; the ring *was* lost! It had fallen, said the
Vicar, through a grating. . . . Another ring was being
fetched from the Vicarage. . . . In the meantime, would
the congregation please wait reverently. . . .

The organist came nobly to the rescue, and plunged
into Handel's 'Largo', thundering out chords and pulling
frenziedly at stops. The guests looked at each other in
silence. A bridesmaid tittered and was rebuked by another
bridesmaid. Mr Ruggles glanced at his watch. There was,
in fact, a general consultation of watches and an air of
mute inquiry. The time was just after a quarter to three;
another quarter of an hour, less – another fourteen minutes
– *and the wedding would not be legal*!

Mr Ruggles grimly whispered this information to his
wife. Other guests were obviously whispering it too, and

the faces of the bride's parents looked very strained and apprehensvie. Only the Vicar remained calm and un-ruffled.

Five minutes went by; then another two. The organist came to the end of 'Largo' and started again. Another minute passed and even the Vicar began to look a little anxious, and then, to the immense and clearly audible relief of the whole congregation, the choir-boy, breathless and scarlet in the face, reappeared. A ring was handed over, and the service continued.

Two minutes after the final words pronouncing Uncle Albert and Miss Whiffen man and wife were spoken, the church clock chimed three!

They were back at The Willows later than had been expected. Grandma Whiffen was sitting at the window looking none too pleased, and the first thing that greeted Mrs Ruggles's anxious ear as the front door was opened was a dismal cry from William. She could hardly wait to reach him.

'What is it, my lovey?' she cried, picking him up from some cushions on the floor where he had been lying, 'What's the matter?' But William only cried louder.

''E don't seem very 'ealthy, your baby,' remarked Grandma Whiffen rather sourly. 'An 'ealthy baby didn't ought to cry like that – and 'iccup – 'E's 'ardly stopped 'iccuping since you left!'

'Not *healthy*!' exclaimed Mrs Ruggles indignantly. 'Well, it's the first *I've* heard of it! Why, he's considered one of the best babies at our Welfare! And perhaps,' she went on, 'perhaps you've not heard as he won a prize at the Otwell Baby Show last year!'*

'Happen he's ate something?' said a kindly but

* *The Family from One End Street.*

simple-minded guest, hoping to smooth matters over.
'They do sometimes,' she added brightly.

''E's not ate anything along of *me*,' said Grandma
Whiffen firmly.

There was silence for a moment or two broken only by
William's wails and hiccups.

'Well, he's not had nothing since his breakfast to *my*
knowledge,' said Mrs Ruggles. 'Except a cup of soup –
and they said as it was home-made.'

'What's that about soup?' cried the bride gaily,
coming in at this moment. '"Home-made" – I should
say it was – I made it myself! Yes, *me*, folks! Leastways,'
she went on, 'I opened the tin and added the water, and
put it in the saucepan. Got to learn to cook now, you know!'

This domestic revelation was greeted with roars of
laughter by the assembled guests to whom, apparently, it
appeared the height of drollery. But Mrs Ruggles was not
at all amused. So that's how it was, was it! A nice look-out
for Albert. . . . Better have given him a couple of tin-
openers than a broody hen! . . . And meanwhile, for all
they knew – or cared – her William might be poisoned! . . .

Mrs Whiffen now waddled forward and suggested Mrs
Ruggles might like to take her baby upstairs and let him
have what she called 'a nice lay down'; and, Mrs Ruggles
having eagerly assented, she led the way, breathing hard
and pausing for rest on every second stair, to an apartment belonging to her younger daughters.

'Just lay him down a bit,' she wheezed, turning back a
very grand silk eiderdown, 'and perhaps,' she added
hopefully, 'you'd like to stay with him a bit? We could
send you up something to eat.'

Stay with him! Well, really! thought Mrs Ruggles,
removing William's shoes, did they imagine she'd leave
her baby alone and crying in a strange bedroom while

she went and enjoyed herself? She thanked her hostess politely, however, and Mrs Whiffen, murmuring she must 'see to things' waddled thankfully away.

Downstairs the other guests were being shepherded across the hall into the dining-room where, in the matter of catering, the Whiffens had certainly surpassed themselves! In the centre of the table was a three-tier wedding cake surmounted by a sugar cupid. A chicken, a tongue, slices of ham and brawn, trifles, jellies, and bowls of fruit salad stood waiting to be devoured. There was port and sherry, and last, but judging from the array of gold-necked bottles, certainly not least, champagne! There were also, for those unable, or unwilling, to touch alcohol, large jugs of lemonade. The table was decorated with sprays of some green trailing plant, there were little dishes of chocolates and other sweets – and there were even crackers!

Lily Rose, keeping close to her father, gasped audibly, but Mr Ruggles tried hard to look as if attendance at such a banquet was an everyday occurrence for him.

Meanwhile, upstairs, William continued to hiccup and wail.

Looks as if he *had* ate something! said Mrs Ruggles to herself. Can't be that soup, surely, or we'd all be queer by now! I wonder ...! Perhaps he's picked up summat when that old Grandma weren't looking and has got it tucked away at the back of his mouth – I've knowed him do that afore now ... I'll just have a good look. And putting her finger into William's mouth she ran it carefully round the furthest recesses. Ah! he *had* got something there! ... And amid terrific wails and screams she presently extracted a pulpy lump of what looked like pink blotting-paper. She examined it carefully. What *could* it be? *Whatever* had he got hold of? ... Goodness! Could you believe it! *If it weren't them return bus tickets!*

For the next few minutes, Mrs Ruggles was concerned only with William himself. Very soon, however, he ceased to cry; his hiccups grew less and finally ceased, and before long he had fallen asleep from sheer exhaustion. She sat watching him for a moment or two, then she tip-toed over to the wash-stand and very carefully washed the half-chewed tickets. But before she had finished she was wearing a very worried expression indeed! For instead of *three* tickets, there were only *two*! Where was the third? Was it somewhere in the house – or – had William swallowed it?

She was standing wondering what she ought to do when there was the sound of footsteps on the stairs and the next moment, balancing a trayful of food, into the room came Uncle Albert. On the tray were two glasses, and from the pocket of his blue serge suit protruded a gold-necked bottle.

'Oh, Albert, *quiet*!' whispered Mrs Ruggles holding up a warning finger and pointing to William; and then, as he showed no signs of waking, 'Oh, Albert! I'm afraid there's a dreadful thing happened!' And she related the fate of the bus tickets.

Uncle Albert grinned broadly.

'Don't seem exactly your lucky day, Rosie!' he said.

'If you ask *me*, Albert,' replied his sister, 'I haven't *got* a lucky day! But what can we do?' she went on, 'The pore l'il mite!'

'You ought to make him sick – that's the proper thing,' said Uncle Albert briskly. 'Tell you what, Rosie,' he went on, 'I've nicked the remains of this bottle,' and he patted his pocket, 'special for you and me. How about giving William there a drop? – it can't possibly hurt him – only do him good – after all it's what millionaires live on when they're ill – him being so young, though, it might make him just a bit sick first. It's worth trying!' And putting down the tray he pulled the bottle from his pocket and filled up the two glasses.

But Mrs Ruggles said firmly, 'no'. She couldn't, no, she couldn't risk it. Suppose it made William really ill? – and anyway it wasn't certain he *had* swallowed the ticket. Best leave things to Nature.

'Well, as you like,' said Uncle Albert, 'but I must be getting back – guests clamourin' for the bridegroom and all that. ... Here's luck, Rosie!' he went on, taking a large gulp of the champagne, 'It's been fine to see you again, old girl, and it's been good of you and Jo to come. Things is going to be All Right now, Rosie – you'll see!' and draining his glass of the last drop of the precious liquid, he kissed her affectionately and was gone.

I'm sure I done right, said Mrs Ruggles to herself gazing fondly at the still sleeping William. It don't never do to go agin Nature – Goodness! I believe that stuff's gone to my head – or rather my feet! I'd best eat something quick! And she attacked the trayful of food. She had just finished and was feeling better when the door handle rattled and in burst Lily Rose, very out of breath, very pink in the face, and wearing a paper hat perched rakishly on the top of her bridesmaid's wreath.

'Mum!' she cried, half-way between a gasp and a giggle, '*Mum*! They wants you to go down! They've cut the cake and they're pulling crackers, and Uncle Albert's going to make a speech! I've had some cake – it were just lovely! And oh, Mum! I've had some champagne – only half a glass – I didn't like it much, and it hasn't half made me feel funny, so I said I'd come and stay with William while you went down – coo, he looks fine now, doesn't he? Hurry up, Mum, 'cos they're waiting!' And Lily Rose paused for breath.

Mrs Ruggles hesitated. William certainly did look better, and she would like to have a bit of wedding-cake for luck and hear Albert's speech. . . . She regarded Lily Rose critically. They'd no business to have given her champagne – even if it was only half a glass – a kid her age.

'Well, you sit quiet and look after William careful,' she said after explaining briefly what had happened – and what might be expected to happen, 'and call me if he don't seem absolutely all right' and she hurried away.

It was a very different company from the one she had left half an hour ago! The guests, replete with food and drink and crowned with paper caps, were now laughing and joking and thoroughly at home. Even Grandma, seated in a corner holding the remains of a glass of port and wearing an orange paper bonnet with green streamers looked mildly benevolent.

Uncle Albert stood making jokes and offering to pull crackers with everyone. The champagne, Mrs Ruggles was afraid, had gone to his head too. He greeted her with wild enthusiasm, holding out a cracker and crying, 'Hi! Rosie, Hi! *Pull!*'

And pull Mrs Ruggles did. There was a deafening bang and she nearly fell backwards as the greater part of the cracker remained in her hand. Inside it was a flaming red cap with silver stars, and down to the floor fluttered a motto. Uncle Albert pounced on it.

' "*A-Big-Surprise-Will-Soon-Be-Coming-Your-Way*",' he read. ' "*A-Big-Surprise*" – I'll make three guesses, Rosie, the surprises you'd like best today!' And he drew her towards him and whispered something in her ear.

'Hush, Albert!' exclaimed Mrs Ruggles, giggling a little in spite of herself '*Hush*! They'll hear!' But her brother only laughed and was about to say something further when he was interrupted by cries of 'Speech! Speech from the bridegroom! Speech!'

Uncle Albert stood for a moment looking rather shy, but after glancing questioningly in the direction of his best man and receiving a nod in return, he seemed to pluck up courage.

'Ladies and Gentlemen; All,' he began and, waving the cracker motto to and fro as he spoke, he went on to say that while his sister might have a surprise coming to her, today had been one long succession of surprises for him! There were the wonderful presents given him and his Winnie by so many kind friends – not least his beautiful broody hen (and he glanced very lovingly at his relatives). ... The surprise of seeing a new nephew (and he was sorry he wasn't with them now but they must save a cracker for him). ... The (at the time) very dreadful surprise when the ring rolled down the grating, and the almost greater (though happy one) of learning that the Vicar kept "spares"! And lastly, the surprise of the really wonderful supply of food and drink provided by his parents-in-law; and he now suggested they should all drink a toast to them and their daughters and of course, he added hastily, Grandma there in the corner.

And though Grandma was heard to remark she didn't want no toast and it were 'just a h'excuse for h'another drink', no one took any notice and, the champagne having given out, glasses were filled with anything liquid that was left.

A toast was next proposed by Mr Whiffen to the bride and bridegroom, and, after that, Uncle Albert looking very serious announced *he* had a surprise.

Oh dear, thought Mrs Ruggles looking anxiously at him, he's never, he's never, surely, going to tell about his Misfortune? ...

But she need not have worried. Uncle Albert's surprise was entirely respectable. Merely a photographer friend who had offered to come and take some wedding 'pictures' and who had now arrived and was ready and waiting outside in the garden.

In company with the photographer a bright interval seemed to have arrived too, and a fitful sun was shining. A rug was hurriedly carried out and spread on the damp patch of grass between the two grave-like flower-beds, and on it Uncle Albert and his bride standing arm in arm and looking intensely solemn were duly photographed.

Mrs Ruggles now hurried away to William in order that Lily Rose might return and appear in a photograph of the bride and bridegroom, the best man, Mr and Mrs Whiffen, and the bridesmaids; and when this had been taken, Uncle Albert said he would now like what he called A Real Family Picture; all the Whiffen family, his own relaytives – including William, and – why not, hadn't she long been one of the family? – his broody hen!

And though Mrs Ruggles, still uncertain of the fate of the bus ticket, was reluctant to include William; and Grandma Whiffen (who had condemned the whole enterprise as 'great h'extravagance') was prevailed on to agree only because the bride showed signs of weeping at her refusal, and 'no one could be h'allowed to cry on their wedding day – no h'indeed,' Uncle Albert had his way.

William and the broody hen were fetched and exactly at the right moment the sun, which had retreated again, came out and shone brilliantly. The broody hen, in the arms of the best man (who seemed to have taken a great fancy to her, and had agreed to 'set' and look after her during the honeymoon), gave a kind of crow; William, in the arms of Mrs Ruggles, pointed joyfully towards her and crowed in return; Mr Ruggles, swelling with pride, almost crowed too; and everyone, even Grandma, smiled! The photographer enthusiastically pronounced it 'a perfect picture' and Uncle Albert recklessly ordered copies for everyone!

It was now almost five o'clock and if the happy couple did not wish to lose their train, said Mr Whiffen, the bride had better hurry away quickly to change.

'And us too,' whispered Mr Ruggles to his wife. 'We haven't a great lot of time neither. And we mustn't miss that bus on no account. Get Lily Rose out of that finery and soon as they've drove away we'll make tracks – you've got them bus tickets safe all right, haven't you?'

Mrs Ruggles hesitated and, fortunately, the next moment the best man came up and hurried Mr Ruggles away to assist in tying a shoe on the back of the bridal taxi.

And when she got upstairs again Mrs Ruggles was glad she *had* said nothing, for from the turn-up of William's woolly cap as she put it on him, pulling it well down over his ears, out fell the missing ticket! It was creased and crumpled and rather sticky but, except for the little piece that had been clipped out by the conductor, *it was whole!* ...

She was just, and only just, in time to join in the throwing of rice and confetti as the taxi moved off; and if the other guests caught the words, 'All's well, Albert! All's well!' and Uncle Albert's, 'What did I tell you!' as he leant out of the taxi, waving and trying to dodge the showers of confetti, they were none the wiser. Nor, when 'good-byes' and 'thank-you's' were said, were the Whiffens – not even Grandma, who remarked of William that 'e seemed to have got over 'is 'iccups nice now 'e'd 'ad a bit of a lay down – but there, you never knew with babies!

And Mrs Ruggles as she shook hands agreed, fervently, you certainly never *did*!

They were in good time at the bus stop but the bus when it came was very crowded and it was with some difficulty they all found seats.

'Hurr-y up! Hurr-y up!' cried the conductor who had had a long, tiring day, his hand on the bell, 'Do you think we can wait for ever while you chooses where you'll sit?'

Mr Ruggles felt like saying there was not much choosing about it but refrained – no good startin' a row. . . . But

alas! he had hardly found a seat and sat down before a row was in full swing!

Asked for her ticket, Mrs Ruggles, to whom a kindly young man sitting near the door had given up his seat, had produced her handkerchief with the chewed 'remains', explaining that her baby here – indicating William – had unfortunately attempted to swallow them – they were a little chewed but the pieces were all there and, she added, smiling hopefully, had been thoroughly washed.

But the conductor was in no smiling mood.

'Oh!' he said, 'thanks for telling me! Thanks very

much! The dirty little brat! Well I ain't a-goin' to touch 'em!' and he waved the handkerchief away.

Mrs Ruggles turned on him furiously.

' "Dirty little brat" indeed! "Pore l'il mite" more like, *I* should say! How could he know as they weren't good to eat? It's plain you've no children of your own, young man!'

'*On* the contrary,' said the conductor over his shoulder as he started to elbow his way up the crowded bus, 'it happens I've got four! Any more fares, please? *Any –* more – fares?'

Mrs Ruggles sat staring straight in front of her, an angry spot of red burning in either cheek, unpleasantly conscious of nudges and giggles. Her William, a dirty little brat! She hugged him more closely, thankful he remained quiet and presently fell fast asleep. . . .

It seemed an interminable journey but at last the outskirts of Otwell came in sight; very soon they were rattling up the steep hill to the High Street, and at the familiar bus office.

They all staggered out of the bus, a weary party indeed, William unfortunately awaking and, though too exhausted for whole-hearted yelling, whimpering continually as they trailed slowly homewards.

'Only another minute or two, my sweet, only another minute, and we'll be there,' murmured Mrs Ruggles endearingly at intervals, while Mr Ruggles sighed deeply and decided Bank Holidays weren't what they used to be and that evidently other people felt the same, judgin' by the few people about and it barely eight o'clock. But as they turned the corner into One End Street, Lily Rose, who was a few paces ahead, suddenly stopped dead.

'Coo! Dad!' she cried, '*what ever's up?*' For instead of

the usual deserted air One End Street invariably wore at
this hour of the day in summer – the hour when teas were
over and suppers not yet being considered; when fathers
were busy in gardens and allotments, and mothers
snatching a few minutes peace and gossip with the

neighbours, and only those children too small or too un-
adventurous not to be far afield, playing in the gutters –
instead of all this – heads at windows, every doorway
crowded – and not a child in the street – not a child. . . .
But yes, there were two. On the steps of No. 1 sat Jim and
John, and standing one on either side of the doorway,
and looking as if they had been there some considerable
time, *were two policemen*!

CHAPTER NINE

Mrs Ruggles Gets a Surprise

THE thoughts that flew through Mrs Ruggles's mind – and for that matter Mr Ruggles's – though his took longer so there were less of them . . . ! Run over! Half-drowned! House on Fire! Trespassing on Railway Line! Damaging Ricks! Stealing! (Impossible, this last, surely, *their* boys . . . !) But when the twins jumped up and smiled and waved and shouted, and as the house appeared to be still standing and intact, it looked as if it could not possibly be any of these things.

'The *key*, Dad!' yelled John, 'the *key, and come quick*! It may be here any minute – it's been seen down London Road way – and the cops can't go till you come!'

Mr Ruggles was running now. People called to him from crowded doorways and windows but he was far too flustered to hear what they said. What on earth! Who – what – had been seen?

The elder of 'the cops' stepped forward. 'Glad you've come,' he remarked. 'It's only a *chance*, 'course, it'll come along here, but we've had instructions to warn every street and see all children's indoors and your boys is locked out, seemingly.'

'But what,' gasped Mr Ruggles, fumbling in his pocket for the door key – good heavens! had he lost it? . . . no, here it was . . . '*What* might come along? For goodness sake,' he cried, becoming angry with anxiety as no one answered, 'explain yerselves, can't you?'

'Thought you'd have heard it,' said the younger 'cop' slowly; 'thought the whole town knew by this time,' he added with a lugubrious sigh.

Now Mrs Ruggles, Lily Rose breathless beside her, had come panting up. So loudly had so many neighbours shouted the news that at first she was unable to make out what anyone said, but when she *did* . . . !

'Jo! Jo! the key! *the key*!' she screamed. 'Open the door! *Open the door!* Get in everyone, *quick*, I tell you, quick, *quick*! *There's a tiger loose! a tiger*, do you hear! ! Oh, my goodness me! my goodness me. . . .'

It was true! Bealby's Super Circus (Animals Humanely Trained and Treated) Featuring Thelma, The Time-Telling Tigress, which had arrived the night before, and was to have given its first performance that evening, was without its leading lady!

Never, even at spring-cleaning time, had so much furniture been moved about at No. 1 One End Street, nor, judging from the lights burning unwontedly late in windows, and the noise of sundry bumps and bangs, at other houses in the street either. The mangle, a table, two chairs, a sack of coke and another of potatoes were wedged firmly against the door into the yard, while the big chest of drawers from Mr and Mrs Ruggles's bedroom was brought downstairs and put across the locked and bolted front door. On it were placed two large and very heavy scuttles of coal, and finally the kitchen table pushed against it as a kind of buttress.

'All the same,' said Mr Ruggles as they stood, rather breathlessly but with some pride, regarding this barri-cade, 'I feel if it comes, it'll be at the *back*. There's *cover* there,' he added in a knowledgeable sort of way, as if building defences against the ways of wild animals at bay was just one of his everyday jobs.

'What do you mean, "cover"?' snapped Mrs Ruggles who was tired to death as well as frightened.

'Bushes,' replied her husband. 'Bushes and . . . and little trees-like. All that tangle between our wall and where the tannery yard begins.'

'I can't see no animal, wild nor otherwise, bidin' long *there*,' retorted Mrs Ruggles, 'the smell's enough at times to drive anything out and they says as animals smells things more nor what we do.'

'But a tiger might *like* tannery smells, Mum,' broke in Jim, 'same as dogs like awful nasty smells sometimes!' No one made any reply to this comforting remark, but Mr Ruggles suddenly clutched his hair as he sometimes did when excited, and cried, 'You've give me an idea! Quick, Rosie! Where's that there big sugar-sifter – him as you won on the Hoop-La once – and the pepper?'

Sugar-sifter? Pepper? 'You goin' barmy, Jo Ruggles?' inquired his wife. 'Let me tell you this don't seem to me the time to be makin' silly jokes!'

'It's *not* a silly joke,' replied Mr Ruggles, faintly offended, 'it's a very serious and sensible idea. You've heard as they uses pepper on dogs in dog-fights? Well, why not on a tiger?' And before Mrs Ruggles had had time to protest again, he had whisked the sugar-sifter from its place on the dresser, emptied it, filled it up with pepper, and, dragging a length of string from his pocket, the next minute was climbing through the back kitchen window.

'Won't half make it sneeze, this won't!' he chuckled as he disappeared into the yard.

But Mrs Ruggles was in no laughing mood.

'You're *barmy*!' she cried running after him into the back kitchen, 'Just *barmy*! For Heaven's sake, Jo, come *in*! It might be out there *now*, ready to spring! It's not *safe* I tell you!'

But Mr Ruggles was not to be persuaded – or hurried

and, while Mrs Ruggles stood watching, her heart thumping against her ribs with terror, outside he remained until, in the form of a booby-trap over the yard door, he had fixed the pepper-filled sugar-sifter completely to his satisfaction. Then he crawled back through the window, latched it securely, and, finally, picking up a big bag of flour, placed it against the catch as a further precaution.

'You're barmy!' repeated Mrs Ruggles once again. 'Barmy!' But Mr Ruggles only grinned.

At long last all preparations were completed and, with the exception of William, mercifully asleep in his cot where he had been put, protesting and fully clothed, immediately on arrival, they all sat down to some bread-and-cheese and cocoa. The twins, full of a delightful feeling – half terror, half excitement – were in the highest spirits, but Lily Rose was so shaking with fear she spilt her cocoa every time she attempted to lift her cup. She wept loudly and declared she was terrified to go to bed – much less to sleep! In vain Mr Ruggles patted her shoulder and assured her nothing – not even an elephant – could get past the barricaded doors. Lily Rose was past reasoning with.

'Just imagine, Dad,' she wailed, the tears rolling down her cheeks and splashing into her cocoa, 'Just imagine it gettin' in – somehow – and . . . and . . . creeping (sniff) up the stairs (sniff) and . . . *crouching* on the top step (sniff) all ready to spring when we comes out of our rooms in the morning!'

Mr Ruggles said he couldn't imagine no such thing – nor anyone else in their senses. But Lily Rose only shuddered and wept still more. Mr Ruggles decided if she was going on long like this – and it looked probable – they'd none of them get to bed that night, much less have any sleep. Mrs Ruggles, beyond saying sharply 'stop actin' like a big baby', said nothing. Lily Rose's feelings were too much like her own.

'Now listen,' said Mr Ruggles presently. 'You stop makin' that hullabaloo – how do you think we'd *hear* if it *did* come, with you goin' on like thàt? And when you're all upstairs *and in bed* I'll make a barricade on the landing. There! I can't say more nor that – can I?'

'No,' sniffed Lily Rose, slightly reassured, and definitely more disposed to silence at the horrible possibility that the noise of her tears might prevent warning of any awful approach, 'No.'

Mr Ruggles was as good as his word, and before the lights were put out all the bedroom chairs stood jammed together in a fine tangle on the top landing.

Comforted, but completely convinced she would stay awake till morning, Lily Rose lay down. In twenty minutes she was sleeping soundly!

Mrs Ruggles said afterwards that she never knew how she slept through that night, but this was only a way of putting things. Far from sleeping through it, she hardly slept at all! Tired – exhausted – as she was after the long day – was it really hardly more than twelve hours since they'd started for the wedding? – her ears were alert for every sound – and how very *many* sounds there seemed to be – both in and out of the house – she had never, she was sure, heard before! Tappings and creakings, and bumpings, so as anyone'd think the place was haunted! She kept sitting up in bed to hear more clearly, and twice, so suspicious were the noises, that she got up and went over to the window. Something scratching on wood? (*did* tigers scratch?); then a *thudding* noise as if a heavy body had hurled itself against a door (was Jo really right about them

barricades standing up to even a elephant?) ... Snakes
alive! there it went again! ...

'Oh, get back to bed, and go to sleep, Rosie, do!'
muttered Mr Ruggles crossly, 'and don't act so daft.
Haven't you never heard the wind before? Believe me,
that tiger's either shot or back in its cage be now; and if
it's not, we can't do no more about it.' And he rolled over,
taking most of the bed-clothes with him, and almost the
next minute was snoring!

Mrs Ruggles was scandalized! She could hardly credit
such callousness. His whole family like to be attacked by
a tiger any minute – and *snoring*!

All the same, she knew her husband was right. What
more *could* they do? She got slowly back into bed, pulled
what was left of the bed-clothes around her and, with a
protecting hand on the bars of William's cot, pushed close
beside the bed, slept fitfully until the alarum went off.

Breakfast next morning, eaten at the kitchen-table still
wedged against the front door, was a strange meal indeed
– but what else could be done? Very early a police-van
with a loud-speaker had arrived in One End Street, announcing the animal was still at large, but adding there
was no need for panic; police and troops would patrol
every street, and children should be sent to school as
usual, though if possible escorted by a parent 'or other
responsible adult'.

'Well, *really*!' exclaimed Jim disgustedly, 'you'd think
we'd get given a holiday – *wouldn't* you! After all, it's
pretty special – a tiger loose!'

'Bit too special for me!' grunted Mr Ruggles, 'but the
idea – warnin' parents to "escort" their children – funny
sort of parents they'd be as didn't, with a tiger loose! A daft
sort of warnin' I calls that!'

'Well, I think it's daft they should go to school – or out of the house at all,' said Mrs Ruggles, 'and what match is you – or any other parent – goin' to be for a tiger anyway?'

'Actually, it's a tiger-*ess*, Mum,' put in John, 'and they're even fiercer – aren't they, Dad?' he asked, enjoying the shudder that went through him at the very thought, and the expression on Lily Rose's face.

Poor Lily Rose! She had been shaking with fright again ever since she woke up, while the very thought of going outside the door, much less all the way to school . . . !

'Oh, Mum!' she cried, squeezing up a few tears, clasping her hands together, and hoping she was looking a little like the picture of Queen Philippa pleading for the Burghers of Calais in her history book. '*Please* let us all stay home, *please*! I could look after William,' she added hopefully. 'You won't be able to put him in the yard now and he'll be awful fretty left alone in here.'

The twins looked at her in disgust. Not to go to school was one thing, but not to go *out* – on such an occasion as this! To miss the slightest chance of seeing anything and everything there was to see connected with such an event! Really, girls . . . !

But before Mrs Ruggles had time to reply, Mr Ruggles, finishing off his third cup of tea, got up from the table. 'Come here, my girl,' he said. And putting down the cup he took Lily Rose by the shoulders and pushed her gently to the window.

'Look! – bottom of street.'

Lily Rose looked. There, one on either pavement, each with a rifle and fixed bayonet, stood two soldiers.

'There's others – in every street – and police,' said Mr Ruggles. 'What animal, do you suppose, is goin' to get past *them* and stay alive?'

Lily Rose didn't know. She only knew, Dad (sniff), she was ter-terribly fri-frightened . . . (sniff).

'Then you comes along a-holdin' of my hand,' said Mr Ruggles, *'but you're going to school.* If you don't, with no proper excuse, like as not I'll get fined and I'm not wastin' no money that way – there's little enough as it is; so pull yerself together and get ready, for it's nearly time to be off.'

When Dad spoke like that, Lily Rose knew there was no more to be said. She looked beseechingly at her mother but Mrs Ruggles seemed to have changed her mind. She, too, had looked out of the window and seen the soldiers and the sight had considerably reassured her. But she had also seen something else. Leaning from an upstairs window her eyes darting in every direction, was Mrs Nosey-Parker Smith. From every house, children escorted by fathers 'or other responsible adult' were pouring forth. It was not going to be said at No. 4 that the Ruggles, alone of all the street, had funked going out, and kept their children from school!

'Your Father's right,' she said, 'there's soldiers every-where. And all the other children's goin'. Get your things at once and get off. But mind!' she added, 'you're none of you not to move *one inch* outside the school – understand – till your Father calls for you – *not one inch*!'

There was no hope for it. Lily Rose abandoned her Queen Philippa attitude, blinked back her tears, and sulkily fetched her hat. As to holding Dad's hand . . . nice silly she'd look! . . . All the same – it was *terrifying* . . . !

The next thing was how to get into the street without disturbing the barricaded doors. Through the kitchen window was the only solution, and Lily Rose hoped against hope that for once her bulk might prove an asset and she would be unable to accomplish this. But alas! pulled by Mr Ruggles from outside, and pushed by Mrs

Ruggles from within, it was easily, if not exactly gracefully, managed, and the only consolation to be had was that she couldn't be as fat as she felt – and people said, and she went off slightly more happily, if no less fearfully than she had expected, in consequence of this. The twins followed, and Mrs Ruggles and William were left alone.

She stood, holding him in her arms, watching from the window, until her family reached the corner of the street, where they all stopped to wave before turning into the main road, and waving back in return.

'Wave!' she commanded William, 'wave, and say "bye-bye".'

William waved vigorously with both hands.

'Say "bye-bye",' repeated Mrs Ruggles encouragingly, 'Quick!' – giving him a little shake, 'say "bye-bye".' William stopped waving. 'Bye-bye,' prompted Mrs Ruggles again. 'Say "bye-bye"!'

There was a pause; then, "Puss-y-cat!' cried William, and he bounced up and down in her arms. 'Puss-y-cat!'

'You and your pussy-cats!' exclaimed Mrs Ruggles disappointedly as she put him back in his high chair and proceeded to give him the remainder of his breakfast. Really, much as she disliked admitting it, there was no denying, as far as talking was concerned, William was undoubtedly a *very* backward baby!

If yesterday had been one of the longest days she had ever spent, this, Mrs Ruggles was soon to discover, was to be *quite* the longest morning! William, his breakfast over, was very quickly aware of some disturbance in his usual morning routine, and was not long in announcing his displeasure.

'Out-door! *Out-door!*' he protested when it became increasingly clear his mother was going about her usual

business, but without installing him in his playpen in the
back yard, where every fine morning, side by side with
the hens crooning in their soap box, crooning back in
return, he grubbed in the dust with an old kitchen spoon
or murmured endearments to a small wooden horse very
much the worse for wear.

'Not today, my lovey,' said Mrs Ruggles for the twen-
tieth time, 'not today. No, I *know* it's not raining' – as a
loud yell pealed forth – '*but you can't go out!*'

Oh dear, what *could* she do with him? . . . No good
tellin' him the real reason . . . he wouldn't understand if
she did. . . . She began to wish Lily Rose, at least, *had*
stayed at home. If only they'd thought to bring in the
playpen last night! However was she to keep him quiet
and safe, and out of mischief, while she got on with her
work? She was all behind as it was, goin' out yesterday –
and an extra large wash this week too. . . .

'Out-door! Out-door!' wailed William, banging on
the table with a spoon. 'Out-*door*!' And suddenly, furious
with frustration, he seized a tea-cup and flung it on the
floor where it broke into half a dozen pieces! He then let
forth one of the loudest of his famous yells!

Rarely Mrs Ruggles lost her temper with him; more
rarely still would she acknowledge he was spoilt. Now,
suddenly, she did both.

'Stop making that noise – *at once*!' she cried, running in
from the back kitchen and giving him a little shake and
pointing to the smashed cup. 'You're a naughty, spoilt
boy! Stop it! Do you hear? *Stop it!*' And then, as William
only yelled the louder, she picked up the remains of the
cup, put it on the table, and smartly smacked both his
hands. 'Naughty, spoilt boy!' she repeated.

For a second, from sheer surprise, William remained
silent; then he opened his mouth and *roared*!

There were few tears – the smacks had not been hard ones; he roared only with outraged dignity, and fury.

'Be *quiet*!' cried Mrs Ruggles, shouting to make herself heard above the din, '*at once*!' But William only roared louder.

Really this couldn't go on; next thing the neighbours 'ud be in to know what was up.

'*Be quiet!*' she cried once again, and she held up a warning finger. But William, now scarlet in the face with rage, only redoubled his roars.

Mrs Ruggles went quickly into the back kitchen. The next minute she returned with his push-chair; picked him up, dumped him into it, fastened him in securely with the straps, and giving the chair a little shake, pushed it into the middle of the room.

'Now stop it!' she cried, '*or up you go to your cot*!' And taking no further notice of him, she collected the breakfast things off the table, carried them into the back kitchen, and set about the washing-up.

For another two or three minutes William howled lustily, kicked, and banged on the sides of his push-chair with his fists, but all to no avail. He remained alone.

Mrs Ruggles finished the washing-up. The noise was subsiding somewhat; by the time she had peeled the potatoes, sorted out the washing, and lit the boiler, there was only an occasional plaintive sniff from the kitchen. A few minutes later, no sound at all. She peeped round the door. Worn out with defeat and tears, William slept!

'Poor li'l mite,' she said to herself as, torn between remorse and relief, she went upstairs and started to do the bedrooms. 'But he's got to learn; can't have him breakin' china and that – a good cup too – not one of the cracked ones of course – and yellin' fit to wake the dead. . . .'

Oh dear, what a mess things were in upstairs! No chest

of drawers, chairs all in the wrong rooms, and her own and
Lily Rose's wedding finery heaped on Peg's bed still
waiting to be put away! Have to stay for now, that would.
. . . Lick-and-a-promise was all she'd time for today. She
sorted out the chairs and began making the beds, going
over the events of yesterday in her mind as she did so.
What a day it had been! . . . Well, tied up good and
proper Albert were now; she only hoped as that Whiffen
woman 'ud be a good wife to him – shame now he'd made
good if he weren't happy. . . . Her folks had certainly done
things a treat – champagne and all, she reflected as she
finished the beds and started on a quick dust round.
Personally, she'd rather have had a nice glass of port or,
if it *had* to be fizzy stuff, cider. . . . Still, it'ud be something
to tell Mrs Smith! . . . 'Very good *the champagne* was – very
good indeed!' Matter of fact, she was afraid it had been
a bit *too* good for Albert! How he had gone on about that
motto she'd got out of the cracker . . . the guesses he'd
made! . . . fancy, she'd almost forgotten about it till this
moment. . . . What had it said exactly . . . ? She went
over to the dressing-table and rooted in her handbag, and
found the little piece of paper where she had pinned it for
safety to the lining.

'*A Big Surprise Will Soon Be Coming Your Way*,' she read,
and then she laughed, a little grimly. Well, a Big Surprise
most certainly *had* – and not lost much time about it
neither! But a tiger loose and prowling around – never,
she was sure, not if he'd been given a thousand guesses,
would Albert have guessed *that*!

The possibility that there could be an even bigger
surprise in store never – perhaps fortunately – entered Mrs
Ruggles' head!

The bedrooms finished, she came downstairs again.
William still slept. She went into the back kitchen and

began to prepare the vegetables for dinner. For a while all was quiet and peaceful, but after a time small, whimpering cries began to come from the kitchen. William was awake again. The cries, however, were subdued ones; William was chastened. Mrs Ruggles, her heart melting but telling herself to be firm, went into the kitchen.

'Out-door!' whimpered William, holding out his arms. '*Out*-door!'

'No, my lovey, *not* "out-door" today; Mum's said "*no*" and she means "no", but if you're a *good* boy you can have these bricks and play on the rug. There!' And she undid the straps of the push-chair and, putting him down on the hearth-rug, produced a box of bricks which had caught her eye in the twins' bedroom. They wouldn't be pleased at this borrowing of their property, but there was nothing to break. She wished she had remembered them before.

William welcomed the bricks rapturously. 'Puss-y-cat!' he crowed.

'Not "pussy-cat",' corrected Mrs Ruggles. '*Bricks*. Say "bricks".' But William only gurgled.

Keep him quiet for a bit, anyway, they will, said Mrs Ruggles to herself, and returned to her work.

She was right; for a long time there was no sound but the ticking of the clock, the bubbling of the copper, and, from the kitchen, low crooning noises of pleasure from William as he successively built up and knocked down the bricks. She had just decided she would make a cup of tea for herself when the crooning abruptly stopped. For a moment or two there was silence. She filled the kettle and put it on the fire.

'Puss-y-cat! Puss-y-cat!' came from the kitchen.

Gettin' bored, said Mrs Ruggles to herself, putting the tea in the tea-pot. No, I won't go, not for a minute or two I won't anyway; I'll just have me tea in peace. . . .

'Puss-y-cat!' cried William again, this time more loudly, and then came gurgles of laughter! 'Puss-y-cat! Puss-y-
cat!'

What made her suddenly rush towards the kitchen Mrs
Ruggles never knew – when William gurgled like that he
was happy – but rush she did, and for a fraction of a
second stood in the doorway unable to move for horror!

The kitchen was curiously dark. On the hearth-rug, his
face wreathed in smiles, waving a brick in either hand at
the window and gurgling delightedly, sat William. Outside, its paws on the sill, its huge head almost filling the
small window-space, and gazing with enormous green
eyes into the room, was the tiger! !

'Big Puss-y-cat!' cried William, turning and seeing his
mother, '*Big* Puss-y-cat!'

Swifter than speech Mrs Ruggles rushed forward and
grabbed him. The next minute, scattering bricks in every
direction, she was across the room, through the door, up
the stairs, and into her bedroom. Putting him down on the
floor, her fingers trembling from fright, she locked the
door and then, summoning every ounce of her strength,
pushed the big double bed against it. Then, picking up

William – till now too surprised to utter a sound, but opening his mouth ready for a yell, she went over to the half-open window and, her heart beating with terror and exertion, peeped timidly out.

No longer on its hind-legs, the tiger stood now on all fours, its back to the house, turning its big head first this way and then that. Shouts and screams were coming from neighbouring houses, and the two soldiers, their rifles at the ready, began to move slowly up the street. The noise seemed to confuse the tiger, it shrank back against the wall under the window.

And now, suddenly, at the end of the street, a man appeared, running, panting. . . .

'Do not shoot! Do not shoot!' he cried, between gasps for breath, and he clutched one of the soldiers by the arm. He was a little, dark man and he spoke very broken English. 'Do not shoot!' he repeated, 'I beg you! I beg you!'

But the soldiers continued to advance slowly up the street.

The tiger, standing stockstill, remained under the window.

'I do believe it's frightened!' said Mrs Ruggles to herself, and this was such an enormous relief that she put William down on the bed and, opening the window wider, leant right out to hear better what the little man was saying. Whatever it was, he seemed in terrible earnest – almost in tears.

'Do not shoot! do not shoot!' he kept repeating, still clinging frantically to the soldier's arm as they advanced together up the street. 'She is most quiet – most quiet! Only some little silly boy leave open her door or she never go out – never! But she is quiet, I tell you – always quiet – and *valuable*! *Very, very, valuable!* If you shoot, never, never,

can I replace her! . . . I beg you . . . only leave her to me
. . . she will come. . . . See, I have a chain . . . only see . . .
but keep back, and do not shoot I *beg* you. . . .'

At this moment an officer appeared at the bottom of
One End Street. There was a hurried command to the
soldiers and, almost before anyone had fairly grasped
what was happening, the little, dark man, chain in hand,
was advancing alone towards the Ruggles's house.

Softly, very softly, in some strange and unknown
tongue he called. Slowly the tiger came forward from
against the wall. It stood for a moment as if bewildered,
and then, its long whiskers twitching and gleaming in the
sunlight, padded softly towards him. He spoke again, so
low no one could hear the words, and the next moment it
was lying sedately, head on paws, at his feet, for all the
world like a domestic cat asleep on the hearth-rug! A
couple of seconds, and he had slipped a steel collar round
its neck, attached the chain, murmured some command
to rise, and the next minute, before the spell-bound gaze of
the inhabitants of One End Street, the officer, the two
soldiers, and a posse of policemen who had just arrived in
charge of a sergeant, it was ambling down the road at his
side as happily as a dog out for a morning walk!

That evening, before the largest audience for a small
town her owner and Bealby's Super Circus (Animals
Humanely Trained and Treated) had ever seen, Thelma,
The Time-Telling Tigress, gave her performance as usual.

And in the very front row of all, in seats sent by the
manager 'as a small return for the inconvenience caused
by a tiger at his kitchen window', sat Mr Ruggles, Lily
Rose, and the twins! Mrs Ruggles, 'thanking you kindly
all the same' having refused, affirming, yes, in spite of
all, 'as she didn't hold with dumb animals behind bars';

while William, who had wailed lustily at intervals all day for his 'Big Puss-y-cat', was at long last asleep – and quiet.

CHAPTER TEN

Mr Ruggles Buys a Pig

Now that the Pig Money was all but gone and there seemed little prospect of adding to what was left, poor Mr Ruggles had almost abandoned the idea of ever trying to buy a pig; and then, exactly a week after the tiger episode, while they were doing their morning round of the dust-bins, his mate, Mr Bird, drew his attention to some notices which appeared to have been pasted up over the week-end on a variety of walls and hoardings. These referred in large letters to a forthcoming sale of 'Prize, Pedigree, and

Other Superior Stock'. Further details, in smaller characters, were revealed on closer inspection. A well-known
gentleman farmer it appeared was selling 'at great sacri-
fice', and 'on account of immediate departure for abroad',
his entire stock of cows, sheep, goats, poultry, and pigs.

'Pigs!' said Mr Bird who had long been in Mr Ruggles'
confidence on this important matter. 'See, Ruggles, *pigs*!
Now's yer chance, mate! Fine pedigree stock this is, and
bein' only just advertised – the sale's next Saturday as
ever is – t'wouldn't surprise me if there were very few
bidders. It's short notice and, this time o' year specially,
most farmers and smallholders has all they can do rearin'
young stock and not particular ready for more. You'd like
as not get a real good pig dirt cheap.'

Mr Ruggles pushed back his cap and scratched his
head thoughtfully.

'That's as may be,' he said slowly. 'Trouble *is*, Bird, I
ain't got a penny – come to that an 'alf-penny – to spare,
and that's the truth; and I owes you for them eggs as
'tis,' he added.

Mr Bird said kindly, 'no need to worry about *that*', he
could wait; and he went on to say that a loan for the price
of what he called 'a nice little shut',* if it went 'reasonable' would not greatly inconvenience him either. He'd a
bit put by and an old widower like him didn't need much
anyway.

'Well, I dunno,' sighed Mr Ruggles, 'I dunno. My old
Mother used to say as 'them as borrers comes to sorrers'
and she weren't never very far wrong, she weren't. Besides
– there's the question of a sty. Can't have a pig and no-
wheres to put it. I'd had a mind to knock up summat on
the allotment if I'd ever decided definite to get one, though
I've a notion some Authority or other 'ud object prompt.

* A very young pig.

Anyway, a sty of any kind is goin' to cost money too – and take time to put up – couldn't possibly be done by Saturday.'

'Ah, that's where I come in!' said Mr Bird. 'I were going to explain but you interrupted. Listen now, it's a real co-in*ci*dence!' And he went on to say that his friend who owned the small-holding and had supplied the eggs and the buttonhole for the wedding, had asked him, this very week-end, did he know of anyone who could do with a pig-sty. He'd one on his land; they could have it for the asking and welcome provided they'd keep it in repair and perhaps lend a hand with his apples in the autumn. 'Lot of cider apples he's got – take a deal of coping with, they do,' concluded Mr Bird.

Mr Ruggles said nothing for a moment or two. He read through one of the notices again, then turning a corporation dustbin upside down, perched himself on it and sat thinking deeply. It certainly did seem to be a co-in*ci*dence. A sale of pigs, a sty offered, and Bird willing to lend the money! On the other hand, his old mother's warning weighed heavily on his mind. . . . Still, he argued with himself, one had to take a risk some time – or never take nothing . . . stupid, surely, to go agin such a provision of Providence as this seemed? . . . And after all, if the worst came to the worst and he couldn't save enough to pay back the money, surely 'a little shut' would double, even treble its weight in no time, and he could sell it for double, even treble, what he'd paid for it? He told Mr Bird he would 'think it over' and let him know 'dinner-time' what he decided.

Twelve o'clock came, they knocked off work, and Mr Ruggles' mind was made up. If Bird was really willing to loan the price of a pig and part of its keep, he, Ruggles, was willing to risk buying one. It was a pity, he continued,

as they began to walk homewards, they'd neither of 'em
be able to go to the sale, being at work Saturday morning,
and the trouble was to find someone to do the buying;
must be a good judge of pigs and the only likely person
he could think of was his neighbour Mr Smith who, as
Mr Bird knew – as everyone knew, having been all too
frequently reminded – had been bailiff to the late Sir Cuthbert Jennings, *M.P.* (Mr Smith was always very particular about the M.P.) He would not, added Mr Ruggles,
have chosen Mr Smith, on account of his Nosey-Parker of
a wife, had there been any choice, but there was not. Mr
Bird nodded sagely and agreed Mr Smith was certainly
the best man for the job – if he could be persuaded to do it.
Mr Ruggles thought there would not be much difficulty
about this, provided the matter could be arranged out of
hearing of Mrs Smith, but, in any case, he asked Mr Bird
to keep the fact he was lending the money a tight secret
between them; and Mr Bird promised.

It really seemed as if Fortune, for once, was smiling on
Mr Ruggles. Whom should they meet round the next
corner but Mr Smith himself. The matter was speedily
settled, Mr Smith being only too pleased to oblige, having
'had a mind', as he put it, to go to the sale in any case out
of curiosity, and for the sake of old times. Oh, Mr Ruggles
could rely on him to pick the best possible animal at the
price. He thought he still knew a good pig when he saw
one, ha! ha! In the old days, of course, Sir Cuthbert had
relied on his judgement *entirely*. . . . Many, many, were the
sales he had attended. He remembered. . . . Here Mr
Bird announced he must be 'getting along' and took
himself off, but Mr Ruggles had to listen to several weari-
some reminiscences of Mr Smith's prowess as a judge of
livestock. He got away at last, however, thanking Mr
Smith profusely, and impressing on him that he would

prefer nothing, nothing at all, should be known of the transaction until it was all over and done. He was not so much as telling his own wife. The pig was to be a 'sort of surprise like'. Mr Smith winked one eye and assured him of complete secrecy, and Mr Ruggles went happily home.

That evening, instead of going to the allotment as usual, he visited Mr Pedler, the owner of the pig-sty; inspected it, expressed his readiness to keep it in repair and to assist with the cider apples when required.

The stage was now practically set for the long-desired animal's advent and that night Mr Ruggles, for the first time for many weeks, went to bed feeling extremely cheerful and confident.

On the morning of the sale it was raining hard. This, said Mr Bird, was all to the good as it would probably mean fewer bidders. Mr Ruggles hoped he was right. He had begun to feel a little apprehensive. 'Them as borrers comes to sorrers' kept ringing in his ears and all sorts of horrible calamities suggesting themselves. The pig would not thrive; he would not be able to afford its keep; it would contract swine-fever and die; he would be in debt to Bird for life. . . . Oh dear – it must be the weather! *Drat* the rain, would it never stop! Apparently not. As the morning wore away it proceeded to come down even more heavily, and by dinner-time, wrapped in many sacks, he was picking his way homewards through streets running like young rivers – and it looked like going on.

'You're never going out again!' exclaimed Mrs Ruggles as, without waiting for his usual Saturday after dinner pipe, she saw her husband making for the door.

But Mr Ruggles muttered something unintelligible and was gone.

He hurried along to No. 4. The door was opened by Mr

Smith, Mrs Smith, fortunately, being busy with the washing-up.

He'd got it, all right! Mr Smith whispered. A beauty! A real beauty! Best little shut he'd seen in many a long day. Thanks to the weather there'd been few bidders and things had gone remarkably cheap. He'd left instructions for old Pat – Mr Ruggles knew old Pat, of course? – Mr

Ruggles nodded – to drive the animal back and put it straight into the sty, and it ought to be there any time after three o'clock.

'Who's that, Herbert? Who's that at the door?' called a querulous voice from the back kitchen, and Mr Ruggles hastily thanked Mr Smith for his trouble and fled.

'Where ever have you been to?' cried Mrs Ruggles

MR RUGGLES BUYS A PIG

crossly when he returned. 'Look at you – dripping all over my nice clean floor! I should have thought you'd had enough wet this morning without wanting for to go out again! I want you to keep an eye on William a while – I've got some laundry as must be finished; Lily Rose is off to the Guides, and the twins must have slipped out while I was upstairs.'

Mr Ruggles glanced at the clock. Five minutes to two. He sat down in the wicker armchair by the kitchen range and resigned himself to amusing his son for the next three-quarters of an hour. He took William on his knee; whistled to him; blew smoke rings; and performed various antics with his fingers. William gurgled appreciatively but appeared less sprightly than usual at this hour of day. After ten minutes or so his eyelids began to droop and very soon, to Mr Ruggles's immense relief, he had fallen asleep. He put him gently on a couple of cushions in his playpen and sat smoking in peace for a while.

Presently the hands of the clock pointed to a quarter to three. Jumping up, and calling out he had 'to see about something', he opened the street door, and before his wife could put down her iron and come into the kitchen, had vanished! And the rain still coming down in *sheets*! Really, *men*! said Mrs Ruggles to herself.

Mr Ruggles arrived at Mr Pedler's premises and sploshed his way down the muddy track that led through the orchard to the pig-sty. The 'little shut' would no doubt be feeling the cold after its trek from the cattle market, he mused. Lucky he'd got a good meal mixed for it last night.

In front of the pig-sty was a small open yard with a gate. He unbolted this and peeped into the covered sleeping-quarters. Alas! No little shut had arrived!

Well, it was early yet. Any time after three, Mr Smith

had said. Mr Ruggles resigned himself to waiting and sat down on an old wooden box inside the sty to be out of the rain. It seemed to be coming down slightly less heavily now, he thought, and his spirits rose. Any moment, and the pig ought to arrive! He pulled out his pipe, lit it, and sat smoking in great contentment. Fancy! after all this time – a pig of his own! Funny, it didn't seem hardly real somehow. He pulled happily at his pipe, looking out every now and then at the weather. The rain was definitely stopping. Time, however, was getting on. Presently the town clock chimed a quarter to five. Could old Pat have made some mistake, wondered Mr Ruggles?

Old Pat – a well-known character in Otwell – though not exactly half-witted could hardly be described as a very intelligent old man. His chief occupation – always accompanied by much shouting and a great deal of arm-waving, was the directing of cars in and out of awkward parking places (in which the town abounded) – usually to the detriment of the cars. At other times he loafed outside the station on the look-out for suitcases to carry, while at every sale of livestock he was present, having an affection for 'the bastes' as he called them, and greatly in demand for holding restive animals and doing other odd jobs among the cattle-pens. Oh, old Pat was all right. No doubt he was waiting till the weather cleared. That would be it, decided Mr Ruggles, and, judging from the clouds, another half hour or so and it would be fine. He'd best be getting back to his tea or Rosie 'ud be asking questions. ...

She asked some as it was and, for once, Mr Ruggles was grateful to William for upsetting his milk all over the table and causing a diversion. Before tea was over the sun was shining brightly, and immediately after it – a fork in one hand, a large vegetable basket in the other, he was off, bound, presumably, for the allotment.

On arrival at the orchard Mr Ruggles found the sty still empty. He felt faintly worried. Vegetables for the Sunday dinner were wanted, however, and he decided he would fill in time by getting them now instead of later as he had intended. The allotment was very wet and he was longer among the carrots and potatoes and cleaning the worst of the soil off them than he had expected. It was after seven when he reached Mr Pedler's orchard once again.

Surely the pig should have arrived by now! He went eagerly towards the sty fully expecting to be greeted by happy gruntings. But not a sound! The sty was empty as air!

Mr Ruggles now began to be seriously alarmed. *Something* must have happened! He considered going down to the cattle market, but there were several roads leading to it and whichever he took, old Pat, if he came, would be certain to take another and they would miss each other. By seven-thirty he was getting frantic! Get back he must for his wife would be waiting for the vegetables – she always prepared them on Saturday evening for the Sunday dinner. He decided to call in at No. 4, risk meeting Mrs Smith, and see if Mr Smith could offer any solution to the mystery. He set off homewards.

'Wantin' Mr Smith?' called a kindly neighbour as he was about to knock on the door. 'I met him and his missis not ten minutes ago – off to the cinema they were.– won't be back yet a while.'

So that was that! Mr Ruggles went on home and deposited the vegetables in the back kitchen.

'Why, Jo, you've forgot the onions!' called Mrs Ruggles a minute or two later. Drat the onions! thought Mr Ruggles. No – on second thoughts – bless them! He could go back for them after supper – *and* to the sty, and no questions would be asked. And although Mrs Ruggles said not to bother – it 'ud be getting dark, Mr Ruggles said cheerfully, no matter, and appeared to be in a singularly obliging mood.

And getting dark it was by the time he had got the onions and reached the orchard once again. But joy! Oh, joy! Coming from the sty were sounds; sounds which, on coming nearer, could be identified with snoring – very noisy snoring. Mr Ruggles put down the onions, unbolted the outer door, and peeped into the sty. The light was fading fast; inside the sty it was almost dark. An animal was lying stretched out, its back towards him, asleep. Even in the failing light he could see by its outline it was a very large animal – most certainly no little shut! He tiptoed nearer, not wishing to wake it. No, it was certainly no little shut! It was an enormous black *sow*!

Mr Ruggles, his breath almost taken away, tip-toed quietly back again, and, quietly too, bolted the door of the yard. *Here* was a nice go! A huge fat sow in his sty! But where, oh where, was *his* pig – his little shut? . . .

'Them as borrers comes to sorrers.' His old mother's warning mocked him as he stooped down to pick up the onions and slowly made his way back through the now almost dark orchard and out on to the lighted high road. 'Them as borrers. . . .'

There was no light in the Smiths' house, he saw as he approached it. They were evidently still at the cinema so any hope of a possible explanation of the mystery from Mr Smith was not to be had that night. As for searching for old Pat, Mr Ruggles had no idea where he lived and anyway was far too exhausted to attempt it. He went on home; locked the front door for the night, and threw down the onions on the kitchen table.

'You looks tired, Jo; very tired,' remarked Mrs Ruggles regarding him with a sympathetic yet critical eye. 'Well, it's Sunday tomorrow so you can have a nice late lay in.'

To her surprise Mr Ruggles shook his head.

''Fraid not, Rosie,' he said.

'What do you mean, "'Fraid not"? What's up with you, Jo?' And then, as her husband made no reply, 'It's my belief you're *hidin*' something – you've been actin' funny ever since dinner-time.'

Mr Ruggles sat down heavily in the wicker armchair. 'Children in bed?' he asked in a low voice.

'They *ought* to be,' replied Mrs Ruggles, 'but there's a deal of noise going on above. Be quiet, up there!' she called up the stairs. 'Dad's tired and don't want to hear no more of you; it's time you were all asleep. Well?' she asked, returning to the kitchen '*Well?*'

'Well is just what it isn't, Rosie,' replied her husband. 'Give me my cheese and cocoa,' he added, more to gain time than because he was really hungry, 'and I'll tell you.'

Ten minutes later Mrs Ruggles had heard the whole unhappy tale.

'I wanted it to be a sort of surprise for yer, Rosie,' said Mr Ruggles sadly, 'but everything's gone agin me.'

Mrs Ruggles regarded him with a mixture of compassion and annoyance. 'A tiger nearly in the kitchen last week were surprise enough for me for a long time,' she said slowly, 'and now you're tellin' me as a sow has come to stay! Really, Jo, I can't think how you come to do such a thing! Borrowin' money! The idea! It's not often,' she went on, 'as me and your old Mother's in agreement about anything, but just for once we *are*. Looks only *too* like coming to sorrers to me!'

And on this depressing note they ate their supper and presently went gloomily up to bed.

There was certainly no 'laying in late' for Mr Ruggles

next morning. He had slept badly anyway and was awake long before it was light. At seven o'clock he was up and clattering about, irritating Mrs Ruggles almost beyond endurance. Such an unusual departure from the normal Sunday morning routine brought the twins and Lily Rose from their beds loudly demanding what was 'up'. By now, thought Mr Ruggles, they might as well know what had happened, but he was unprepared for the wild whoops and shouts of joy that greeted his news.

A pig! *A pig! At last!* The fact that it was the wrong pig bothered them not at all! *A* pig had arrived and none of them could bear to wait another hour, hardly another minute, before seeing it. They threw on their clothes, fought to be first to wash under the kitchen tap, and rushed out of the house banging the door 'fit to wake the whole of One End Street', as Mrs Ruggles, trying to snatch a few more minutes' sleep, muttered bitterly to herself.

Mr Ruggles meanwhile had gone on ahead and was knocking at the door of No. 4. After some minutes a window was thrown up and the furious face of Mrs Smith, her hair in a myriad curling-pins, looked forth. Wanting her husband – *At this hour!* Did Mr Ruggles realize it was *Sunday?* she exclaimed. Would he kindly go away – at once. The idea! Knocking at the door like that, fit to wake the dead! And she slammed down the window, making twice as much noise herself. Mr Ruggles muttered something not at all polite under his breath, and the next minute the twins, followed by Lily Rose, came rushing up.

'Quiet!' cried Mr Ruggles, '*Quiet* – can't you! Remember it's Sunday and everyone's asleep. If you makes any more noise you won't come and see the pig at all!'

There was silence after that, and subdued, but walking briskly, they all set off for Mr Pedler's orchard.

It was a lovely morning. Birds were singing and the grass, still wet from yesterday's heavy rain, sparkled in the sun, while every little pool in the rutty track among the apple trees shone like a small mirror.

'Now stop there – where you are – all of you,' said Mr Ruggles as they approached the sty. 'I don't want the animal frightened – you can see it presently.' And he went forward and unbolted the door, closing it carefully behind him.

The sow was evidently awake. From the inner part of the sty came a kind of subdued grunting – a satisfied, contented sort of sound; the sound of an animal at peace and well-pleased with itself. Mr Ruggles peeped in. The sow was still lying with her back towards him as she had last night; but hearing footsteps she turned her head, flapping her large ungainly ears. At the same moment there was another sound – several sounds; a series of high-pitched little *squeaks*! The next minute the sow stumbled clumsily to her feet. She stood blinking at Mr Ruggles with her white-fringed little piggy eyes, while away from her rolled squealing into the straw, six, seven, eight – he had difficulty in counting them – nine? ten? – yes, *ten* pitch-black little pigs!

Mr Ruggles came out of the sty and leant against the wall. He felt dazed. The sow advanced to the doorway and stood there blinking and grunting while the little pigs squeaked and plunged blindly about in the straw.

Lily Rose and the twins could wait no longer. They came running up. 'Coo!' they exclaimed in chorus as they leant over the pig-sty wall, '*Coo* – ain't it a whopper! Oh, Coo! *Dad* – there's little ones – *little ones*! You never said nothing about *them*!'

'No,' replied Mr Ruggles. 'I didn't.' But I could say a lot now, he added to himself. 'No – you're not to go in,' as

John laid a hand on the latch, 'she might go for yer. You can help me get her feed – it's in the shed behind here. . . .'

The amount that sow ate! Three times Mr Ruggles filled up the trough and still she seemed unsatisfied. At this rate, he thought, the money he'd set aside for keep 'ud be gone in a week! The sooner her rightful owner was found and she and her family removed the better! Meanwhile, surely there was a clue – a label or ticket of some kind that would show who that owner was?

Looking closely at the sow he noticed a piece of string round her neck and dangling from it a very crumpled piece of paper that looked as if it might possibly be the remains of a label of some kind. Risking a bite he grabbed it, and then, regarded with a very baleful eye by the sow, grubbed among the straw and the piglets and eventually

succeeded in recovering three further scraps of paper.
They were wet and sticky and the writing on them had
'run' considerably.

Mr Ruggles spread them out on the pig-sty wall. When
pieced together they formed what appeared to be the
remains of two labels. After a time, with some difficulty
and the assistance of Lily Rose and the twins, the words
'Susannah of Sandwich' were finally deciphered on one,
while on the other, which was less damaged, there was
an address which read clearly as follows.

'Lord Glenheather, Glenheather Towers, Strathglenheather,' followed by the mysterious letters, 'N.B.'

A lord's pig, by gum! thought Mr Ruggles; but how in
the name of fortune – or rather misfortune – had it arrived
in *his* sty! And where, oh where, was his little shut? Enjoying his lordship's hospitality at – where was the outlandish
place – Strathglenheather – wherever that was? Sounded
a bit Scotch-like. Anyway it was a clue, and Mr Ruggles
felt slightly happier; but the sooner they all got back to
breakfast and found old Pat and learnt what had happened, the better.

But Lily Rose could hardly be dragged away! She had
caught but the fleetingest glimpse of the baby pigs but
she longed, fiercely, to hold one in her arms; to kiss it;
play with it. . . . They were too *absolutely* sweet, didn't
Dad agree? . . . Were there really *ten* of them – and all
quite, quite, black?

'Yes, *ten*,' replied Mr Ruggles gloomily. 'Ten Little
Nigger Boys,' he added with a rather wry smile. 'Come
along, do.'

The twins shouted with joy, and immediately began to
sing and, Lily Rose having at last been prevailed upon to
move, 'Ten Little Nigger Boys' accompanied the party
the whole way back to One End Street.

CHAPTER ELEVEN

Ten Little Nigger Boys

INSTEAD of lingering happily, as he usually did, over his Sunday dinner, Mr Ruggles ate it hastily, and a few minutes before one o'clock was knocking once again at the door of No. 4. It was opened by Mr Smith and before Mr Ruggles quite realized what was happening he found himself being ushered into the Smiths' very superior Front Room. He had barely told his troubles, and found Mr Smith as mystified as himself as to what had happened, when in sailed Mrs Smith, her hair well repaying the torture of a night in curlers, arrayed in her Sunday best, and carrying an incredibly superior-looking wireless set. This she put down on a small, highly polished table evidently specially dedicated to the purpose, giving Mr Ruggles a curt nod of recognition in passing.

Almost immediately sounds began coming from the wireless set. 'The One o'clock News,' announced Mrs Smith, and she held up a finger which said plainly, 'Silence, both of you!'

'Sit down, Mr Ruggles,' she remarked graciously, 'no doubt listening to the wireless is quite a treat for you?'

Mr Ruggles said nothing. He sat down, very gingerly, on the extreme edge of a mustard-coloured plush-seated chair, his hat held firmly in both hands, and stared at the Smiths' richly patterned mustard and blue carpet.

The news seemed to go on for a long time. Items of national and international interest wafted about the room. A threatened strike in Wales; political disturbances in Germany; tension in the Far East; a hurricane in the West Indies; and apparently desperate doings at a place called Wall Street. Mr Ruggles's mind began to wander.

His eyes roved round the room taking in the plush up-
holstered chairs, the superior wallpaper and curtains, and
the numerous little silver cups and bowls – doubtless the
fruits of Mr Smith's prowess as a judge of livestock – on
the very elegant sideboard; and coming to the conclusion
that he preferred his own kitchen, steam, airing clothes
and all. Suddenly the name Otwell caught his attention.
... What was the bloke saying ... ?

... 'An outbreak of foot-and-mouth disease has been
confirmed among cattle at Otwell-on-the-Ouse ... an
order has been circulated, and is now in force, prohibiting
the movement of all cows, sheep, pigs, goats, and deer
within approximately fifteen miles of the infected premises. ... That is the end of the news.'

Mr Ruggles felt it was almost the end of him too. He
looked at Mr Smith, and Mr Smith looked at him, while
Mrs Smith, with what he couldn't help feeling was a gleam
of malice in her mean little eyes, looked at them both.
Mumbling something that sounded like 'Thank you', he
put on his hat, made for the door, and the next moment
was outside in the street.

'All movement prohibited within fifteen miles ... all
movement prohibited within fifteen miles. ... Them as
borrers ... them as borrers ...' murmured poor Mr
Ruggles as he went slowly homewards to break the news
before hurrying away in search of old Pat.

Old Pat was finally discovered sitting outside the C
Dragon Inn, awaiting opening time though th'
for another three or four hours.

Yes, 'twas himself had druv home
affirmed in the accents of far-
baste 'twas!' What was th
pig he was asked to d

on to explain how 'a gentleman who checked what was druv away', had tied a label round the pig's neck, and how another gentleman had come and taken it off, and finally a third had tied on another – *and* pasted one on its back as well. Not he added, that labels meant anything to him, as he couldn't neither read nor write. Fair moithered all the officials were, what with the weather and getting the animals away; and fair moithered he was himself. Never, even in County Donegal, did he see the like of yesterday's rain. . . . 'Indeed,' in reply to a question from Mr Ruggles ,'a hundred labels might have been washed off a hundred pigs and no one a penny the wiser.' After he'd started, he went on, the rain came down so heavy that he'd had to take shelter in the Masons Arms – putting the pig in an empty shed at the back. And in the Masons Arms, it seemed, he had fallen fast asleep and so remained till opening time. And then, well . . . he nodded his head several times. . . . Mr Ruggles knew how 'twas. . . . But the pig he had druv back were the pig he were asked to drive *and no other*. . . . And with this explanation from which, with all the obstinacy of his race, he stubbornly refused to depart, Mr Ruggles had to be content.

Meanwhile, there seemed nothing to be done but to keep on feeding Susannah of Sandwich.

The amount that pig consumed! Already, thought Mr Ruggles, she had eaten nearly three days' rations, and his old mother's warning kept ringing in his ears. Most of the neighbours, when they heard of his predicament, had offered him scraps and potato peelings and, later in the evening, the twins, each with a bucket, went collecting from house to house. Being a dustman for once had its advantages and next morning Mr Ruggles was able to get what Mr Bird called 'the pick of the bins' in the way of stale bread and scraps.

Mr Bird was very sympathetic and helpful. He felt faintly responsible for the transaction though as he said, who on earth could have foreseen the way things had turned out! He insisted on making inquiries at the cattle market on Mr Ruggles's behalf, only to find, however, that owing to the foot-and-mouth restrictions no market was being held; few officials were on duty, and no one could give any helpful information. He returned very disheartened, and between them they decided the only thing was for Mr Ruggles to write to the address on the label he had found, as soon as he got home that evening, inquire if his pig had arrived there, explain about 'the foot-and-mouth', and ask what he was to do with Susannah of Sandwich – *and* her family.

Letter writing – or indeed writing of any kind, was never Mr Ruggles's strong point. As he said, the very sight of a pen and a bottle of ink seemed somehow to put every idea clean out of his head!

If only his Kate had been at home! She, no doubt, would have been able to write it all out for him in next to no time. As it was, starting immediately after tea, it was supper-time before he had got much further than 'Dear my Lord Glenheather', and even that didn't seem quite right. However, fortified by bread-and-cheese and several cups of cocoa, and after wasting many sheets of Mrs Ruggles's best professional note-paper, the letter was written. And, declaring it had taken more out of him than a week's overtime, he hurried out and dropped it into the pillar-box round the corner just in time to catch the last post out.

Three whole days went by and then, on Friday morning, the postman delivered a letter with a very Scotch-looking postmark. Mr Ruggles seized it and eagerly tore it open. It was headed 'Glenheather Towers, Strathglenheather', and began 'Dear Sir'. After thanking Mr

Ruggles for his letter, it went on to say that a small pig had arrived by rail two days earlier. Although correctly labelled and addressed it had been assumed some mistake had occurred as Lord Glenheather had telegraphed a sow was to be expected. There could be no doubt it was the animal about which Mr Ruggles was inquiring and the pedigree sow delivered to him was the one purchased by Lord Glenheather. His lordship was away from home but had been informed and his instructions were awaited. In the meantime, owing to the outbreak of foot-and-mouth disease in the Otwell area, nothing could be done at present in regard to the sow, and no doubt Mr Ruggles would prefer not to have his own pig returned until all danger of infection was over? The letter was signed, 'Angus MacKenzie, Factor' (whatever that was?) 'to Lord Glenheather'.

Except for the knowledge that his little shut was safe and sound, it did not seem a very helpful letter, and it looked as if nothing could or would be done until his lordship returned home or wrote – and how long might that be? In the meantime, Susannah of Sandwich had to be fed – and she was consuming no less as time went on – if anything, rather more. . . . And the foot-and-mouth sometimes lasted for *weeks*! . . .

The same afternoon, Lily Rose came home from school, threw off her coat and hat, and set about laying the table for tea – Mrs Ruggles being out shopping. She had just finished when there was a knock at the door. Not, *not* Mrs Smith, she hoped fervently. No, it was not Mrs Smith. A tall, thin man, dressed in a very old and rather dirty tweed coat, grey flannel trousers, and a very battered-looking green felt hat, stood on the step and inquired whether Mr Ruggles was at home?

Lily Rose regarded him a little doubtfully. His shoes –
like all the Ruggles children she was an expert on foot-
wear – however, looked good. She came to the conclusion
that he was not a tramp; decided he might be a prospec-
tive customer or a sanitary inspector, and, remembering
her instructions in regard to such persons, asked if he
would 'care to come in and wait – Mr Ruggles would be
home any time now.'

'Thank you,' said the stranger coming in and removing
his odd-looking hat, 'but I'm afraid you're just going to
have tea?'

'We don't have it till five,' replied Lily Rose, 'I've
just got it ready to help Mum – she's extra busy today.'

'You're Mr Ruggles's little girl, I suppose?' asked the
visitor ducking under some airing sheets and nearly
falling into William's playpen. Lily Rose gave a sup-
pressed giggle. She certainly never thought of herself as
little!

'I'm his eldest,' she said. 'There's seven of us!' she
added proudly.

'Good gracious! That's a very large family!' said the
visitor thoughtfully and as if he were genuinely concerned. 'It must cost something to feed and clothe
you!'

'It *does*!' replied Lily Rose in a heartfelt way, 'and it's
going to get worse, and worse, and worse!' she added
dramatically.

'Dear me! How is that?'

But Lily Rose felt suddenly shy, and that she had said
too much. She hesitated a little but the stranger looked
at her so kindly that she felt encouraged to go on.

'It's along of a pig Dad's bought,' she said. There was
silence for a moment or two, then, 'It's like this, you see,'
she went on, standing first on one leg and then on the

other, and fiddling with a saucer on the table as she talked. 'Dad bought a pig a while back – a quite *little* pig, but he couldn't fetch it home himself and someone made a mistake and it got sent all the way up to Scotland . . . and, and, an *enormous* sow come to him instead. . . . And now she's got ten babies – fancy, *ten* – they're just too sweet! But you wouldn't believe what she *eats*! she's costing pounds and *pounds*; and now the foot-and-mouth's broke out and she may have to stay for weeks! It's just terrible!' Lily Rose paused for breath.

The visitor looked sympathetic and seemed to be about to speak when she went on.

'This sow really belongs to a very grand gentleman. He's a lord! Lord Glenheather's his name. Dad's wrote to him but he's away from home and no one don't seem to know what to do. . . . You simply couldn't *believe* what that sow eats – it just never stops!' She sighed deeply. 'If only we knew where this here lord *was*!' she concluded.

'Well, as a matter of fact,' said the visitor slowly, 'He's here . . . I – er – I mean, *I'm* Lord Glenheather.'

Lily Rose looked at him incredulously. *Him!* It couldn't be true! It was a joke. He was 'kidding' . . . And she glanced again at his old tweed coat and funny round hat that somehow reminded her – and she almost giggled – of a badly-made pork-pie.

'It's quite true, really,' he said seeing her hesitation, 'and it's the sow I've come about.'

There was silence for a minute or two. Lily Rose stood on both legs and stopped fiddling with the saucer.

'I never thought a lord 'ud look a bit like you!' she said slowly, 'sir', she added as an afterthought; and there was no denying she sounded very disappointed.

'What did you think they looked like?' asked the lord in question curiously. Lily Rose hesitated. She felt suddenly

shy again. 'Well – I – I – dunno . . .' she said, then,
plucking up courage – 'I think I always thought of 'em
wearing those tall shiny hats – and them funny plush-four
suits – and – and driving around in *enormous* posh motor-
cars – or – or standin' about with guns on their shoulders
and *huge* big dogs at their sides.'

His lordship smiled. 'You've been looking at the picture
papers,' he said. 'I'm not at all that sort of lord. It's true
I do wear a shiny hat occasionally though I hate them,
and – er – plush-fours – though never together, I hasten to
add! And I do drive about in a car though it's certainly
not enormous, and no one could honestly describe it as
"posh". I suppose I might be said to "stand about with a
gun",' he added thoughtfully, 'and I've certainly got some
dogs – lovely dogs, bless 'em – but not "huge". Labradors.
Do you like dogs?'

'Oh, *yes*!' said Lily Rose losing her shyness again, 'and
we'd love to have one but we couldn't ever. Why, the
licence costs 7s. 6d. a year – unless you're blind or keep it
for sheep and you couldn't very easy in One End Street –
keep sheep, I mean.'

His lordship nodded gravely, and he looked a little sad.
'I wish –' began Lily Rose, but what she wished will never
be known for at that moment the door opened and in
came Mrs Ruggles, William in her arms.

'Mum!' cried Lily Rose darting forward before she was
barely inside the door, '*Mum!* This – this gentleman is
Lord Glenheather. He's come about the pigs!'

Mrs Ruggles almost dropped William. Goodness! The
unexpectedness of things! Now it was a lord in the kitchen!

'Take William!' she commanded, holding him out to
Lily Rose. '*Careful*, now – don't bump him down like that!
How often am I to remind you as he's a baby and not a
bundle of washing!' Then straightening her hat and

attempting to tuck in a floating wisp of hair, she turned to her distinguished visitor.

'Excuse me, your lordship, but it's all rather a surprise like! Won't you please to sit down – my husband'll be in directly. Lily Rose, why ain't you offered his lordship a chair?'

A chair was brought and his lordship just begun to explain how he had arrived at Otwell, when the door handle rattled and in burst Jim and John, closely followed by Mr Ruggles. Seeing a stranger the twins quietened down and slipped away into the back kitchen. Who was that bloke, their eyes asked each other? . . . 'Coo!' as they heard the introduction to Mr Ruggles being effected. 'Coo-*er*!'

'Listen!' said John, 'what's he saying?'

His lordship was saying that he had happened to be stopping in the neighbourhood – with Admiral Mellish, whom no doubt Mr and Mrs Ruggles knew as he was the Member of Parliament for the district? And Mrs Ruggles nodded and said '*Oh, yes*', as if she and the Admiral were on the friendliest terms (as indeed they had been on his brief house-to-house visit to One End Street at the last election). A letter, went on Lord Glenheather, had come from his factor – 'I think that's what you'd call a bailiff down here' (*that* mystery was solved!) – enclosing Mr Ruggles' letter and asking what had best be done. 'Being so near,' he concluded, 'I thought it was simplest for me to come and see for myself and talk things over – so here I am!

'And I hopes,' said Mrs Ruggles a little shyly, 'as your lordship'll accept a cup of tea – the kettle's just on the boil.'

His lordship said it was just what he would like, and after it perhaps Mr Ruggles would spare time to take him to see Susannah – and her family.

Leaving the two men to talk things over, Mrs Ruggles
hustled Lily Rose and the twins upstairs, hurriedly tidied
herself and William in the back kitchen, and opened the
pot of jam she had just bought for Sunday. She *did* wish
she'd had out the best cloth and china but there, there
was no time now. . . .

Five minutes later, Lily Rose and the twins, their hands
washed, their hair neatly brushed, William, wide-eyed
and for once subdued, in his high-chair, they were sitting
round the table 'all', as she afterwards put it, 'as matey as
could be!'

His lordship enjoyed his tea immensely and told Mrs
Ruggles it was the best he'd tasted since leaving home
adding, confidentially, that he was sure that Admiral
Mellish's butler never warmed the tea-pot first – and
didn't Mrs Ruggles agree that was half the secret?

Mr Ruggles, at first almost overcome with shyness,
gradually plucked up courage and asked a question or
two about Scotland, and Lord Glenheather, his face
lighting up as he spoke of his native land, told of mists and
mountains; of brown salmon rivers, and dark fir forests;
of the shining bog-cotton in summer and the pink and
purple heather in autumn; and of the deep, deep snow
in winter. He spoke also of his farm; of his shaggy Highland
cattle, and his long-haired, long-tailed sheep, while Lily
Rose kept wishing and wishing Kate were there to hear it
all.

'And if you ever come to Scotland,' he concluded, 'any
of you – yes – ' as Mr Ruggles smiled and shook his head
at such a remote possibility, 'you never know! remember
to call at Glenheather Towers. In the meantime, perhaps
three or' – glancing at William – 'should I say three-and-
a-half? nice-mannered children might like something I
got at the Bank this morning? And now, if Mr Ruggles

can spare the time, I think he and I had better make tracks for the pigs.' And picking up his pork-pie hat he put four large silver coins on the table.

'One each,' he said.

'Crown pieces!' exclaimed Mr Ruggles, wonderingly. "'Tis a long time since I saw any of they! I doubt the children have ever seen one afore. Thank you, my lord, thank you very kindly indeed.'

'And thank you, Mrs Ruggles, for that excellent cup of tea,' said Lord Glenheather holding out his hand as they stood for a moment outside in the street. 'Good-bye, children – and don't forget – if you ever come to Scotland – Glenheather Towers!'

'Thank you, my lord,' said Mrs Ruggles as she shook hands. 'We won't forget. Say "thank you" to his lordship, children, for . . .' she began as they crowded the doorway. But so excited with the crown pieces were Lily Rose and the twins that instead, led by John, they lined up on the step, waved wildly and shouted, 'Three cheers for Lord Glenheather! Hip, hip, *hurray*! Three cheers for Lord Glenheather. . . .' And continued until he and Mr Ruggles had turned the corner of One End Street!

And when Mr Ruggles returned home an hour or so later, he was nearly as excited.

'It's *good* news for a change, Rosie,' he cried as he came in. 'He's a-going to pay for all the sow's keep till the foot-and-mouth's over; then she's to go up to Scotland, and we're to keep two of the little 'uns – *two* – instead of my little shut bein' sent back. There, what do you think of *that*?'

'I'm thinking what your old Mother would have said!' replied Mrs Ruggles with a laugh.

Mr Ruggles looked a little sheepish.

'It's learned me never, never to borrer again, Rosie,'

he said. But he had been thinking the very same thing himself – all the way home!

The first thing Lily Rose saw when she awoke next morning was her crown piece sitting on a corner of the chest of drawers.

Five whole shillings to do just what she liked with! How *should* she spend it? There were such dozens of things she wanted! And she didn't want to spend it all on herself either. . . . She lay for a long while thinking deeply. She would like to give Mum a present, she decided, though it wasn't her birthday or anything. Something ... something to wear perhaps? ... Some beads ... or a brooch ...? She'd go to Woolworth's, this very afternoon! And then how about something special – very special, for tea, the day Kate and Peg and Jo came home – how many days was it ... ? She began counting them up ... only six – seven if you counted today, now! ... She was beginning to look forward very much to Kate's return. *What* a lot had happened since she went away! What a *heap* there'd be to talk about! And how thrilled, how absolutely *thrilled* she'd be with the Ten Little Nigger Boys!

But alas! Kate never saw them!

CHAPTER TWELVE

The Return

THE day that Kate, Peg, and Jo returned to One End Street was a long, long, day. There were the early-morning good-byes at Upper Cassington: to Mrs and Miss Midgley; Mr Shakespeare and Mr Milton; Sam and Mr Digweed, and many other friends – even a message was left with her daughter for Mrs Megson on her return. (Good-byes to Miss Alison had been said the day before and a letter in Kate's very best handwriting, thanking for Cuckoo-Coo, left with her for Mrs Ayredale-Eskdale.)

Next there had been the difficult business of coaxing Cuckoo-Coo into a straw-lined hamper from which, on no account, must he be taken out until they were safely indoors at home. Cuckoo-Coo had shown his displeasure in no uncertain manner, clawing at the hamper and mewing in a most distressing way, but finally falling asleep.

Then had come the dreadful moment of parting from the Dew Drop Inn; from Mr Wildgoose, and from Elsie. Everyone *tried* to look cheerful, Mr Wildgoose whistling and cracking jokes, Elsie bustling and smiling as ever, but inwardly everyone was very sad. Of course they *were* all coming back One Day, and Mrs Wildgoose was coming to see them 'for certain' as Jo put it – and Mr Wildgoose if he could get away, and perhaps Elsie too. . . . All the same . . .

And then, while Mr Washer's taxi was ticking at the door, Kate had disappeared! She had suddenly felt she must run upstairs for a last look out of her window and to say good-bye once more to her little room.

Mr Washer had grumbled horribly and said they would miss the train – for 'certain sure'.

During the drive to the station everyone tried to be brave, while at the station itself there was not much time to be brave or the reverse, for the train came puffing in; there was only just time to hurry across the bridge after George and the luggage, be given a hasty hug each by Mrs Wildgoose, and be bundled hurriedly into a carriage. But as the train steamed away and they stood waving, waving, very large tears indeed were rolling down all three faces.

The journey itself was uneventful. The train was very empty and they had the carriage to themselves. Cuckoo-Coo slept peacefully, never even waking when they had to change at Haywards Heath. This was successfully accomplished though the hour they spent sitting on a bench waiting for the train to Otwell, 'not moving an inch' as they had faithfully promised Mrs Wildgoose, was surely the longest hour anyone on earth had ever known!

Once safely in the Otwell train, however, everything

was forgotten but the thought of seeing their mother once more. They had a carriage to themselves again and per-haps this was as well for as the miles to Otwell sped by they became more and more excited, Kate singing, and Peg and Jo jumping up and down on the springy, velvet-covered seats. They made so much noise that Cuckoo-Coo at last woke up and began to mew wildly.

What *would* Mum say to him? They kept asking themselves and each other over and over again!

And when at last the train steamed into Otwell station what a thrill it was to see her on the platform! *How* she hugged and kissed them all, exclaiming again and again at Peg and Jo's bright eyes and round, fat, sunburnt faces – so different from the pale, skinny little creatures she had seen off six long weeks ago! Grown too, she was sure, while even Kate, who seemed never to add an inch to her size in any direction, was surely the tiniest bit fatter and taller? And *what ever* was in this hamper? . . .

The longed-for moment of introducing Cuckoo-Coo had come, and the mingled expression of horror and surprise on Mrs Ruggles's face at the prospect of this addi-tion to the household left nothing to be desired! And, before she had time to speak, quickly, joyously, all three together, they explained about the kind arrangements for his keep. But Mrs Ruggles made no difficulties. Truth to tell, she was so glad to have them back that at that moment she would have welcomed even a mastiff to One End Street!

And how happy and excited Dad and Lily Rose and the twins – and even William, who crowed with wide-eyed joy – were when at last they reached home! While Cuckoo-Coo, released from his hamper, was almost smothered with kisses and allowed to lap up nearly half a jug of milk!

And the tellings and the listenings as they sat round a

late but almost party tea! *A pig! A pig at last!* And *little* pigs! Kate could hardly believe it; it was almost as if they had brought some of the country back with them! She sat clasping and unclasping her hands, gazing round on all the familiar, loved, but now somehow strange surroundings. She was not a bit hungry although it was ages since dinner and Mum had got such a lovely tea for them. . . . She felt unbelievably tired, and only too glad when, Mr Ruggles having suggested she should go with him to see the pigs 'afore it were dark', Mrs Ruggles said sharply, 'Certainly *not*.' And when at last she went up to bed instead of the long, long talk with Lily Rose they had both planned, she fell asleep almost the moment her head touched the pillow!

She woke up the next morning feeling Rather Queer. Her head ached, she felt hot and cold by turns while the trellised wallpaper seemed to be behaving in a *very* peculiar manner. . . . (Yes, it almost seems as if we were back at page one again!)

'Measles,' said the doctor a couple of hours later. 'Definitely. No – no connexion with the first outbreak at all . . . she must have been in contact with a case while she was away. . . .'

'So much for country air!' said Mrs Ruggles to herself as she stood at the door with William in her arms watching the ambulance drive away an hour or so later.

'Don't seem very lucky, *do* you!' called a voice, and there, shaking a duster out of a window at No. 4, was Mrs 'Nosey-Parker' Smith!

'Puss-y-cat!' cried William, waving his fists towards her, 'Puss-y-cat!'

Mrs Ruggles carried him inside and shut the door firmly.

'You're right!' she said, sitting down on the nearest chair. '*Big* Pussy-cat!'

Poor Kate! (And so she thought herself as the ambulance rolled away!) She would never see the little pigs; she would miss still more school – and she felt – just *frightful*!

But she was only really ill for a few days (though they seemed very, very, long ones), and the first morning she was able to sit up and *enjoy* something to eat, there was a letter from Mrs Wildgoose. Inside was an absolutely staggering surprise! Nothing less than an invitation to spend the whole of the summer holidays at the Dew Drop Inn! She was to be Mr and Mrs Wildgoose's own guest, and they were even sending the railway fare!

It was incredible; unbelievable! She lay back on her pillows gazing blissfully at the high ceiling of the ward, completely oblivious to anything going on around her.

The whole of the summer holidays! Oh, it was worth having measles; worth missing almost a whole term at school; worth not seeing the Ten Little Nigger Boys! It was worth *anything* – almost!

*Some other Puffins you might
enjoy are described on
the following pages.*

TOMMY MAC

Margaret Stuart Barry

'Do we *have* to have Aunt Lil, Dad?' moaned Tommy Mac, hardly able to bear the thought of her ministrations while his mother was in bed with 'flu, unable to look after her six children. 'Nothing lasts for ever,' grinned his father, so Tommy could see that the only hope now was to think of some scheme to get her off the premises. But what? Nothing he planned seemed to work, and in the end it was his little brother Charlie who solved the problem, though nearly at the cost of his life.

Tommy Mac, the schoolboy hero created by a new writer for children, who is herself the mother of three and teaches at a school in Liverpool, is one of those fictional characters who make friends instantaneously wherever they are read.

THE DRIBBLESOME TEAPOTS AND OTHER INCREDIBLE STORIES

Norman Hunter

'Oh, oh, oh, oh! This is terrible,' cried the Queen. 'Not a teapot in the Palace that can be used. Oh, disgraceful! I must have a teapot that doesn't dribble, I must! I must! Half the kingdom as a reward for anyone who can bring me a teapot that pours without dribbling!'

'Here, here, half a mo!' cried the King, getting all agitated. 'You can't do that. What do you think's going to happen to Sypso-Sweetleigh if you go offering half of it for teapots?' But it was too late, the Royal Herald had shouted the proclamation all round the city.

By the author of *Professor Branestawm*, this is a marvellous collection of outrageous fairy tales, where the characters struggle against problems that are not nearly as simple as the old legends suggest.

THE SATURDAYS

Elizabeth Enright

It was Randy Melendy who first had the idea of the Saturday Afternoon Adventure Club. She and her sister and two brothers were tired of wasting good Saturday afternoons because they hadn't enough pocket money to do anything interesting, so they decided that they'd pool their money and take it in turns to spend one Saturday afternoon in four doing what they particularly wanted. The result is a series of funny, exciting and often unexpectedly rewarding adventures.

PROFESSOR BRANESTAWM'S TREASURE HUNT

Norman Hunter

When it was a case of inventing an unspillable teacup, a collapsible-cum-expandable house, a liquid carpet to be applied with a brush, a machine for peeling and pipping grapes, a bomb or a fire alarm, Professor Branestawm was the man for the job. His interests were wide, and his intentions excellent, but it simply isn't any joke to be an inventor, or to be anywhere near one, as the Professor's military friend Dedshott and his long-suffering housekeeper Mrs Flittersnoop well knew.

Readers who first met this eccentric genius in *The Incredible Adventures* of Professor Branestawm will find the new adventures in this book just as hilariously impossible.

ROYAL HARRY

William Mayne

'Letters are private,' said Harriet furiously. 'PRIVATE!'
And she tore the two mysterious letters across again and again
and watched the pieces blow away under the bridge and into
the water.

Now, just because her father had interfered, she would never
know where they were: the house and the mountain that had
been left to her. But her father knew where the house was, and
he marched her off there in double quick time, to a peculiar
house where perfect strangers kept popping in and out of a
secret passage in the spare room cupboard, and everyone
treated her with a funny kind of respect, even to accepting
orders from her.

This is as original and unexpected as all William Mayne's
stories are, and funny too.

STIG OF THE DUMP

Clive King

Barney is a solitary eight-year-old, given to wandering off by
himself. One day he is lying on the edge of a disused chalk pit
when he tumbles over, lands in a sort of cave and meets 'somebody with a lot of shaggy hair and two bright black eyes' –
wearing a rabbit skin and speaking in grunts. He names him
Stig, they learn to understand each other, and together they raid
the rubbish dump at the bottom of the pit, improve Stig's cave
dwelling, and enjoy a series of adventures that are sometimes
wildly improbable and sometimes extremely practical. One day
they discover how to make a chimney with a batch of old tin
cans, another they rescue the family silver from burglars, and
on another they capture an escaped leopard.

MY FRIEND MR LEAKEY

J. B. S. Haldane

Mr Leakey was the only magician who could bring a sock to life, or bewitch a tie-pin and a diary so that he could never lose them. He wanted to run over to Java after lunch, and was going to use a touch of invisibility in the morning to cure a dog that was always biting people.

If you want to know more about Mr Leakey and his household jinn and the octopus who served his meals and the dragon (wearing asbestos boots) who grilled the fish, you must read this book to find out.

For readers of eight and over, especially boys.

JOE AND THE GLADIATOR

Catherine Cookson

How do you manage to look after a horse if you have no home or money? This was the problem that faced Joe Darling when his old friend Mr Prodhurst bequeathed to him The Gladiator, the ancient, intelligent horse which had once pulled a rag-and-bone cart.

But it was a challenge he had to meet, and by sheer determination and with the help of some very surprising friends, he managed to keep the old horse and his efforts are rewarded in ways neither he nor his family would ever have guessed.

This story, which has been dramatized for television, will be enjoyed by readers of nine and over.

CARRIE'S WAR

Nina Bawden

When bombs were falling on London, Carrie and Nick were war-time evacuees billeted in Wales on old Mr Evans, who was a bit of an ogre, and his timid mouse of a sister. Their friend Albert was more lucky, living in Druid's Bottom with Hepzibah Green and the strange Mister Johnny, and Carrie and Nick were happy to visit him there, until Carrie did a terrible thing, the worst thing she ever did in her life . . .

Recently serialised on television, this is a book full of all the right ingredients – plot, characters, and suspense – to be read over and over again with increasing pleasure.

WHAT THE NEIGHBOURS DID

Philippa Pearce

What is it like to be a fly on the wall in our neighbours' houses, to see their real selves at home, instead of the polite people who say good morning and disappear through the front door to who knows what? Without fuss or drama, Philippa Pearce lifts the lid from our neighbours' houses, shows us the feeling lives within, and helps us understand them. There's the story of a family blackberrying expedition that might have been fun but is no such thing when Dad is bossing the troops, another about a never-to-be-forgotten midnight feast, and a boy's thrilling afternoon exploration ruined by a little girl tagging on.

Simple things, told with the sincere, simple artistry expected from the author of *Tom's Midnight Garden* and *Minnow on the Say*.

If you have enjoyed this Puffin Book and would like to read about others which we publish, why not join the Puffin Club? You will receive the club magazine, Puffin Post, *four times a year and a smart badge and membership book. You will also be able to enter all the competitions.*

For details of cost and an application form, send a stamped addressed envelope to:

The Puffin Club Dept. A
Penguin Books Limited
Bath Road
Harmondsworth
Middlesex